THE
REST OF
YOU

ALSO BY MAAME BLUE

Bad Love

THE
REST OF
YOU

MAAME BLUE

AMISTAD

An Imprint of HarperCollins*Publishers*

THE REST OF YOU. Copyright © 2024 by Maame Blue. All rights reserved. Printed in the United States of America. No part of this book may be used or reproduced in any manner whatsoever without written permission except in the case of brief quotations embodied in critical articles and reviews. For information, address HarperCollins Publishers, 195 Broadway, New York, NY 10007.

HarperCollins books may be purchased for educational, business, or sales promotional use. For information, please email the Special Markets Department at SPsales@harpercollins.com.

FIRST EDITION

Library of Congress Cataloging-in-Publication Data has been applied for.

ISBN 978-0-06-337596-3

24 25 26 27 28 LBC 5 4 3 2 1

CV 07.24.2024 0945

For my sisters, and the sisters that came before us

Part 1

CHAPTER 1

London, Present

Whitney

The second time you lost yourself, you were in the Tuck Shop. But you were no longer a child, no longer scraping coins together for a Crunchie bar or stealing Chewits from a friend. You were out on a Saturday night, in a club named after a shared childhood sanctuary, promising sweetness in name only, as music encased you in that place—a sultry, regular vibration that had a way of soothing all of life's ailments. Blue lights lit up the dance floor, and the gimmick of the club meant an assortment of penny sweets in bowls scattered across the gleaming limestone bar. Everyone scrunched up their noses at their first sight of that candy, but bottomless glasses of clear and brown liquids that passed across that same bar hours later led to empty bowls, the sweets having disappeared into drunken mouths and into the pockets of people riding highs to the moon.

You rarely took part in the pill-popping festivities, but this night was different. When midnight hit, you had officially turned thirty, joined by a group of friendly strangers jump-dancing around you as Stevie Wonder's *Happy Birthday* spun loudly under the DJ's careful fingers. You had danced for what felt like hours, feeling elated and a little tipsy from the pearl you had placed under your now-tingling tongue, though it had long since dissolved. Fingers dragged themselves in multitudes in front of your eyes as the buzz took hold and you swayed to the rhythm, hoping you weren't missing it in inebriation. You looked to your kin for validation, your best friend and flatmate Chantelle holding on to both your hands, dancing with you, laughing, swinging with you to the same rhythm, even if it differed from everyone else's. She really was a ride or die, you remember thinking, or some approximation of that thought as the drugs slipped into phase two and suddenly all you could think about was the sensation of fingertips against each other and on skin.

Ma Gloria always said that you held your feelings in other people's touch. It was only when you became a masseuse and began to feel the strength of skin on skin and all the things you could communicate to strangers without words that you started to understand her meaning. You wondered often if one or both of your parents had been the same way. Your mother, Tina, had been the youngest of three, after Ma Gloria and Auntie Aretha. But Tina had died in a Kumasi hospital while bringing you into the world, and your father—Bobby—passed away soon after that from an unknown illness when you were still a toddler. There was something particularly difficult around losing him that you never completely understood. Ma Gloria wouldn't talk about it, and you'd long since given up trying to find out more. Naturally, you had become a quietly curious person because of it, always hovering in between the gaps of things you didn't know about yourself. You rarely asked things out loud anymore, even when questions constantly ran through your mind, even when you wondered why people did the things they did, why they hurt each other—or you. Your mouth remained closed. Perhaps that was why, when the

Bard called yesterday, you did not say what you needed to say. You did not ask the question.

"I wanted to wish you happy birthday. Can't believe you picked up. Finally."

"It's tomorrow, actually."

"Oh. I mean, yeah, obviously I knew that."

"What do you want?"

"Whitney. Don't be like that. You never called me back. I was worried something had happened. But you're good, yeah?"

You could feel his question on the back of your tongue as if you had asked it yourself. It was for him, not you, and it tasted like tin, metallic like blood coming or recently spilled. A reminder of the *first* time you had lost yourself, underneath him.

"Don't call me again. I mean it."

It was the most you could say—to question out loud would be to request answers you were not ready to hear. So you hung up the phone before he could reply, his words still ringing in your ears. And he liked to talk; it was how he had endeared himself to you in the first place and why you had nicknamed him the Bard. He'd had an unhealthy obsession with Shakespeare and thought reciting sonnets in the shower was all a woman could ever want. For almost two years you believed that to be true, and then three months ago, he told you he just wanted to worship you, so you let him, unsure if you really liked him getting that close to you, lips in places you'd only recently geared yourself up to glance at with your makeup mirror. You ended up on top of each other; that's how it felt, anyway. Rolling around, you were always somehow looking *up* at him, though his words implied you were the goddess he knelt to. And underneath him his sonnets felt quieter but pointed, and you couldn't tell if he was trying to pierce your heart or the whole of who you were. At the time, your unwitting submission seemed to propel him onward inside you, and he took on a speed that was displeasing, almost unhinged in its rapidity. So you whispered into his ear with an adopted gentleness.

"Slow down."

Because suddenly there was pain around the edges of you that was coming into clear focus in the midst of his thrusting. But his ears were closed to you, as he continued his incessant journey, as if trying to burrow, and you wondered if you should have been louder. So you pushed a hand into his chest and used your other to hook a finger under his chin, bringing him eye level to you, just to break what felt like a ferocious concentration on his main task. Then you spoke with volume.

"Go. Slow."

And he looked at you with ice-blue eyes, sharp like a knife edge, and replied, "No."

And then your hands were gone from your vision, held securely by his own over your head as you shook and were shaken through the rest of it. You knew what it was, the refusal to let you be an equal partner in a shared activity. He was all-powerful, a terrifying giant, an overseer of your faculties, ones you had previously thought you were in control of. And you were shrinking beneath him, becoming small and incoherent, your language suddenly simple and new; you no longer felt you had the capacity to verbalize what was happening. But worse still was that it felt familiar, like the ache from an old injury, a scar that sometimes pulsated at night, at odd times throughout the year.

The leather sofa creaked and squealed beneath you, your head bobbing from side to side as if you were a rag doll, and you glimpsed the sides of his clenched muscles holding your wrists firmly. You kept your eyes on Rudolph's red nose on the sofa blanket behind him, coming in and out of focus with each new motion. And you counted backward from one hundred until it was over, because you didn't really know when it would be over. Afterward, he kissed you goodbye as if you had shared a meaningful encounter, and you pulled that same Christmas-themed blanket off the sofa and stuffed it into a black bag. Then you showered cold and stopped returning his calls. That was winter.

The memory of him stayed with you, of course. It was the smell at first: Giorgio Armani layered over the faint sour scent of sweat because he was always running somewhere, always late. You tried in the weeks following not to think about him, not to look at his name in your phone and ponder, not to sit on the sofa. You were washing your hands too often; it was standard practice after each of your clients left, oily and relaxed, your palms still tingling from the deep sensory work. But there was a slight increase now, a running of each finger under the tap, soapy and twisting aggressively against a finger on the opposite hand, as if there were a layer of filth you just couldn't quite get rid of. When you closed your eyes, you felt it all over you, hovering on top of the tiny hairs that covered your body. You spent the days trying to ignore it, to get on with things. But at night, he was on top of you, the heavy beat of his chest against yours, and every sensitive touchpoint was connected with him in your mind.

That was when the nightmares began, with a rhythm and a story. You always ended up in a coffin, buried in dirt, in a body-shaped hole with the earth being thrown upon you too quickly for you to find your way out. And even if you could, your limbs were frozen. You began to wake up that way, paralyzed from the neck down for seconds, sometimes minutes, searching the corners of your room for him, for monsters. You spent all of those stuck moments imagining what it would be like if you screamed, if you let Chantelle hear you across the hallway and finally rescue you from something you couldn't really explain. But she was a deep sleeper, and you knew it would end eventually, so you rode out the storm alone.

Chantelle had never liked him for you; she'd told you numerous times. He was "too up himself" and treated you as less than, which to her was unforgivable. She assumed you had dumped him because you had gotten tired of his starving-artist lifestyle and his inability to pay for anything.

"You work for yourself," she told you. "You ain't got time to take care of someone else."

Chantelle had been seeing a man—Paris—for the last three years, in a relationship that they had recently decided didn't exist if they weren't both in the same city. You didn't understand it; their silent agreement of a mutual wandering eye, but you left the judgment at the door of your mouth because what was there to say about your own situation?

Spring sunshine had already begun to melt away the frosty mornings, but after the Bard's surprise phone call it was as though you had been dunked in ice-cold water, and the feeling hadn't left you since. So, perhaps that was why you took the pill offered to you by the redhead with the pixie cut, who was giving them out to all the women around her on the dance floor. You wanted to forget, just for one night. To be truly in the moment. At first your mind was still yours, but quickly the crevices became bigger, and older thoughts began to push their way to the surface. Now you swayed on the dance floor, trying not to let the darker things consume you in a place of elation, though it was already too late. You were powerless. The Bard flashed up, and you could smell the leather of the sofa, his aftershave, the dusk of his voice when he wanted something from you. You thought about banging your head somewhere, to knock the memories out, and then as if on cue the drugs changed your focus. New threads began to weave around your mind. They came in a series of absurd sensory snapshots: the salty taste of a rough hand in your mouth, the smell of smoking charcoal on the breeze, the feeling of dirt between fingertips pressing deep into the earth. Your heartbeat was quickening too fast, as if trying to escape what you couldn't see, and that's where you became stuck, the moment not quite on a loop but rather a freeze-frame jerking at the edges every few seconds so that you could never quite capture the truth of it. But you felt it in your legs and between sweaty palms that pushed against an invisible block.

Maybe you weren't even in the room anymore. The rhythm wasn't rocking you in the same way; something else was pulling at you, that cracking thing that whipped you to another place. You found yourself standing at the bar suddenly, the party raging behind you, bodies moving as one big sweat lodge of youth and pride. Your vision bouncing around, locking and unlocking eyes with the bar staff at uneven intervals, causing confusion in your desire.

"Do you want a drink or not?"

The bartender looked annoyed, and you wanted to call out to Chantelle, to let her know that you needed to leave and you wanted her to come with you so that you didn't have to take a bus home with strangers and deal with the dead-drop comedown of whatever this trip was. But your heart rate was speeding toward a level that might be considered alarming, your palms were slick with sweat, and the bodycon dress you'd successfully slipped yourself into earlier in the night now felt like a straitjacket. You gripped the bar, leaning awkwardly against a stool rather than attempting to sit on it, avoiding that climb to what felt like a great height. You managed to focus on your hands at least, a step toward feeling still. You noticed your nails, a star painted on each tip, bright white against a blush pink background. Chantelle was getting really good at doing them, and you'd already had so many compliments. You tried to make a mental note to tell her, to suggest she add some satisfied customer quotes to her nail art Insta, because it made good business sense. But your thoughts were crickets, hopping through the air, bouncing off the ground, disappearing into the atmosphere. Nothing remained in place. You felt like you were vibrating, the music adding to the pounding in your chest, but something else internal, unseen and not quite known, flitted around your stomach and twisted itself into anxiety. You were no longer trying to hold your stomach in. Its fullness gave your dress a different shape now, one a bit more dynamic and human than at the beginning of the night, when you'd managed to present a smooth surface to anyone looking at you from the side. Your mouth was dry because you were taking too many deep breaths in a place where no one inhales too hard for fear of what might enter their nostrils. If you could just have a drink of water or something soothing, sweet on your tongue, you might feel better, like dealing with sea sickness. It was only then that you glimpsed a moment of clarity and reached toward the bowl of sweets on the bar to your left, barely keeping upright as your fingers extended themselves as far as they would go to find a sugary salvation. You brought the bowl toward your face, and your blurry eyes investigated as best you could; some sweets were naked and not to be interfered with; others were wrapped safely in plastic.

You ripped open a packet of strawberry laces with your teeth before your brain could question it, as if you'd not eaten for days, starving and desperate for sustenance. You were suddenly so hungry for the sweet redness of the licorice to slip down your throat that you ignored the tiny piece of plastic wrapper that you were sure went with it. You swallowed and then took a deep breath, then another and another. You wondered if this was truly breathing for the first time, whether you had been doing it all wrong until now. Your thumping heart's slowing rhythm finally suggested something was right, but your head was still fuzzy, still white noise with no remote. You realized you were not yet in control, that you needed something else on your tongue. You reached for the bowl again, but you'd had the last of the laces. Your heart sank to an unreasonable low, and the fizzy feeling in your nose made you think tears were coming. You searched frantically around you for more because there were always more. And then your eyes caught a second bowl of sweets down the other end of the bar. You practically launched yourself at them, ripping open three more fun-sized bags of the red licorice, each one a chaser for the one before it until you felt a small wave of nausea hit your stomach. You flipped around awkwardly so that you were facing the crowd again and belched loudly into the air, equal parts amused and disgusted with yourself. You felt a little better, less loopy. After a few minutes you even managed to flag down another bartender and order a pint of tap water. You sipped it slowly and felt yourself sobering up, certain you wouldn't be taking any more pills from strangers for a while.

But you hadn't been alone; Chantelle had been there when you'd tossed the little gift into your mouth. In another setting that wasn't on this day of all days, she might have lectured you about taking a pill, assuring you that you couldn't handle it. Only then did you realize how much time had passed since you'd seen her last. You scanned the crowd for her, sure she was probably wondering where you were too, but you didn't want to be subsumed back into the masses, exposed to wandering hands, unwanted strokes, and men feigning dance moves in order to rub themselves against you. Suddenly the dance floor felt like a scene from *Battle Royale*, and you weren't ready to face that sick feeling of emotional gore just to find a fun moment again.

You turned toward the exit, where hefty bouncers surveyed the room with beady eyes. To you they looked like pillars flanking the

doors to freedom. You made a beeline for the cloakroom, mag-
ically finding the ticket for your jacket and scarf still safe in the
front pocket of a crossover bag too small to actually carry anything
substantial. You reclaimed your things and finally made it outside,
gulping down the fresh air, a comfort and a relief. You turned back
toward the club when you felt a presence behind you, one of the
bouncers closer than you'd expected.

"Dropped this, love. Cold as shit out here tonight. Gotta stay warm."

He held your scarf out to you, almost smiling, gritting his teeth
because of the aforementioned cold. You hadn't even noticed the
new chill. You thanked him quickly, trying to smile him away, turning back toward the road and wrapping the viscose scarf around
your neck obediently. You looked down at your fingers; they were
wrinkled, clenched into fists to indicate that some part of you was
feeling the cold. You moved to the side and sent what you hoped
was a coherent text to Chantelle, just as a few more people exited
the club behind you. Every new person passing by too closely sent a
shiver down your spine, and you felt your heartbeat vibrating heavily against your chest, trying to steady itself. After a brief moment
of calm, you jumped out of your skin at the sound of a booming
voice to your far left—a handsome, dark-skinned man in an electric
blue shirt slapping his friend on the back in greeting, the sound
cracking so hard that you winced.

"BRUV! DID YOU SEE THE BEAUTY I WAS JUST
WITH?!"

He spoke at a volume that could only be described as "too loud."
He was a dapper dresser, perfectly shaped up, a crisp line of a
beard, but something off with his eyes. Not quite trustworthy. You
averted your gaze, pretending to be engrossed in your phone and
hoping the battery wouldn't die before Chantelle's name popped
up. Nothing had come through yet, and you tapped lightly with an

open-toed shoe at the chewing-gum pavements of Brixton, seeing little clouds of air escaping your mouth already. Chantelle warned you that your coat would be too small, hence the last-minute addition of the scarf. Eventually you heard that *ping* you'd been waiting for, your friend letting you know her ETA, asking where you were exactly, why you were by yourself. You hadn't felt alone until she'd inquired about it. Or you hadn't noticed that you were standing by yourself, that no one had come along to ask if you were okay. Perhaps if your insides were showing, people would notice how disrupted you felt, as though you were stuck in a conversation loop and had long since lost the thread of the exchange. For a reference point, your eyes found Blue Shirt Man again; all done boasting to friends, he was now chatting up a woman who had just left the club and was making her way to the bus stop across the road. She looked tired of his talking already. You wondered if he actually had any real game, or if every woman who talked to him just got hassled into handing over their details, real or not. His confidence spilled out into the streets around him, an attractive and dangerous combination depending on who was passing by. You pondered over all the attention he garnered, and your mind went to the usual place. Had he ever taken advantage of his power? All that height and depth of voice up close, delivered from a pretty face. Even the way his gait begged you to watch him until he was watching *you*—it was enticing. The way his eyes felt like they were eating you when caught in his sights, trying to make you all his. You wondered after the women, if it ever felt all the way good under that piercing gaze?

Chantelle would say this wasn't a healthy way to think about men, especially the ones you didn't know. And the staring too, that didn't help. Blue Shirt turned toward you, the two of you locking eyes suddenly. You readied yourself for an approach, unsure if it was in excitement or fear, but then a finger hooked into your little one from behind, causing you to whip around and face the physical intruder. Chantelle's custom-made Brazilian wig swished over your shoulder as she grabbed your waist from behind and pushed you forward.

"There you are!"

She grinned as you turned around to face her, and then she grabbed both your shoulders, staring you dead in the eyes suddenly.

"Whitney Appiah! What did you take?"

"Whatever everyone else took."

"Those weren't for you. You know you can't hang, yeah?" You screwed your face up at her but stayed quiet. Chantelle knew you too well. She didn't seem to notice your annoyance and pulled out her phone. "Uber's here in two minutes. How long you been out here?"

You shrugged, feeling a bit like a child who had been scolded by a parent and now wanted to sulk. Chantelle kissed her teeth.

"Don't be mad at me because you had a bad trip."

"No, it wasn't that—I'm cool."

"Oi, you! You owe me one a' dem, yeah!"

Chantelle had turned to yell at someone behind you, and you followed her gaze just in time to see Blue Shirt approach, holding an unlit cigarette in one hand and a lighter in the other.

"Y'alright, beauty? I was *literally* coming to bring you this, promise."

He flashed a smile at Chantelle, and she took the cigarette out of his hand without saying thank you. He leaned in to light it, but she waved him away.

"Nah, I'll smoke it later."

She made a small head nod in your direction, and he nodded back in response as if he understood exactly what was being said. You had never felt so invisible and in the way, all at the same time before.

"Maybe I can get your number?"

You heard Chantelle scoff as if his request were ridiculous, and then her phone buzzed to say the Uber had arrived. With that she took your hand and led you into the back seat of the taxi, aware that Blue Shirt was watching dumbfounded, unable to argue with thin air.

"Did you see his face? Boy was confused!"

Chantelle was laughing to herself as the Uber rejoined the road, and you wanted to laugh along but you could only muster up a grin. You tried a question instead, hoping she wouldn't notice your own lack of mirth.

"What's with the cigarette exchange?"

She frowned at you, only one eyebrow raising quizzically.

"*That's* the question you wanna ask?" You nudged her playfully, and she sighed in hesitation, as if you were dragging an important secret from her. "I bummed him one earlier, that's all."

"And then?"

"And then we made out for a bit. It's not a big deal."

"And . . . what about Paris?"

"Nope. Not doing this with you again, Whit. You know what it is with me and Paris. Please just leave it."

You leaned back, frowning, ready to explain that you weren't asking about her new foray into an open relationship. If anything, you were hoping it meant she was single again, but your brain was a bit too tangled to articulate things properly. You didn't know how to say it in the moment, so you said nothing and let the rest of the journey back home be soundtracked by Kisstory on the driver's radio. The night was already blurry around the edges, spilling into the dozens of other nights you'd spent out together. Nothing special except that you were officially three decades old. You turned from the window after taking in your birthday view of the city and met Chantelle's peculiar gaze.

"You okay?"

She showed concern on her face rarely; it was oftentimes reserved only for her aging grandmother, her favorite person in the
world, who taught her the "proper way" to make Jamaican rum
cake. But tonight she lent that care to you, and you decided to
reply with another smile, although slightly less enthusiastic than
the last. You could still taste the licorice of the strawberry laces
on your tongue, paired with that extended moment of abject and
unexplained fear. You didn't say this to Chantelle. You couldn't.
She just kept looking back at you, obviously with something to say
but unsure how to speak it. Silence followed you the rest of the
way home, returning to your shared flat in Camden with the early
hours of the morning touching the bottom folds of the sky.

In the kitchen, both of you now in pajamas, you took a deep
breath, readying yourself for her to say whatever she had been
holding in on the drive home. You turned to face her, and she
placed her tea down immediately, her words poised.

"What happened to you tonight? One minute we're dancing,
next thing you've disappeared, and I thought I saw you scoffing
down those *dutty* sweets at the bar, but then maybe I imagined that?
I just wanna make sure you're okay. So . . . are you?"

The answer echoed in your mind, so inexplicably complicated
she might as well have asked you to recite the theory of relativity.
You weren't okay, and you couldn't tell her why, so what could you
tell her instead?

"I think . . . I shouldn't have had that pill. It was just a bad trip,
like you said."

You couldn't even keep eye contact with her. You could tell she
wasn't buying it, but she didn't push.

"You know you're my number one, yeah? If I'm off with someone else, I will always dash them for you."

"I know."

You said it quietly, though her words were breaking through some of the cold, heating you up a little on the inside.

"Just thought it was worth saying. Like, I don't often worry about you, Whit, but if you need me to, I can."

It was a strange thing for her to add, and now you were sure you had once again lost hold of the conversation taking place.

"Listen, I'm officially old now and no longer able to function properly past like two a.m. Can we go to bed, please?"

You tried to sprinkle a little laughter over it, make it sound less desperate than it felt. Chantelle nodded at you, also visibly relieved that the conversation was over. She picked up her tea again and then raised it, ready to cheers, requiring you to raise your own mug too.

"BERT-DAY WEEK!"

"BERT-DAY WEEK!"

You replied back with the same energy because there was excitement around it. And maybe tonight was just a blip, a precursor to a good night's sleep, the bit before everything else got better.

CHAPTER 2

Kumasi, 1995

Gloria

Gloria felt the full possibility of the day in her body. Until now things had been heavy, as if she carried weights on her back and chest. She would wake up every day with this feeling of being underneath her grief. It had lightened a little every year since Bobo was born, but finally she felt things shift properly. Perhaps because she really wanted to remember this day, the first in a long time that Paa Kweku had requested a meeting with her. Just the two of them.

"There's something I want to tell you. Can I pass by later today?"

"I'll come to you."

Gloria had replied quickly as he stood outside the gate, suddenly too shy to step through the opening as he had many times before. But it was early in the morning, he was on his way to Holy Grace Church, and she was not properly dressed. They said their good-byes, and she listened to his footsteps fade away as the guard closed the gate behind him. She tried to tell herself that Paa Kweku's request meant nothing, that she had not been hoping for it or something like it for many years, even after he had pledged himself to a life of godliness.

She had always known he would take that path, and once they

became teenagers, he went away for a handful of years to train in a seminary in Ejisu. During his stay, they wrote many letters to each other; he told her about his daily life, how different and difficult it was there, how he missed home and the taste of his mother's cooking. And that he often wished he could walk over to the Sarpongs' home for the Friday night meal, a coveted get-together that only happened when Daddy returned to Kumasi from overseas, shedding his moniker of Sergeant Sarpong for them, and went back to just being a father to his three daughters. Paa Kweku was the only guest allowed who wasn't a blood relative, and Daddy reminded him often that when he was away, Paa Kweku was to be his eyes and ears, watching over Gloria, Aretha, and Tina. Paa Kweku did not take the responsibility lightly.

But once he had taken his vows, things inevitably changed. He was still close with the family, but the expectation that he and Gloria would get married flitted away into nothingness. It wasn't a question of permission—his faith was such that he *could* get married, but he was just not sure that he wanted to, that perhaps it would compromise his ability to devote himself fully to God. That was what he had told his best friend at the time, who happened to be Gloria. That day was burned into her memory, the flames of it still licking at her every so often. She had no scars from it—just open, tender wounds every time he came by the house to see her, to go with her to the market, or to simply sit in the pews on Sunday after service, talking about the week behind them and the one ahead. She would grab at all those moments, becoming used to having fractions of him at a time, even if most people thought waiting for him was a fruitless venture.

At twenty-nine, she was the eldest, tasked with taking care of the family when Daddy wasn't around. Mommy—Ruth—had given birth to the youngest of them, Tina, and then rejoined God in heaven one week later. Aretha was two years old at the time; Gloria was eight. Daddy wouldn't entertain the notion of remarrying, despite pressure from the wider family. Gloria thought perhaps he was married to his work, as her American cousins might say. She did not like to think that he had always been that way, even when Mommy was alive. But she was older now, and she knew him well. She knew what he was and what he could never be. He found it difficult to be present, to stay home for too long. So she worked hard to fill those gaps. Her sisters were too young to know what they were missing; only Gloria had full, bulbous memories of Mommy.

She returned regularly to the memory of Mommy teaching their house girl, Maame Serwaa, how to make kontomire stew the Sarpong way, using fresh spinach from the garden, the best spices. She remembered the way Mommy would carefully do Gloria's cornrows when it was time to sleep, singing gospel songs to her as she sectioned out each piece of thick hair, soothing her scalp with shea butter. And sometimes Mommy would slip from loving the lord to crooning softly to Aretha Franklin's "I Never Loved a Man," the melody splashing into Gloria's sleepy mind, so that often as a child she dreamed the songs as if they were her real life. Mommy's love for soul music—the old and the new, the pitch-perfect voices that began in the church and ended up shaping rhythm and blues—was well documented. Once, Gloria had witnessed her parents slow dancing to the Supremes, late at night after returning home from a celebration of someone's life, thinking their children were asleep, that they finally had a moment to themselves.

Later, Gloria wondered if she had created the scene in her mind, to retell a different story of her parents' relationship, one with a stronger bond, despite its short life. She would never know for certain. But she had watched Mommy put away her "secular records" when the older aunties came to visit, despite her obvious desire for

all her daughters to feel that same music in their bones, evident in
the names she had given them: Tina, Aretha, and Gloria. All three
sisters had found their way into the church choir as children, but
Gloria's focus eventually shifted to other types of service, from her
training as a nurse to taking charge of Sunday school. Aretha too
had lost interest in singing by then—and in church. Tina was the
star of the three, taking solos when she was only six; Mommy never
got to witness any of it, of course. But Gloria still had the childish
hope that she was watching them all from above and that she was
pleased.

Gloria wasn't a child anymore, but she allowed herself a day-
dream or two about a future with Paa Kweku. What would it be
like if he decided that he loved God but also loved her? It didn't
have to be a competition. But then guilt would follow. She loved his
devotion to his faith, even if it remained the reason they could not
be together. And yet things had felt different between them the last
few months. They had gotten closer, if that was even possible. She
knew that there was something he was not telling her, something
he was struggling with. She supposed that he was either about to
explode with his feelings or break her heart somehow. She was not
sure which, but she was prepared to hear him out, whatever the
outcome. Even if it broke her. What else did she have to lose? And
there was nothing wrong with hoping, after all.

A lot of the things Gloria had felt she always wanted had shifted
since Bobo had come along. But Bobo had changed things for everyone. Her arrival was not unwelcome among the sisters, but it
was unplanned. Gloria still felt a squeeze in her heart when she
thought of Tina, Baby-Last as they used to call her. Gloria recalled
the stoic look on Tina's face when she told Gloria she was pregnant
at just eighteen. Even then, Gloria watched her trying to relay the

news as an adult, prepared for motherhood in a way Gloria had never been. Gloria leaned into it now, but the reality of it felt thrust upon her. Tina was different.

"It will all be well, Glory. I know it. It's okay."

Gloria remembered watching her with curious eyes, this new, more mature Tina having returned from seeing Daddy in Copenhagen three months prior. Gloria had suspected her bright new attitude had something to do with a boy, and she had been right in her assumption when she found out about Bobby, a nineteen-year-old Ghanaian who had grown up in Denmark. Immediately she played devil's advocate with Daddy, reminding him that Bobby was *his* apprentice, a young man who had just completed his Danish military service and was recruited by the Sergeant for his language proficiency. This went some way to calm his fears about Tina's future as a young mother, and Gloria tried to reassure him about the rest. She had been taking care of Tina since she was a baby, after all.

But in secret she was filled with anxiety about having failed her baby sister. And not just her, but the whole family. It was her job to protect them, make sure they followed the paths to the bright futures laid before them by the hard work of their elders. Yet somehow Tina had slipped through Gloria's fingers when she wasn't paying attention. She had seen the three of them at a crossroads; Tina pregnant, Aretha going into her final year of university, and Gloria a newly trained nurse, already a witness to too many teen pregnancies gone wrong, when the young mothers-to-be had no family support and shame was a rope around their necks. It was that thought, that knowing, that made her determined to put everything she had into making sure Tina was looked after, able to bring the baby to term, able to thrive. Daddy talked of a wedding happening as soon as Bobby was granted a visa and was able to fly to Ghana from Denmark. Gloria was not convinced that marriage would solve any of these problems, but she kept quiet about that one—it was not *her* main concern. Instead, for six months, she gave all her time to Tina, and not much at all to Paa Kweku—though he rarely demanded it. And the next time she saw him, everything was broken again, after the tornado of Bobo being born and Tina dying. That one terrible day.

Gloria considered this meeting with Paa Kweku now, three years later, as a reclaiming of that lost time. Of taking back some small thing for herself. She should be allowed to do that, at least.

She was already walking out of the gates of her home when the driver, Prince, poked his head out of the car window to ask where she needed to be taken. She told him in Twi that she was going for her daily walk and waved her hand at him gently to confirm this, even though it was already late afternoon and the Kumasi sun was giving everyone on the road its menacing glare. She dabbed her forehead with a handkerchief—Paa Kweku's, in fact—as she walked past his family compound where she had spent many afternoons playing after school, when their mothers would sit and talk together on the balcony.

Finally she came upon the small house, next to Holy Grace Church, where he now resided as a young pastor. For a while she couldn't bring herself to cross the road. It felt symbolic, as though to go ahead would mean a willingness on her part to approach the line they had silently agreed to stay away from. She stood frozen, looking at the house for so long that taxis going by kept slowing down to honk at her and offer their services. She knew that she looked lost, and she felt that way too. But to turn back was not a better option—she was already acutely aware of what haunted her back home. Her house had changed shape somehow; maybe the ghosts were taking over. She shuddered at the thought and made a mental note to put her hand on the Bible when she entered Paa Kweku's house, to settle herself. Then she crossed the road.

There was a small fan whirring above their heads, spinning warm air around the room in a useless fashion. Gloria stared at it in mild frustration, seated somewhat uncomfortably on a straight-backed chair Paa Kweku had pulled out for her when she entered his small living room. She continued to look up as he busied himself in the kitchen, eventually bringing through a tray with two cups, some tin milk, and a china teapot she recognized from his mother's kitchen. Gloria smiled at the memory. Their histories were interwoven. It made her chest hurt to recall it, to see what they were now. Friends definitely, but no one had said out loud anything else. Not recently. These were the times Gloria felt foolish, as if she were walking a road she had walked her whole life, but every time she walked it, her shoe got stuck in a small pothole. Every day she knew it was there, she even looked out for it, and every day her shoe got stuck.

"I brought everything so you won't say I've ruined your tea with too much milk."

Paa Kweku gave her a small smirk as he placed the tray down in front of her. She leaned toward it and began to pour tea into both their cups. He sat opposite her, the small wooden table a carpenter friend had made for him years earlier, serving as a sturdy dining table for one. Well, two today. She wouldn't meet his eye just yet. She had to take her time, approach things with a clear head. He had already made two holes at the top of the milk can and she deftly tipped it into her cup, favoring the left opening over the right. He watched her silently. They were comfortable in most rooms together, but now the air was full, like an expensive pillow, and Gloria couldn't decide if she felt suffocated or comforted.

"Have I done something wrong?"

His question shook her out of her own thoughts.

"Wrong? No, why?"

"You don't seem yourself. Is all okay at home?"

She shrugged again, as if she were always an uncertain mess, which she was not, usually.

"It is well. You know, Bobo's birthday party was last week, three already, walking and talking and running into everything. Bobby and Aretha get to just make the fun, and I am the disciplinarian. Mabrɛ."

His brow narrowed in concern at her brief confession of tiredness, and Gloria heard her own words as slightly resentful. She closed her mouth, lest anything else fall out of it without her thinking. This was how it always was with him. He did not have to try very hard to get any kind of truth from her. He knew what each of her looks meant. When she was upset or quietly pleased. When there was something she wasn't saying.

"Don't worry. That baby knows who her mother is." Gloria's head whipped up at those words, and Paa Kweku corrected himself quickly. "I mean, everyone is there, but it's you she runs to. Is it not?"

It often felt like men were asking her questions that didn't require an answer. She sipped her tea and tried to relax back into her chair.

"And how are you? Did the reverend find the bread thief yet?"

Paa Kweku smiled as Gloria gave a mischievous grin, hoping some church gossip might break the tension still sitting between them.

"Ah, he knows who it is, but he won't say. I'm staying out of it."

"Even though you also know? Just say it's Auntie Millicent and move on."

"Me? Accuse a seventy-year-old woman of something like that? Hey! I want to keep my new job, okay. I'll pick a better battle."

They both laughed, and Gloria felt that soothing softness on her skin again, of being around him, the sky through the window glowing orange with the setting sun. These moments felt sweet. But something bit through her mind and pulled her out of it.

"Wait. What new job?"

His face changed in a way she wasn't expecting, and Gloria realized she needed to gather her own self, quickly.

"Reverend Addo has chosen me to open a new branch of Holy Grace. In . . . London."

It was the pause that she would remember. The small breath he took before he said "London." The word was carefully curved around his tongue so that the pronunciation was that of the Queen's English. He had been practicing how to say it to her, *for* her.

"When will you go?"

He hadn't been expecting the question so soon, she could tell.

"I—we have some things to arrange before that but, God willing, one month's time?"

Was he asking her, as if she would know? Gloria felt the anger in her calves, her muscles tensing and readying themselves to either kick him or run screaming from the house. She did neither.

"Well. Congratulations. Are you happy?"

On the surface the question was innocent, but it was a jab from her, directly for his sternum, so that the reply became a choke in his throat. He had to cough through it before finally speaking.

"I am happy to do what God wants me to do. Always."

She kissed her teeth and for a second regretted it when he raised an eyebrow. But only for a second.

"Don't say that to me. You know what I mean. I don't want your 'pastoral answer.'"

She made air quotes with stiff fingers, irritated by the stoic look he now wore.

"Glory, what should I say? That I'm not happy to be leaving? That I will be facing misery without you, my closest friend since childhood? What good would it do?"

"Your closest friend. Hmm."

She had been a fool after all, and who could blame her? There had seemed no harm in hoping something for herself; it had kept her from spending her days and nights at those headstones. Her mother and baby sister, side by side in a way no one ever wishes to see. She had shared her grief, her abject sadness with Paa Kweku at the time, and he had provided something more than a rock; he was an anchor for her so she did not get lost at sea. Now she felt as though she had concocted it all—the way he looked at her sometimes, the longing she felt, how it seemed to have grown since Bobo came along. He looked at her differently, yes, but it wasn't bad. It was deeper, somehow. Now he was taking it back, rescinding his affection, and she needed to know why.

"Is that why I am here? For you to tell me goodbye?"

"Ah! Why are you always so quick to the negative thing? I can't just tell you this big news and you be—"

"What? Happy for you? You didn't hear my congratulations?"

He scratched his head in irritation, leaning back into his chair, trying to gather a calmer demeanor at the same time.

"So, this is how it's going to be until I go? You're going to fight with me?"

"You picked a fight when you invited me here."

They were on their third cup of tea when Paa Kweku started up again.

"Will you miss me, then?"

Gloria scoffed into her cup, and then, seeing he was serious, earnest even, she rolled her eyes.

"Ask a better question, PK."

"There's no better question."

"One you don't already have the answer to, eh?"

The sharp edge of her voice took her by surprise. She was angrier than she had expected. She wanted to understand his news, to accept it so that she too could finally move on without him. A bead of sweat appeared suddenly on his temple, and he used a handkerchief to wipe it away. It was warm in the room, but he was used to it; they both were. He didn't sweat often, unless he was ingesting her pepper soup too quickly or he was nervous about something. Gloria noticed but chose to hold back her comments this time.

"I wanted us to start everything again, you know? To wipe the plate clean."

"Aye, you mean slate. Wipe the slate clean."

He chuckled as if she had made a joke.

"Even your corrections, I'm going to miss them."

She could suddenly no longer stand the sight of him.

"Merekɔ."

The switch to Twi was natural but strange between the two of them. They spoke English with each other often. He frowned as she followed her announcement to leave by standing up. She looked down at him with a challenge—he could let her leave or say whatever else it was he wanted to say. She expected he would say nothing, as he had done for so many years. The sun was beginning to set, and she was sure Aretha could use a break after having Bobo all day. Not that she was a problem; but Bobby's constant involvement and questions about every decision could make even the calmest person a little crazy. Even if his heart was in the right place.

She would not tell either of them about what had transpired. She was embarrassed by it and was not blind to the way Aretha looked at her sometimes, with pity and regret, as if Gloria did not know how much her heart was wasted on Paa Kweku. But secretly, Gloria did not feel it was a waste—she loved him because he was hers to love, no matter what happened between them. The rest was just logistics. Except now he was leaving, and the pain from that was unexpected. Her legs were trying to save her from more heartache, but she had not made it very far before he was standing too, blocking the door. She clutched her handbag to her side, waiting for him to speak, but nothing was happening.

"I can't do this for you, PK. This thing you want. Absolution? I don't know. Maybe you want me crying on my knees before you go? That one I won't do either."

He dabbed at his forehead again as she spoke. Exasperation marked his face.

"You and I, we don't have any more time left. In one month, I will be gone, Glory. Doesn't it mean anything to you?"

"You're asking me? Am I the one standing in *your* way?" She pointed an accusing finger at his chest, the tip of her nail grazing his cloth shirt. "Have I ever blocked you from doing what you want? Even if it means I am without?"

"Without what? Heh, without what?"

Paa Kweku let his words bolster him a little and he stepped toward her in a challenging way, just as she took a step back. Gloria was ready to really give it to him this time, to say out loud all the angry words she had swallowed with each tiny rejection. But they wouldn't come. Something was losing in her, deflating. She no longer had energy to fight. So, she stepped back further and sat down in her chair, turning away from him. Her face was forlorn and unmoving. Paa Kweku dropped his shoulders immediately, kneeling at her feet as if about to beg her for something. He put his hands together almost ready for prayer, but then she spoke again.

"You. I have been without you. And I'm tired, PK. So, maybe it's best that you're going."

She felt his hands in hers, lifting them gently from her lap. She felt the rough ridges of his palms with her index finger. Her thumb found the fine hairs that ran up the back of his wrists. He moved both hands up her arms, grazing them gently before gripping her biceps and pulling her up to standing with him. It was swift and she had a moment of lightheadedness as she looked into his eyes. He wasn't sweating anymore.

CHAPTER 3

London, Present

Whitney

You could still feel the night before on your skin. The bass, the pills, the twist of your mind on the dance floor. You had hoped your memories of the Tuck Shop had been exaggerated by intoxication. But the reality of it stuck to you when you woke up this morning. Your senses were dulled by the after effects, your mouth almost bone-dry. It was as if you had taken a paper towel and scraped it across your tongue one too many times, like when you were a kid, trying to remove the too-hot taste of the scotch bonnet pepper that infused Ma Gloria's light soup. You hated it back then, like so many things with heat. You made it to the kitchen after a quick shower, spooning organic instant coffee grounds into a cup, pouring the just-boiled water in after it, your tired eyes taking in the brown puddle with the almond aroma. The coffee always helped wake you up, slipping down your throat like morning salvation. You moved toward the small dining table and nudged your phone awake as you sat down, scrolling with finger and thumb, some cooking show on the TV in the background. Chantelle was showering and taking her sweet time. You were supposed to be at Sunday brunch already, and you felt like you had been up for hours. Your dreams, the bad ones, were tiring you out, causing you to emerge from your bed as if you'd gone ten rounds with someone much more athletic than you. You'd mentioned once having recurring nightmares as a child to Chantelle, when you first lived together and your menstrual cycles had collided, both of you huddled under a blanket on the sofa at midnight, restless, temporary insomniacs. You each talked about sleeping patterns, and then your memory of bad dreams slipped from your lips in a tired confession. She didn't say much, only that it sounded "tough" before voicing an open question about what the true meaning of nightmares was, for which neither of you had an answer.

You couldn't tell her now that they had returned and were rattling you harder than before, that they were still snippets of fear strung together in one long and nonsensical film in your mind. To admit it would have been more cause for concern. Chantelle was always quietly worrying about you even when she pretended not to, and you figured that it must be exhausting. But that's what it was to be close to someone. And in fact lately, you'd begun to wonder if you were too close; if your life would be easier if you weren't so attached to people, didn't feel so accountable to Chantelle specifically, so invested in her feelings about you, about everything.

You looked up to see that she was fully dressed, asking why you weren't wearing any shoes. Somehow your coffee had already gone cold, and time had drifted away from you again. You slunk away toward your bedroom to finish getting ready.

Your second caffeine hit was delivered by Hal at the Coco Cafe a few minutes' walk from the flat. You considered him kindly because he always kept the table in the corner free for you and didn't fuss when you only ordered a lemonade during a three-hour session of reviewing your finances and completing other tasks to keep your freelance masseuse work going. You'd recently begun a subscription service, which meant you had to keep on top of how many massages were paid up versus how many you were still to perform. Hal had even joked the other day about getting you to tip him in back rubs. You laughed along at the time but felt a line of fear tingle your spine when you thought about it later, alone. It was an exchange of services you felt uncomfortable with.

Ten years prior, you had just completed your masseuse training and you tried an effleurage technique on your first client. He told you loudly that you needed to "give it some more." You told yourself you were trying to begin gently, but really you were afraid of him, of the room, of what his presence implied. You had considered yourself a tamer of fears and ailments, that you would be a magic fix to everyone who needed it when they lay on your table, under your inspired hands. But this was only the beginning of that journey. And then he stalked in. Six foot something, bearded, hairy back and front; dark lines of DNA that covered milk-pale skin. Harry, he said. You immediately thought of *Harry and the Hendersons*—Ma Gloria loved that film—and bit your tongue. His eyes were wide, and he stared at you expectantly, already in a fluffy robe provided by the spa reception, waiting for you to instruct him on his next position in the room. You obliged and pointed awkwardly at the massage table, laden with fresh white towels carefully placed and leaving a gap for the face to sink into. You'd been told by the spa owner to anticipate needs, to make the client feel as though they might want for nothing, to embody the calm and relaxation they had been promised.

You moved away to turn the music up on the portable speaker you'd had to bring with you, and then you heard the clump of something on the floor. You turned back and your eyes flashed across his bare buttocks; the hair had decided not to bother him down there and instead stopped dead at his waist. You were watching his naked cheeks now, somehow noticing the finer hairs that trickled down into his crack and—you laughed. It burst from you, short but uncontrollable. You watched him whip back around, expecting anger on his face but finding that a smile had arrived instead—a chipped tooth as the opener, before all the other teeth with a slightly yellow hue joined in. You searched quickly for the extra towel and held it high up, fanned out in front of you so that it completely covered your mortified face.

"This is uh, just so, once you get on the table, I'll just put this, yep."

He seemed to understand, immediately climbing onto the table and placing his face in the hole. You lay the towel across him from the waist down, wondering faintly why he was already naked. It made your skin bristle, asking that question, but you pushed it down. This was a part of the job, they had told you. It was an intimate thing that everyone had different boundaries for; you just had to navigate that. You didn't learn until much later that you needed to know what yours were too; you needed to establish your own line that shouldn't be crossed.

But you were young and new to all of it. You'd landed the job because your college tutor had taken an interest in you, said you had a gift of sorts, that you might have found your "vocation." You had wanted to laugh then too; it sounded so mechanical, so tickboxy. Yet you let it make some sense to you—there was something about getting close to another person that couldn't be replicated when it came to guiding them into a soft feeling with your fingers and thumbs, or waking up aching muscles using tapotement. You excelled in class, practiced heavily, sent Ma Gloria to sleep proudly as you worked on your skill at home.

You considered yourself more than ready for the real world. So you took your tutor's glowing reference to a popular day spa in Kensal Rise and started the following week. You'd never had a real job before, never had to navigate the politics that come with simply working face-to-face with salaried strangers like yourself. You were amenable, though, shrinking when you needed to, joining in when it seemed safe to do so. You were inducted for a week, shadowing a senior massage therapist—Sandra—before it was time for your first client. You had gotten the room ready just so, taking note of each detail, from the choice of oils to the scent in the room and the music that would be playing.

You were going through the steps in your head, using the heel of your palm and the ridge of your thumb to glide across Harry's back, the oil slick and plentiful to also tame the lawn of hair that covered him practically head to toe. That was when he suggested you do more, go harder. You had missed a step, hadn't asked about the pressure, if it was okay. You felt like the complete novice that you were, tried to use your best calming voice to respond and let him know you'd heard him. You pressed harder, eventually moving to compressions, listening to him grunt approvingly. And then it was thirty minutes later and his time, your time, was up. You walked to the other side of the room and used some wet wipes to remove the oil from your hands. You would wash them later, once he had left.

"I hope it was okay. I'll leave you to get dressed. Just shout when you're done."

"No need."

He pushed himself up and off the table and swung his legs round so that he was sitting at the edge facing you momentarily. Then he stood, making no moves to grab the towel that was now bunched up beside him. You were stock-still, his height meaning his semi-erect penis was almost at your eye level. You wanted your head to twist away, to look anywhere else but there, to not witness the way his face was changing from mild amusement to pride. You felt something dripping on your trainers, right through the thin fabric. It took two more drips before you broke eye contact with him, before you noticed you had practically squeezed the wet wipe dry in your fist, the remaining liquid now just a gray blotch on your trainers. You heard him scoff, followed by the rustle of fabric from his robe, but you didn't look up again. You continued to stare at your shoes, focused, the scuffed edges and worn laces saving you from further confrontation. You heard the door click behind him as he left, and you stayed standing there for an unknown amount of time before Sandra knocked on the door, excited to know how your first client had gone.

"He was a looker, weren't he?"

She was buoyant as you let her into the room, your hands now dry from the antibacterial solution of the wipe. You still hadn't washed them, so you walked back over to the sink in the corner, turning on both taps, waiting for the warm combination to be right. She went into autopilot, throwing the used towel into the basket for you, turning down the music, clicking the lids back onto the oils, and lining them up in a neat row. You watched her from the side, pressing the soap dispenser over and over again until you were sure you could have taken a bubble bath with the amount you'd pumped out of it. You scrubbed like you had been taught, singing half of Whitney Houston's "Saving All My Love for You" before you were done with your two minutes of washing. Sandra waited patiently for you to finish, standing now in the corner of the room, where the fresh towels were stacked up. She watched you quietly as you dried your hands, her face giving nothing away.

"The first time's nerve-racking, I know. You'll be alright. He seemed happy, wanted to leave you a big tip. . . . You didn't—I mean, you only did what you've been taught, right?"

You looked up at her, a glimmer of recognition in her eyes at a thing you couldn't associate with the truth just yet. You wondered if you should be offended, or if she was just looking out for you. Maybe it was neither of those things, and you simply didn't understand.

"I forgot to ask if he was comfortable."

At the Coco Cafe, Chantelle was giving you another reason why she thought Hal was weird.

"He's always just standing too close, you know?" She had whispered it to you across the table out of his earshot, and you shrugged because it was eleven thirty in the morning and your brain still hadn't recovered enough from the night before to fully engage. Chantelle looked at you incredulously, and you realized that she was especially stunning today, with a full face of immaculate makeup. You sat across from her, your foundation hastily applied before you left the house, bits of your tightly coiled curls sure to come away in your hand if you ran your fingers through them one more time. You needed a trim. "Hmm, maybe he likes you," she said.

You shook your head, and she frowned like she didn't believe your disagreement, forcing you to push the accompanying sound out with effort.

"Nah."

"You're always smiling at him. He probably thinks you're interested."

"I'm friendly, that's all."

Chantelle burst out laughing and then saw that your face hadn't changed.

"You're many things, my sweet, but friendly? No."

"I'm nice! What do you mean?"

That eyebrow went up again. You were both just making words, saying very little. She chuckled and looked up at Hal, who was now behind the counter ringing up someone's takeaway order. Then she tipped her head to the side as if she were looking at an abstract painting, trying to make sense of it.

"I mean, he's not *my* cup of tea, but that don't mean he couldn't be yours. If you squint, he's kinda . . . cute?"

She grinned, but you couldn't even fake your enthusiasm. You hoped you were passing it off as a hangover. Chantelle leaned toward you. "So, Hal ain't it?" You shrugged again, aware that you weren't being great company, that Chantelle was doing a lot of the legwork. "Don't give the Bard any more thought. He was a loser."

You reached for your almost empty coffee cup in lieu of a reply, and she slid it away from your grip to her side of the table. You sighed.

"Yeah, but I fell for him. Doesn't say much about me."

"Except that he's still a loser, and you're not."

You both laughed quietly, even though it didn't feel real from either side. Hal arrived with brunch. For Chantelle, it was a poached egg and smashed avocado, with an assortment of spices and flourishes. You'd ordered scrambled eggs on toast. Hal had made a joke about the uncharacteristic simplicity of your order, and you'd explained just how hungover you were. His belly jiggled in rhythm with his thick beard as he laughed at your exaggerated-suffering face, and for a split second you wondered what it would feel like to tug at it while running a palm across his closely shaved head. Chantelle told you once that she thought he looked like Rick Ross had absorbed Common and then found himself on hard times. Your lemonade came out of your nose that day as you snorted through an ugly laugh in response. Now she looked at him with open disdain as he stood at the table for longer than she was comfortable with. But you felt differently about him. His eyes revealed an innocence that you recognized, and you wondered if he had a secret, a sad thing that was violating and crippling, making him open to the wrong people, inaccessible to the right ones. He smiled at you as if hearing your thoughts, and you focused your eyes back on your eggs. He moved on to other customers.

Afterward, you and Chantelle jumped onto the Tube heading toward Waterloo, to see her friend's band playing at a small music festival at the Southbank. You had told her that all you had wanted for your birthday was food and entertainment, but mostly food. She insisted this was a necessary stop, so you followed, reluctant and slightly distant. At moments throughout the day you felt you were watching yourself, existing just slightly outside of your own body. You hoped she didn't notice.

CHAPTER 4

Kumasi, 1995

Gloria

It had been many years since they had been together like this. Gloria had spent the better part of a decade trying not to think about that first time. Paa Kweku had returned from Ejisu after four years away, leaving as a sixteen-year-old with oily skin and heat rash, returning as a twenty-year-old man. Tall like his father had been, lean because of the seminary's strict diet. Strong because of the four years of manual labor the students were assigned, learning how to build and plaster and maneuver concrete with swiftness, in between countless hours of Bible study. They had both changed so much, and in that giddy state of youth, their reunion became something that cemented an already close connection. He hadn't known what to do with her body back then, and neither had she, but they tried to learn together. It was awkward and sweaty, and Gloria spent many nights afterward thinking about the curve of his back under her fingertips.

Almost ten years later, they knew each other better. Neither one was shy. There had been a few other men for Gloria during her nursing studies, before Bobo arrived, before responsibility became her full-time job. She suspected the same of Paa Kweku with other women, but they never discussed it. Now he lifted her dress over her head as if it were something he did every day. She unbuttoned his shirt just as she had imagined doing hundreds of times before. Even on his bed, there was no negotiation about who would go where. They flowed together like the tide, limbs tangled, lips on lips and shoulders and necks. It was slow, steady, and all-consuming. All affection and no hesitation. There was sweetness in the air afterward. Gloria tried to explain it—or understand it.

"What is this thing?"

Gloria leaned on her elbow, one side of her face resting in an upward palm so that she could look at him as he lay on his side, facing her. He smiled in a way that only she knew the meaning of.

"I don't know. But I know you, Glory. Just like you know me."

He ran a playful finger along the crook of her nose as he spoke, which caused her to chuckle and bat him away gently.

"Stop." She took his stray hand in hers and held his palm against her cheek. "Just this. This is all I want."

He wrapped his other arm around her bare waist and pulled her toward him. She buried her face in his chest, feeling the soft coils of hair tickle her nose. She did not want to move, to face anything that came after this thing they had put off for so long. She listened to him take a deep breath and then sigh, his arms still holding her tightly. She could feel the strain of his muscles as he squeezed her, and she felt her breathing muffled for a moment. She went to tap his back, to tell him he needed to ease off. But when her fingers connected with his skin, the sound was like a drum. They both jumped at the *BANGBANGBANG!* that intensified her tapping, quickly realizing it was his front door. A strained voice quickly followed. It was the driver, Prince.

"Pastor P! Please are you home? Something has happened at the Sarpongs! Pastor P? My God, hey!"

Paa Kweku sprang out of the bed and disappeared from the room. Gloria had shot up after him, listening to him struggle with the lock on the door after throwing his shirt back on with the khaki trousers that had been discarded when they entered his bedroom. He exchanged a few words with the driver once the door was opened, and Gloria heard her name once or twice. She was dressed by the time he returned to the room, the color drained from his face, the buttons on his shirt closed up incorrectly, so he looked lopsided.

"We need to go. There's been some kind of fight at the house. They're looking for you."

He had adopted his pastoral voice again. It was calm and level and only caused Gloria to panic more. Then she felt a new worry.

"Wait, did Prince see—"

"I told him to wait outside and take you. That you had only just arrived for a visit."

"Are you not coming?"

"I will follow. I need to make a phone call first."

They exchanged a look that meant different things to each of them. He looked down and squeezed her fingers, then brought them to his cheek this time.

"Just this."

She tried to smile, finding herself nodding instead. Then she left his house and greeted Prince. Climbing into the back of the car, she sat facing the front, refusing to look behind her.

The first thing Gloria saw when they arrived at the house were the crowds of people. Shapes shifted in the dark, the red gates of the compound wide open as people were standing around, talking, walking in and out, some wailing loudly. It was that sound particularly that caused her stomach to drop. Prince had said little to her beyond a greeting, even when she questioned him.

"Please, Ma, when we get home, please."

His voice was still strained as it had been at Paa Kweku's door, as if he had been shouting that whole time. Now he honked on his horn at regular intervals to disperse the peering crowd, who moved slowly to the side so that he could drive onto the grounds. As soon as he did, the guard, Kwame, jumped out of the security booth and went to close the gates behind them, but he was met with shouts of irritation and anger from the crowd—local neighbors who knew the Sarpong family well. Prince's car had barely come to a stop when Gloria jumped out and told Kwame to leave the gates as they were. Kwame nodded but did not return to the booth, holding place instead by the gates themselves, trying to take a mental picture of everyone who stood huddled together. They watched Gloria walk past them as she discovered the scene they were already familiar with.

No one had to tell her it was Bobby; she already knew. It was too dark to see the blood, but someone had covered him with a piece of cloth from the clothesline. Only his boots stuck out from underneath, as if it had been thrown over him carelessly. Coal and ash was scattered on the ground, still sending smoke signals up to anyone who hadn't heard the news yet. Viktor was sitting in the corner, hands out of sight, his shirt dirty and one side of his face still red from the ground. He stood out—the *obroni*—the only white man, almost ghostlike among the rest of the bodies around her who faded into the dark and revealed themselves at will. One of the dark figures was walking toward Gloria, and she froze for a second until he came into view under the single light in the entrance: a young police officer. He spoke to her in rapid Twi, adding a timbre to his voice that she recognized as fake—something to give him authority.

He explained that Viktor was cuffed while they waited for the military police. She asked if anyone else was hurt, her throat suddenly dry as she waited for an answer. Relief came when he confirmed that no, no one else had been hurt, that Aretha and "the little one" were inside the house. He asked if her father was around, and she realized she needed to telephone him. Paa Kweku arrived at that moment, walking through the crowd as it parted for him. He had spoken to Daddy, who had booked a flight home from Denmark. He would arrive in the morning.

She still hadn't seen Bobo or Aretha, and she hesitated. What would she say to them? How would she explain her absence this particular evening? And Bobby—what had happened to Bobby? The pieces were not there; no explanation had been given yet for why they were fighting in the first place. That's when she turned back to Viktor. He had been sitting still, head hanging like a scolded dog since she had entered the compound. He would not look at her—or at anyone. He stared at the floor. The man who had just killed Bobo's father.

CHAPTER 5

London, Present

Whitney

You had been leaning against a pillar for too long as you waited for Chantelle, and now your shoulder buzzed with pins and needles. You had only just reentered the lobby of the Southbank Centre, its artsy community atmosphere airy and colorful. The band's music had not quite been your cup of tea, but it had an edge to it that you could appreciate. Still, you breathed easier away from it, and seconds later Chantelle had spotted someone else she knew waiting in the toilet queue and stopped to chat with them. You didn't know the woman personally; her appearance was vague, almost forgettable. But you wondered how many times Chantelle had frequented the Southbank Centre without you, and your stomach fluttered with annoyance at the thought. It had always been a place you'd visited together; the second home of your friendship because of all the afternoons and evenings spent drinking, laughing, and feigning interest at art installations neither of you understood. You looked around, unsure if you still belonged to this crowd, to the same people willing to pay too much for a brownie, perusing the free art lining various stands or drinking mediocre wine in front of a good view of the river Thames. If you were honest with yourself, you'd acknowledge that you too had visited the place without her once or twice, but you always went alone. You were drawn to it; a place to be with people without having to *be* with them, to feel meaningfully guided by the creativity that surrounded you, with the option of walking toward the core of the city and getting lost in it at a moment's notice.

Chantelle finally emerged from the line of people, and you felt a cold snapback to the present.

"She knows how to chat, that one." It took you a second too long to realize she was talking to you, as if the words had not hit your brain yet. "What d'you think of the band?"

"Yeah, they were cool."

"Really?"

She was looking at you suddenly with a face full of doubt, like you had said something ridiculous. Something had been in the air since brunch, since you had tentatively brought up Paris after the Bard conversation. Chantelle had swiped the topic away, as if your mention of him was an argument waiting to happen. Perhaps it was. But now something sharp was between you, piercing friendship clouds.

"Can we go?"

You hadn't meant to sound impatient, eager suddenly to leave a place that was so familiar, but you were feeling funny around crowds now, wary of new bodies that you didn't have command of. A new band had taken the stage downstairs, and you stood at the top of the steps looking into blank space, listening for the first sound of a chord, some indication of genre. You wanted it to matter suddenly, to have your interest piqued, to be distracted by someone else's story in the music. And you felt like you were widening the gap between you and Chantelle with every missed word, unsaid apology, and white lie. If you looked behind you, you were certain you might find it all gathered there at your feet; if only you could pick these bits of your friendship up and put them back into place. But the bending felt too hard sometimes, and you couldn't work out exactly why.

You headed down the steps and Chantelle followed, looping her arm into yours easily, squeezing your forearm a little as you walked. You felt yourself getting more rigid on the inside. You wanted to disentangle yourself from all feelings. You wanted an escape. But she kept her arm cradled into yours as if she were afraid that you really might let go and run free, straight into the Thames. What a thought.

You spotted the exit you wanted and reached toward the handle on the glass door, releasing yourself from Chantelle to pull it open energetically. The call of seagulls hit your ears, along with the fresh air, seconds before you collided with someone marching through the doors from the other side at that same moment. You caught a blur of deep brown curls and a Paco Rabanne scent as Paris's shoulder hit yours and you rebounded off each other in confusion. Chantelle had been walking closely behind you and jumped out of the way before she got caught up in the crash. But Paris grabbed you at the last second, stopping you both from falling, causing you instead to twirl around as if you were dancing with each other. You found your balance and stepped backward away from him. You felt slightly dazed, reflexively rubbing the arm he had hit while he let out a big belly laugh, bending forward and pressing his palms into his thighs to slow the curdles of laughter coming from his throat. Chantelle glanced at you with an embarrassed look as he stood up straight finally, wiping at his eyes. Then he looked past you at Chantelle, stepping toward her and pulling her into his arms. She looked uncomfortable but then immediately relaxed into the hug as if she had been expecting him.

"Finally I find you! How are you doing?"

"I'm—we're good. When did you get back from Lyon?"

Chantelle tried to increase the gap between them slightly as she spoke, but Paris held firmly onto her waist, twisting his body so that there was only a small triangle of space between them.

"This morning! I make it to the flat, but you're not there, then I use that app thingy *et voilà*! So we can go for lunch now?"

"What, did you put a tracker on her or something?"

The words came from you, but you looked around as if they hadn't. Paris's face switched so quickly into a severe question that you felt awkward bubbles of laughter trying to get out of your throat, attempting to place a balm on the moment. He turned to look at you like it was the first time and not the one hundredth since he and Chantelle had gotten together. His arm never dropped from Chantelle's waist, but he locked eyes with you, and that coldness you thought you had shaken earlier made a sudden return.

"Oh please! It's me that's got a tracker on him. He's just tryna get the upper hand."

Chantelle spoke at volume suddenly and laughed in Paris's direction as if he were in on the joke. He flashed her a smile and finally stepped away, sliding his fingers down her waist and finding her hand instead. All the while he kept you in his sights, his face changing softly into what you imagined was supposed to be concern.

"I am sorry, Whit-er-ney. Did I hurt you?"

He was gesturing with his free hand toward your shoulder, as if he intended to physically examine it himself. You fought the urge to step back further by standing your ground, shaking your head.

"No, I'm okay, I'm good."

He put his hand to his chest as if your words brought him great relief, and you noted how all his movements felt melodramatic and over-practiced. Just as swiftly, he was turning back to Chantelle, looking at her impatiently as if she were running late for the lunch date he had only just suggested.

"I told you, P. It's Whit's birthday today. We're doing our own thing. But I'll come check you later."

She squeezed his hand and he looked surprised again, but this time with a line of disappointment. He wasn't used to not getting his way. You knew that about him at least. You gave him a cursory wave goodbye before finally making it to the other side of the exit, not waiting for a response.

The invisible line between you and Paris had been drawn long ago for reasons that piled up every time you were forced to engage with him. You never properly spoke about it with Chantelle, believing she would see it when she was ready to. Or perhaps, as you'd begun to suspect, there were things between them that you would never be privy to, so it might always be this way when it came to him. You refused to even call him by his real name—assigning him instead the nickname of his hometown after their first date when you were certain they wouldn't last. Everyone had taken it at face value as if it were a term of endearment, and now he wore the moniker of "Paris" proudly. So, you continued to hide your secret hope that they might falter as a couple, burying it three-years-deep under your guilt at not being a more supportive friend.

You watched them through the window as Chantelle was saying her goodbyes. You could never tell when seeing them like this, whether they were fighting or sharing words of passion. Perhaps it was one and the same, and you just didn't get it.

Once on a night of too much drinking, Chantelle had suggested that maybe love had to feel like a battle, to make it worth fighting for. You told her that it was the dumbest thing you'd ever heard, and she laughed until there were tears.

CHAPTER 6

Kumasi, 1995

Aretha

Aretha was not the squeamish type. She even considered herself courageous at times. Which was why she didn't understand the numbness that had taken over her body since she had reclaimed Whitney from the ground, crying and covering her face with tiny hands, her nightdress a dusty mess. Aretha didn't know why she would wander outside so late at night, except perhaps because she had heard her father's voice. After one or two drinks of beer, Bobby tended to hum tunes from his childhood in Copenhagen, songs that no one in the house recognized but that soon became a familiar soundtrack for the evenings. Whitney was always spellbound by the melodies, finding him wherever he was in the house, sometimes waking up when she heard him. Aretha would chuckle at his pied piper powers, the ones that reached beyond Whitney to everyone in the house. He was a walking, talking heart of a man. Not particularly tall in stature, but his joyful energy felt large. So to see him cut down, his body quaking almost as if the earth itself were breaking apart beneath him, Aretha could not stand it. She could see him in her mind's eye as she stood over him, frozen in place and clutching Whitney, wanting to run but unable to take her eyes away from him. All she could focus on were his hands, covered in his own blood as he grasped his stomach, trying to stop his own life from leaving him. And briefly Aretha's eyes went to the other man, to Viktor lying on his back too, a few feet away but breathing strong, his hands by his sides, trying to catch his breath with his own eyes shut tight. Unwilling to face what he had done.

The scream that escaped Aretha came unbidden, shocking herself and eventually those who appeared around her. The pitch of it curdled blood, and she did not stop until people began to bang on the gates and the security guard had run toward the commotion. She glimpsed Maame Serwaa somewhere nearby, but after that, things became a blur. In sudden silence Aretha walked back into the house as shadows of people began to move around her. She heard the distant blare of a siren, something like police. She could not take it all in. Something in her switched off. Her thoughts became ordered again, and she moved into autopilot. She called for Maame Serwaa.

"Bring warm water. I want to bath Whitney again."

Aretha tried not to notice the furtive glances Maame Serwaa was giving toward the open door that led back outside. Her face was full of worry at the commotion that was happening, but she nodded curtly and disappeared through another door in the opposite direction. Aretha began to bounce Whitney in her arms. Though already three years old, she still liked to be held from time to time. Ordinarily she would be running around, and at hearing the word "bath" would have wriggled out of Aretha's arms to be chased, giggling in what always felt like a fun game. But Whitney was quiet, holding on tightly to Aretha, her face buried in Aretha's small chest. *Gloria has a better bosom*, Aretha thought. She compared herself too often to her older sister. Gloria just took to things more easily; she adapted quickly and took control of a situation. Aretha always felt as if she were trailing behind, still trying to find her feet, figure out what it meant to be a person in the world. Whitney's arrival had forced her to reassess, to step up and support Gloria in a way she hadn't needed to before. She had even deferred her plans for the military. It had become a duty, and she understood the parameters of what that meant.

Aretha was comfortable when there was a plan in place. So, what to do now? When everything had gone awry and sadness hung in the air? And Whitney, already without her first mother, and now her father. What could be made from that?

Aretha looked down at Whitney, who was still cradled in her arms. She was sniffling, a small sound piercing through the hard shell Aretha had been trying to form around her heart, so that she could do what needed to be done and not think about the way Bobby lay there, staring up at the night sky, life ebbing away. Why hadn't she noticed sooner? Why hadn't she stayed with him as his soul left the earth, one last time? Didn't she owe him that much?

Aretha was very discerning when it came to making friends, and Bobby had not been exempt from her disregard. But he was persistent. Most of the time she was good on her own, always had been. People assumed that, because she was between two sisters, she was always surrounded by people, laughter, camaraderie. But she didn't see it that way. For Aretha, a lot of it was just noise. She was out of step with the two of them—Tina had flights of fancy about getting into a university abroad, hoping to enter medical school and become a surgeon. Gloria had an equal desire to help, "to set the world to rights," as she used to say, putting on her best British accent when she talked about her nursing training. Aretha would laugh at them both when she was alone.

No manner of entering the health-care world was going to bring back their mother. At least Aretha knew that.

She didn't entertain the imagined ways of things like they did. She chose to study business administration because it made sense, and it would propel her forward when she officially enlisted in the Ghanaian Armed Forces. She was driven, just like the Sergeant had been when he had joined. She wanted to be the daughter who lived up to what he had worked hard to build. Maybe her singular focus sometimes came across as self-involved, even dismissive in her delivery, but that was how she had to be if she wanted to succeed. Direct, real, unafraid of things that others might be. She already knew what it was to hold back parts of herself, so sometimes her words were not quiet; they were loud, intrusive things that revealed to others what they were too afraid to see in themselves. She was used to hearing that she was too much. Or not enough of what someone else wanted.

So she was skeptical when Bobby would call on her to share a meal or show him where to buy the best fruit, to get cloth made to send to his mother in Copenhagen, or some other such thing needed to survive a new life in Ghana. He rarely asked Gloria to help him; she was a mother in the house, and he treated her as such. But with Aretha, he made it clear that growing up as an only child, he saw her as the sister he never had because they were so close in age, and they shared a love of languages and travel—even if she talked about it more than she had yet experienced. She also knew that he needed all the friends he could get since moving from Copenhagen and since losing Tina. They had all needed something since she had passed.

"Heh! Fufu *again*? You want the look of a wealthy man, eh?"

Bobby had been unperturbed by Aretha's words almost a year earlier. Instead, he patted his gently protruding belly and shook his head, laughing. They could both hear Maame Serwaa outside behind the kitchen, pounding the cassava and plantain into their combined elastic form to eventually become a substantial meal, her visiting little brother Yaw outside, in charge of pushing his small palms against the ball to help shape it, retracting his fingers swiftly before the mortar came down again. The *tak tak tak* of it fell in step with the fan above them every so often, mimicking the opening of some new Highlife song. Aretha had found Bobby in the living room, seated comfortably on one of the chairs, Whitney on the floor at his feet, enthralled by a new doll he had brought her from Accra. Aretha plonked herself down beside him in a tiresome way, and they watched Whitney for a few silent minutes.

"My mum never makes it. Fufu, I mean. She hates it." Bobby spoke wistfully and Aretha sat back, listening. "The first time I had it was at my one other Ghanaian friend's house, as a kid. I told her afterward, I said, 'Mummy, this one is my favorite now. Can you make it?' but she refused."

"Well, maybe she didn't know how. Me, I won't make something that I cannot also enjoy."

"You lie. You make gari for Bobo all the time, and I've never seen you eat it."

"That's different—Whitney is a child." Bobby held out a palm to her as if she had just made his point, and Aretha huffed and tossed her head back in annoyance, turning her face away so as to hide the smile trying to crack across it. "Anyway, when are you leaving?"

She tried to ask it softly, because she didn't want him to think he wasn't wanted, but he had a way of disrupting Whitney's routine with his bimonthly visits. He had only been able to find work in Accra when he had first arrived in Ghana, the day after Tina had died. So every few weeks he would sit on the bus to Kumasi, traveling the 150 or so miles to stay for a weekend and spend time with Whitney, before returning to the bustle of the city again. But a schedule was important to Aretha, and that was why this arrangement—of her and Gloria and sometimes Bobby—made sense. She made herself available at specific times per Gloria's requests, Gloria fancied herself the glue holding Whitney's life together, and Bobby could be the fun one if he wanted. But lately he had been trying to get more involved than was needed—asking about what Whitney was eating, what time she was sleeping, what other parts of Kumasi she had not seen yet. He insisted he wanted her to know and understand her surroundings, her history, to know where she came from. He had even begun talking about taking her to Copenhagen to meet her grandmother, but Gloria was so strongly against her traveling so young, that Aretha didn't even open her mouth to referee on that one.

"I'll head back tomorrow, God willing. But then I won't be back until next month."

Aretha felt her stomach drop. Despite the effects on Whitney's routine, the house looked forward to Bobby's visits. And Aretha had to admit she felt a little lonely in those days without him. Gloria was either working at the hospital or busying herself at church when she wasn't taking care of Whitney. The family, what they had left, didn't sit together or spend time in the same way as before. And Tina had been a buffer too, the thing that they could all agree on. But Aretha and Gloria didn't understand each other, not really. And since Whitney's arrival, they had united only over her care. That was all. They couldn't even agree to call her the same name.

Bobby took over as the mediator—it came naturally to him— and Aretha allowed him to do that. It made for an easier life in the long run, even if it meant she had to listen to all of *his* opinions on who Whitney should and should not be. These things irritated Aretha but not enough to not be grateful for his company when he was around. He at least took the time to ask her about herself.

He was still looking down at Whitney, but Aretha knew he was waiting for her reaction. She tried to focus her gaze on the child too, hoping it would settle her stomach and stop the anxiety that was trying to make its presence known. Whitney cooed and gently stroked the doll's hair, making it dance around and whispering instructions into its ears.

"Is that not too long for Whitney to go without seeing you?"

"Ah you'll miss me too much, eh?"

"You wish, *little* brother."

"Well, you're the first to hear it—I got a new job here in Kumasi. So, soon I will be here *all* the time, just enough for you to get really sick of me, right?"

He gave her a gentle nudge of his elbow and she revealed her smile this time.

"So the Sergeant finally arranged it? That's good news, bro."

"Actually, I found this one myself, with Danida, but his reference didn't hurt at all. Anyway, enough about me. What's going on with that friend of yours—that one," He clicked his fingers trying to remember the name that had briefly escaped him, "Mabel! Is she still being funny with you?"

Aretha tried to hold the smile on her face but felt it falter.

"It will pass. It always does."

"Then you're not worried about it anymore?"

"When did I say I was worried? She's just an emotional woman, that's all. She's always been that way."

"Ah, I see."

"You see what?"

Aretha frowned at him, the knots of skin above her eyebrows

scrunching closer together the longer she waited for his answer. Bobby shrugged before speaking again.

"There are too many emotions flying around. That's why you're always fighting with this girl."

Aretha paused for a second and then kissed her teeth.

"Of course you, a man, would think that the only reason women fight is because they are just emotional."

"It was *you* who said she was emotional!"

"Listen. I am not a robot. But I also don't need to share every little thing I am feeling every second. I don't expect those things from her, and she has a lot of . . . life happening too. She always wants more from me than I can give."

"As a friend?"

Aretha opened her mouth to respond but seeing Bobby's face, the openness he wore, his words considered and never quite as naive as he seemed, she clenched her teeth together and tried to turn toward smiling instead. Silence was better here. Bobby continued to watch her until they were both pulled out of the moment by a small voice down below.

"Daddydaddydaddydaddydad—"

"Yes, Bobo, what is it?"

"Refa wants water, please."

Aretha pointed at herself and looked down at Whitney.

"*Auntie* Aretha nsuo, Whitney."

But Whitney shook her head, obviously annoyed. She pointed at her doll.

"No, Refa nsuo, *medase*."

Whitney's Twi "thank you" caused Bobby and Aretha to lock eyes and burst into laughter.

"Heh! So the doll Aretha is just as demanding as the real one." Bobby stood up to obey his daughter's command. Aretha stayed

seated, now that her legs were the doll's catwalk, as decided by
Whitney suddenly. Bobby let his smile linger, watching them.
"Thank you." He said it to the room, to no one in particular, and
Aretha watched him leave, puzzled by it.

Sleep came to Aretha easily more often than not. Most days she was
in bed by nine, awake at four for a morning walk. She had managed
to turn Whitney onto her daily routine quickly, sometimes taking
her as a baby on her back, the cloth wrapped comfortably around her
waist so as not to impede her quick pace. Whitney was content with
it too, and Aretha knew Gloria was grateful for it, though she never
said it. Aretha fashioned her whole life around being on time, around
schedule, precision, things that could be relied upon when nothing
else could. So her frustration was high at still not being asleep at ten
thirty, demonstrated through the constant shake of her left leg in the
bed, under the thin blanket she should have been snoozing beneath.
Perhaps she had been naive to expect rest to visit her, on this night in
particular. It had not been simple to even make it into her bedroom,
to close the door behind her, to stand alone for a moment and gulp
back the sobs that had been threatening to expose her all evening.

It was Gloria's return to the house that had done it, that had
moved this invisible lump of pain from Aretha's stomach up to her
chest, her sternum, her throat, and soon her mouth. It always ended
up being her tongue that carried the weight of things, throwing
words out with such a force that unsuspecting passers-by were sure
to get hit. And sisters.

"He's dead, and you were not here."

Aretha had answered a question of Gloria's. It was the only response she had, no matter what the question might have been. Gloria looked at her as if Aretha had grown four heads, one for all the
ways she could be cruel.

"I was—I don't understand. Aretha, what is this? What happened?"

Gloria was standing behind her asking searching questions, while Aretha stayed seated at the dining table, holding Whitney who had fallen asleep in her arms. The child was heavy, warm, and breathing rapidly into her chest, her life force flowing into Aretha's own. It was something like love but much bigger and harder to label—a flourishing thing that sustained Aretha—and her thoughts played on like this until Gloria's presence cut through, as she placed a rough hand on Aretha's shoulder, attempting to shake her gently but only causing Aretha to flinch away dramatically. She shot up quickly, stirring Whitney, and Gloria's eyes traveled to her arms when she realized that she was still holding the child. Aretha practically hissed at her.

"You were not here. Where were you?"

"I was only with PK. We were just—"

"You were enjoying your life, eh, Glory? Must be nice."

"Hey!"

Gloria's voice took on that deep trembling tone, the one that appeared rarely, when she wanted to remind everyone in the room that she was the eldest, that she was the reason for everything being as it is. And so, Aretha felt right in blaming her for being absent for something she could never have stopped. No one could have. She scowled at Gloria, baring her teeth as she watched Gloria's own face change in sync. Both squared off, their emotions already shattered into shards of hurt to throw at each other. It was Maame Serwaa who inadvertently stopped any further bloodshed happening.

"Please Ma, Bobo's water is ready for bathing."

Gloria whipped round at Maame Serwaa, but seeing that she wasn't the enemy her eyes were searching for, she relaxed. Like most who had grown up in the house, Maame Serwaa had already seen all the sisters at their worst. This was not new. And perhaps that was the saddest part of it.

"She's asleep. Just take her to bed, please."

Maame Serwaa nodded at Gloria, gently peeling Whitney away from Aretha, who didn't resist but held the toddler a few seconds longer before releasing her. Then she turned to Gloria, all the energy suddenly drained from her, the little body taking all the fire with her into Maame Serwaa's arms. Aretha sank back into the dining chair she had pulled out roughly, placing both hands on her cheeks, staring at Gloria as she pulled out a seat opposite her.

"He's gone. He's gone-o, he's gone. He's gone-o, he's—"

Gloria jumped forward to wrap both arms around Aretha, to stop her from shaking the table any further, to rock with her as they let their tears spill for a few minutes as her speech turned into a cry and then a song, until it felt like silence had fallen over the whole house except in that room.

CHAPTER 7

London, Present

Whitney

Chantelle liked to take her time with a cigarette. She enjoyed watching the circles she made with her O-shaped mouth after every puff, the vapor wafting up in wisps above her head, into the atmosphere, disappearing into the clouds. She took in deeper and deeper breaths as you stood on the Golden Jubilee Bridge, until the cigarette disappeared from her fingers as if it had not been there in the first place. In the last few weeks, you'd caught yourself watching her, trying to figure something out, the answer to an unknown question hovering around your five years of friendship.

More than a handful of years earlier, you had spent a week interviewing housemates, but none had felt right.

"You're too particular."

Ma Gloria had told you this over the phone when you updated her on the failings of your search.

"Other people aren't particular enough."

You were pleased with the quickness of your reply. And you knew your landlady was happy to give you free rein because you paid your bills on time and kept the place clean. But her patience only stretched so far. You had interviewed three potential flatmates that morning, all of them self-labeling as "quirky," "a clean freak," or "easy breezy." You were about ready to give up completely and let your landlady choose when Chantelle arrived. She floated into the flat as if she'd been there before, greeting you just after you'd finished off the Madeira cake Ma Gloria had given you: a leftover from an elderly church member's funeral. You had said you would attend the farewell service but canceled at the last minute. Something about showing up felt false—a platitude you woke up to that morning without the energy for. It was on your mind and inevitably spilled into your conversation with Chantelle when she mentioned recently losing an uncle. You ended up talking about it, about the uncomfortableness that followed you when you stepped into those funeral spaces, often in a hired-out school hall somewhere with faces you recognized vaguely as Ma Gloria's church family. Black, white, and red kente cloth splashed around the room in the shape of people. You moved through these spaces as if you were ready to leave at any moment, your coat never too far away. Eventually, you would soothe your anxious hands by heading to the kitchen, offering to help serve food to other guests, hiding behind a plastic apron and no-name aunties barking orders at you. It was oddly comforting being there, being useful. It made sense to you. But you hadn't turned up this time, to Ma Gloria's disappointment. She reflected her feelings back to you when you went to your childhood home in Golders Green to receive the cake wrapped in foil.

"It's not something to be afraid of, you know."

You had frowned at Ma Gloria, not completely listening as you sliced the cake, wanting to taste it before you took it, to make sure it was worth the transportation.

"Afraid of what, cake?"

You scoffed at your own joke, randomly placed, uncalled for, as you would have realized if you'd been paying proper attention.

"No, Bobo. Death."

You turned to look at her, hearing the reverberation of your life-long nickname followed by a word that felt like a cold splash of water in your face. Nothing else was said afterward that you can recall, only a look exchanged.

You didn't share that part of the story with Chantelle, though she had been easy to talk to during that first meeting: laughing at your jokes and quips, ones you'd been delivering confidently to each new prospective housemate all day to see how they would react. You had the script down by that point, and you watched curiously as she leaned toward you from across the room as if you already had years of friendship behind you, rather than ahead. But her responses to your monologues had been different; she pulled the conversation toward the deeper things, like death and family, and then back out toward working life, so that you were gently skimming the surface of meaningful topics.

"So, you feel people up for a living?"

Chantelle grinned as she said it, cautiously though, unsure if you would accept the joke or take it too seriously. You laughed.

"That's not what a massage therapist does . . . I mean it is! But less creepy than that."

"Okay, so what is it *exactly* then?"

Her words echoed like a challenge.

"It's just another way of giving people a bit of relief, a break when things have gotten so hard that they physically show up on your body."

"And you like it? I mean, I dunno, oil and strangers? That's just too much for me. Freaks me out thinking about it."

"Yeah, I get that. For me, though, being in service sort of connects me to people. And it's different because they've asked for it, given me permission to do it . . ."

You trailed off because you'd never described it like that before, not out loud anyway. But Chantelle tipped her head to the side as you spoke, her eyes widening slightly at receiving this information, this other perspective. You got the sense she liked to be challenged, only appearing stubborn to those who didn't have the patience to wait for her, to go a little deeper. You told her the room was hers if she wanted it, and she accepted on the spot. You knew you'd be friends before you really knew each other. She was the push to your pull, opposite but complementary.

You looked back out across the bridge, leaning over the edge slightly, tourists littered around you, stopping every ten seconds to take photos. Chantelle stood beside you, no longer surrounded by smoke, mints on her tongue to remove the tobacco taste. She whispered "Happy bert-day" into your ear and then pulled you onward to your next stop.

It was already late afternoon, and you both entered the restaurant with your stomachs growling. You'd picked a place in the middle of Soho with Neapolitan food on the menu and dance music splashing into the room, drowning out the conversation. Except that it was only five thirty, and you were already reconsidering your dining choice, trying to decide if it was too late to leave and find a better, quieter restaurant. But Chantelle was looking at you and reading your mind with impatience.

"We literally just got here. You wanted gnocchi, Whit. We're having gnocchi." You stared at her, wondering if she was angry at you or the restaurant DJ. Or maybe she was joking? You decided on the latter and tried for an overly dramatic sigh. "You know what, it's *your* birthday. We can leave if you want?"

Her voice quivered slightly. You tried to laugh it off, waving away her concerns with your hand. You weren't even big on birthdays, but you'd had numerous people say that this was the one you *had* to celebrate, so you let their excitement infect you until you too were excited. When you were a kid, you would jump out of bed the morning of your birthday and stare into the mirror on your wardrobe door. Had you grown taller? Maybe your hair was thicker? Or your fingers, were they longer? Something had to have changed, to mark another year of your life, otherwise what was the point? You found yourself again, at thirty, investigating your hands, wondering if you'd finally see the changing of time. Instead, it was marked in Chantelle's face and all the things she knew about you.

She scrolled for a minute or so on her phone, then looked up to see that you were looking at her. She gave you a public smile as if you were a stranger. When she glanced back down at her phone, her eyes lit up.

"Caine is going to that place in Shoreditch, the one that plays "Pony" at least ten times a night. You wanna go later?"

You felt confused. Why was she mentioning her dealer? You took a second to breathe, to try not to be immediately angry at what she was really asking you.

"So, Paris is gonna be there, then?"

She hesitated. You recorded that pause in your mind for later.

"It's not a big deal, Whit, come on. There'll be people there that you *do* like."

"I thought we were going to the Prince Charles? For that showing of *Labyrinth*?"

"Ugh, you know that film is a lot for me. His trousers are too tight, man."

It was funny and you both knew it, but neither of you laughed, and you thought you tasted iron in your mouth.

"If you weren't into it, why didn't you just say?"

"It's your birthday, not mine."

You felt frustration cross your brow. You'd eaten too many

breadsticks already without ordering anything else, and now you could see the waitress on the edge of your periphery, pen ready so that she could do her job, if only you didn't keep avoiding her eye. Chantelle was still staring at you, waiting for you to let her off the hook so she could go meet Paris, with or without you.

"It's cool. You go hang with Caine and—whoever. I'll go to the Prince Charles on my own. Sorted."

"I'm not letting you go sit in a nasty old cinema in the middle of the night by yourself."

She grimaced at the thought.

"It's fine. And I won't be alone; Jak will probably be there."

Chantelle nodded but said nothing more, the matter supposedly resolved.

CHAPTER 8

Kumasi, 1995

Aretha

Morning arrived without hesitation. There was only the crowing of cockerels in the distance and, later, the bleat of wandering goats traversing their own paths, shared with early morning drivers navigating big wheels along the mountain-like rockiness of the red ground, searching hopefully for smoother lanes on concrete roads that might get them to work faster. Aretha lay still among all of it, only listening. If she didn't move, didn't show life as the sun shone boldly through thin curtains, then perhaps time too would stop. And if she closed her eyes fully, maybe she could muster the power to reverse it, to undo yesterday, the party, the fight, the anger of men, all of it.

She had not slept at all, and she knew the day was only going to get more exhausting. She considered hiding in her room, but that only conjured memories of Tina, who regularly used Aretha's bed and bookcase to indulge her quiet time, especially when chores needed to be done.

She did not want to think about what Tina would have made of the day Bobby died. Aretha suspected they had been in love, though Tina never told her that outright. They did not often share

that kind of thing, but being close in age, they did move toward de-
veloping a friendship when they were still teenagers. Tina at thirteen looked up to her fifteen-year-old sister and did well at trying
to be her shadow. Aretha pretended that it irritated her, but she
looked for Tina when school was over, made sure they were side by
side on the walk back home. These were the obligations of having
their remaining parent regularly working out of the country; each
of the sisters was responsible for the one that came after. And then
there had been one day, a Friday afternoon when Tina was to be at
choir practice and would be brought home by the driver, Prince.
So, Aretha walked home with her best friend Mabel instead.

"You'll really travel to the US this time? Or is this another
Anansesem?"

"I did not make it up last time. The trip was just canceled,
Adwoa."

Mabel always emphasized Aretha's day name—given because of
her Monday birth and assumed peaceful nature—like it was something special, a thing to be handled delicately. Aretha shrugged as
if she still didn't believe Mabel. When they had been younger, in
primary class, Mabel had gotten a reputation for telling tall tales.
A growth spurt in Class 5 had also meant she towered over everyone with her new, long, spindly limbs—the same ones that would
become the envy of other girls when they came into their teens. At
the time, it added to her tongue that was quick to fib, earning her
the nickname Ananse. Even at fifteen, she couldn't shake the remnants of having an active imagination as a child.

"Anyway, America is okay. It's cold in Boston though. You'll have
to buy a scarf and hat and wear those puffy gloves for warmth, I'm
telling you."

"*Adwoa?* What do you know about America, really? You've
never been!"

Mabel threw her head back in laughter at her friend's indignant words, the confidence she always spoke with, especially about things she had never experienced herself.

"My father has told me."

It was all Aretha felt needed to be said to prove she knew what she was talking about. Mabel shook her head as they walked, squinting briefly as the sun caught her eye.

"It's warm there now, my cousin has told *me*, because it is spring. Ooh, I'm going to eat so many chocolate eggs for Easter! Shall I bring you some back?"

Aretha shrugged, adjusting her backpack. Her mind felt cloudy suddenly, gray even.

"I'm getting coconut. You want?"

They had stopped on the corner where the freshest coconut was sold. It was a regular stop of theirs when Tina wasn't trailing behind, unable to keep up with the longer strides of her older sister.

"I'll just have the meat."

Aretha nodded and relayed the message to the fruit seller, who had already stuck a straw into the green geometrically cut shape of the fruit, pocketing the money that Aretha handed him quickly, turning back to his paper as if the two girls were no longer there. Aretha sipped the cool, sweet liquid before passing it back to the seller. He took the makeshift cup, used a small knife to extricate the meat into a piece of his newspaper, and handed it to Mabel. She began to chew, offering a piece to Aretha, who shook her head again and quickened her pace toward home, so that Mabel had to skip suddenly to keep up.

"What should I bring you, if you don't want chocolate? Some American candy instead? I know you don't have a sweet tooth like me, but I'll bring some anyway."

Mabel's voice had taken on a soft lilt, as if trying to endear

Aretha back into the conversation, noticing that her mood had changed.

"I don't want anything. The Sergeant brings things all the time. It's not special anymore. When will you come back?"

Aretha tried to ask it in a nonchalant way, even though she was poised to record the exact date and time of Mabel's return.

"I will find something to bring that you'll like. You know I'm good with presents!"

Aretha stopped in her tracks and turned to Mabel, who walked ahead a little further before realizing Aretha wasn't beside her anymore.

"You're coming back, yes?"

The words sounded hard coming out of Aretha's mouth, but the conversation was suddenly important, and there was no time to soften things. Mabel looked at the ground, stuffing another piece of coconut in her mouth, buying some time before having to deliver an answer.

"I am but . . . *Adwoa*, I don't really know. Mommy is talking about looking at private schools there, because you know I want to study law eventually and she wants to give me the best chance and so it might make sense if I am there to finish high school, you know? It won't be forever, and it's not yet decided . . ."

Mabel's words were running into themselves, into one simple truth. Aretha's best friend was leaving her all alone. She swallowed down the thought, knowing she would let it digest in its own time. For now, she had to protect herself from its impact.

"Well, it's not a surprise. You want to move there, don't you?"

Mabel's face creased for a moment, as if Aretha had her hand raised, ready to physically slap her, though both were only standing on the road with their hands by their sides, their uniforms slightly crumpled from the day on their bodies. Neither was sure why they both suddenly felt a lot hotter than before.

"I am only excited to visit. It won't be the same without you."

Mabel put her hand out and Aretha took it, like she always did. They stared at each other, not saying anything for a while. No one else was on the road then, so Mabel moved closer to Aretha until they were eye to eye. There was only the distant honking of cars in traffic from the main road and someone with their radio on at full volume, Kojo Antwi blaring from the speakers.

"I want you in my heea-art, I want you in my heea-art . . ."

Mabel leaned her head forward, and Aretha did the same so that their foreheads touched. They balanced against each other as they looked down at the ground between them, their combined shadows creating a new shape at their feet.

"Make you run, make you run your sweet love to me, make you run . . ."

The radio was slowly being drowned out by more honking that neither Aretha nor Mabel was paying any attention to. Their heart rates were slowing, and the sun didn't burn as hard then.

"All I need is you! All I need is you! All I need is you!"

Aretha felt at peace with Mabel like this, when time was allowed to stop for a few seconds. It was only later that day, at home, when Aretha scribbled notes down for some math homework that she felt Tina's smaller frame plonk down beside her.

"Did you know that love is just a chemical reaction?"

Aretha turned to the voice beside her, confusion marking her face. *This child is strange*, she thought to herself, then tried to hide a smirk.

"And where did you hear that one from?"

Aretha was feeling generous enough that afternoon to humor

Tina, which she rarely allowed herself to do. Tina nodded matter-of-factly.

"I read it! You know being in love can affect your appetite?"

Aretha put down her pen and turned fully to Tina, realizing quickly that this wouldn't be a short exchange.

"Tina, what are you talking about?"

Tina smiled softly, staring at her sister intensely.

"It can affect our appetite, can show in the food we eat or *don't* eat. I've seen it."

"You? What have you seen?"

"You don't eat whenever Mabel is around. You did drink the co-conut juice today, but you refused the meat, even though it's your favorite thing."

Tina was smiling at Aretha as she spoke, unaware of the way her words were dropping onto her older sister's head like tiny anvils.

"So you followed me home but did not make yourself known? Are you a spy now?"

Aretha could hear her voice getting harder and tried to temper it, lest she alert one of the house staff who would immediately tell Gloria when she came home. Tina looked scared, not understanding what she had done wrong, clearly planning for the conversation to go a different way. She shook her head and stood up from her chair, ready to run away if she needed to, if Aretha's lightning-fast right hand made an appearance.

"Choir was canceled because Auntie Evelyn is not well, so I ran back to catch up with you and . . . and . . . and I didn't mean to spy but you were talking to your friend and I thought you would be angry and I'm sorry, Aretha . . ."

Tears did not arrive in Tina's eyes very often, so Aretha took a beat. If the Sergeant called and Tina was still upset, Aretha would get the blame, as she often did when there were disagreements between the two of them.

"Ah, there's no need for crying. Just . . . don't do that again, okay? You can't watch people without telling them. It's not kind."

Tina nodded again, vigorously this time, certain that she would never forget that lesson for as long as she lived. She was still staring at Aretha, waiting for permission to keep going with life, so Aretha sent her to the kitchen, to bring some of that coconut meat she loved so much: a peace offering that Tina gladly accepted, leaving the room quickly. Aretha tried not to think about what Tina had said and what she had seen.

Aretha's teenage years were long gone, even if the memory was still fresh, of Tina and how astute she had been, trying to reach Aretha on a more personal level. What might she think of things now, as they were? Mabel had returned to Ghana from the US almost three years ago. It was not long afterward that she contacted Aretha, and their friendship was rekindled as if no time had passed. Aretha could even admit to herself that she hoped for more, now that they were both older and could make their own decisions. But Gloria had put a stop to all that. She introduced Mabel to someone at Holy Grace Church, the son of a pastor, one of PK's friends. Within a year, Mabel was married and pregnant with her first child. Aretha could not turn from her friend then, as she took her first tentative steps into motherhood. Now they talked weekly about Mabel's baby son, Malcolm, and of course, Whitney. But there was no going back for Aretha, no more pieces of her left to give over to Mabel now. And for Gloria, Aretha still held an anger she couldn't shake. Once again, Gloria had intervened in Aretha's life and taken her choice away.

Yet it was still easier to think over those things than what was currently happening in the house. Aretha was sure no one had slept all night, and the day had well and truly broken by now. At five thirty a.m., it was too hot for a walk or a chance to straighten out her mind. All she could do was get up.

"And so what? She wants to send him back there, like a, like a cargo or something?"

"She's his mother. I cannot refuse her."

"But it's too much. We haven't even located his father for that, er, that decision to be confirmed!"

"Ah, Uncle, he didn't even know the man. He is more at home in Denmark, you know this."

"I know that *his* child is here, that the family is here. That is what I know."

Aretha had stopped herself from entering the room when she heard her granduncle Christopher conversing with the Sergeant, who had returned home on an early morning flight. She was sure he had had no sleep, and usually she would check on him, but she wanted no part in this conversation, one that referred to Bobby not as a person anymore but as a thing to be dealt with. She wondered for a moment if he was still lying out there, on the ground in front of the house, waiting to become dust, the proof of his life spilled out around him, dried now in the heat of the morning sun. She felt sick suddenly, her stomach a churning mass. But she stayed by the open door, out of sight, knowing that she had to keep listening to what the Sergeant would never tell her if they were face-to-face.

"Anyway, it is already done. They have him at the morgue. I'm going now to start the paperwork."

"Hey, Nana. You know this isn't how we do things. You said he was looking for his father, that he had located him somewhere in

Tema. If we can just wait a week, I will send someone to get him and then at least all the family can have a say. Even the girls—"

"Uncle, respectfully, you will leave my girls out of this. It has already been too much for them. That Aretha was even here with Whitney when he—"

Aretha heard her father's voice crack for the second time in her life. The first had been three years prior, at Tina's funeral.

She felt her ears prick up, waiting for more to spill from him that might indicate some emotion beyond anger and irritation, but he only cleared his throat before telling granduncle that arrangements were already being made, that a boy needed his mother, especially now. Aretha stepped back then, heading outside to expel what she had been holding in since she'd woken up. Her chale wote kicked up red dust around her feet as she quickly crossed the courtyard and yanked open the wooden door to the toilet. She knelt in front of the toilet bowl and waited for something to rush forth, hoping the scent already filling her nostrils would be a catalyst to rid her of all the bad things that had been coming toward them all in the last few years—or perhaps most of her life. It was often these times when she tried hardest to remember her mother.

Her memories were of a maternal feeling, shrouded in music, melodies flowing throughout the house. Everything on the periphery was a different color of warmth, and Aretha thought of it as the last time she felt at ease with herself. Perhaps she wasn't always so concerned with time, perhaps she liked to mess around with her dolls like Whitney, perhaps she had imaginary friends and made up songs with Mommy and smiled a lot. At least this was what she was told by aunties when she was a teenager. By then, the memories were already becoming music notes and splashes of color, and her mother's face had gone from a moving image in her mind to a static one that was a picture, a photograph she saw every day that sat on the desk in the Sergeant's study. No longer a memory that belonged to her, it had been taken over by whatever she was told now, subsumed into the annals of her subconscious so that all there was left was a faint tinkling of a song she couldn't recall the words to. And when their mother was all but faded to a feeling, and Tina had given birth to a new life sooner than anyone could have planned for, they were visited by death again in that same way, as if their mother had agreed to some otherworldly relay race that no one else had a say in. Her life ends. Tina's begins. Then *her* life ends. Whitney's begins. And before the cycle can continue, Bobby's life is taken from him. But that talk of recurrent loss—of what was happening to their family—apparently it had begun long before their mother had died.

Aretha had listened to Auntie Vida—the Sergeant's cousin—tell the story when Whitney was just a baby. She was visiting from Accra, six months after Tina's funeral. Gloria had been quieter in those days, but Auntie Vida's excitable energy and matter-of-fact attitude seemed to bring Gloria out of herself a little more. At least, that was how Aretha saw things.

"You know your family's connection to the king, to the Asantehene, yes? Don't look like that, it's not some tall tale. Your father has a good friend, Benjamin Frimpong, who is a historian—he will tell you! You ask him the next time he comes to visit, eh? The only thing I know about it is that someone in your family worked at the palace in Kumasi, maybe a great-great-great uncle, I think. Anyway, he was a scholar, trained at some fancy university in London, and he came back to Ghana to be an adviser to the kingdom on some legal things that were changing at the time—"

"Okay, Auntie, but what time is this exactly? Eighteenth, nineteenth century?"

Gloria was finicky about those things. She didn't like vague stories; she always wanted detail. It was one of the few things she and Aretha had in common. Auntie Vida had kissed her teeth in annoyance, the flow of her story interrupted.

"Oh! I'm talking about the late eighteen-oh-oh, okay? Nineteenth century, for your British Empire–educated ears." Gloria frowned but hid this reaction from her auntie; she and Aretha were aware that they were never too old to receive some small violence from an irritated elder. "Anyway, as I said, this great uncle, he was working in the palace and struck up a friendship with a princess, one of the Asantehene's nieces. She was already promised to some big man in another clan, as was the way back then. But she was young and fell in love with him—he was a young lawyer, worldly about things and such, you know. But he didn't come from wealth, as the royal family would have expected, so they ran away together and got married in secret. She absconded from her duties—just like that!"

Auntie Vida snapped her fingers, and Aretha watched Gloria cringe from the other side of the room, waiting for the yell of baby Whitney from the bassinet nearby, potentially rattled by the surprisingly loud sound made by just two fingers. But no cry was heard. Aretha was sitting beside the baby, with her hand on Whitney's belly, gently soothing her back to a peaceful slumber before a ruckus could be made. Auntie Vida nodded satisfactorily at not disturbing the peace before continuing her story.

"Of course, they located the couple soon enough, and they were brought back to the palace to face punishment. But this niece, she was a favorite of the Asantehene, like a daughter to him in fact, so her life was spared, and so was her husband's. And if the story could have ended there, it would have been fine. But when the young couple had run away, the mother of the girl, the Asantehene's younger cousin, had been *so* angry that her own child had brought shame on the family. So she consulted a witch doctor to bring her daughter home because she was convinced this young lawyer had put her under some kind of spell. This mother agreed a pledge with the witch doctor that nothing her daughter created with this man—that is *no life, no children*—would prosper. That *anything* they did together would not succeed. You understand?"

Auntie Vida looked from Gloria to Aretha, aware that she had her audience hooked. They both nodded in unison.

"Eh heh, so what happened next, it won't be a surprise. The niece, the young woman, she became pregnant, and there was rejoicing because Asantehene had forgiven everything. But her mother was afraid, of course. She knew what she had done in a time of desperation, and she knew the child would be lost. She tried to undo this thing, but of course the witch doctor could not be located. So she confessed to her daughter what she had done, hoping that speaking it aloud might undo some of the spell somehow." Auntie Vida shrugged, resigning her voice to the fate of her own story. "A mother will always hope. And somehow it worked! The baby was born healthy and happy, the young mother pronouncing that she willed it herself, that she gave all her love so that the baby would survive. And then a few days later, with love on her breath, the young mother died."

Aretha gasped even though she had expected a grim ending: some moral tale about being careful what you wish for and what you put out into the world. She wanted to brush it off as just a story at the time, but Gloria spoke up.

"Auntie, that was a very sad story."

Gloria sounded disappointed, but Auntie Vida raised her eyebrows, indignant about the point she was trying to make, the warning she felt she was rightfully imparting to them.

"Listen, the baby survived, raised by the father—she was still part of the royal family, eh? One of your great-great aunts, I don't know how many greats, but the relation, it is a direct line to your father and the three of you. A blessing and a curse."

"Why a curse?"

Aretha felt the need to ask it, whispering loudly across the room, one eye on Whitney, making sure she didn't stir. Auntie Vida held out both her hands, as if her point were abundantly clear.

"Because when new life comes, death follows soon after. It's something we've always known in this family, and you girls have already seen it. Maybe too many times." Auntie Vida suddenly became quiet, realizing what she had said to them and what it had left behind. Before they could really react, she stood up. "Anyway, ladies, I have to go. The tailor is waiting to fit me for a wedding in a few weeks. *Everybody* wants marriage-marriage, but it's us who suffer the cost, eh?"

She tried for a lighthearted exit, but the weight of her words hung in the air long after she had left the house.

These were the things coming back to Aretha now, as she hunched on the floor trying to make sense of these past stories, to link them with the present. Nothing ever seemed to stay the same in that house. There could be a handful of years when things were okay, even when Ghana was finding itself, clutching onto independence and trying to move away from bloodshed. Even when the news screamed treason and murder and protest, the Sarpongs remained resolute, steadfast. Only, it wasn't true. Aretha was seeing that now—that was the gift of the Sergeant, letting his children believe that even in loss and death and what felt like endless grief, they would be okay, eventually.

"No matter what, you can always rely on this home."

It often formed part of his Friday night speech, though it had become infrequent, along with his visits, and sometimes Aretha spoke the words to herself for comfort or some reminder of him, of what she and Gloria were trying to keep together. Only now, something else had happened to shake them all. In the house that had kept them safe for so long. Perhaps it was a curse that would chase them until their final days, finding them in their beds or stumbling outside innocently, faced with fire and anger and the crimson of their insides.

The contents of Aretha's stomach finally made a violent exit, and she watched helplessly as some of it caught the edge of the toilet bowl, ricocheting onto the beige stone walls, leaving unpleasant trail marks in its wake. She clenched her eyes shut and resumed her seat on the ground, trying to remember what yesterday was, what she might have missed. And then a familiar voice rang through from the other side of the door.

"Sister Aretha, are you okay? Sorry to disturb you but—your daddy is asking for you. Should I tell him you're—"

"I'm coming. I'm coming."

Aretha felt the croak of her voice reach Maame Serwaa and listened as her feet flitted away from the door. *She's like a ninja sometimes*, Aretha thought. Maame Serwaa could appear and reappear at will without you noticing her in the room, until she wanted you to. She was stealthy. And Aretha began to wonder if maybe Maame Serwaa had seen something she had not.

CHAPTER 9

London, Present

Whitney

Jak was sitting behind the ticket counter at the cinema when you arrived, cracking monkey nuts between two teeth, chewing the contents and then spitting the shells expertly into a plastic cup to their left. They spotted you making a face at the door on the other side of the glass and grinned as you walked in.

"Whit! You're early, man."

"Yeah, dinner was short."

"With Chantelle?"

You nodded. Jak raised their eyebrows but said nothing more. Something had happened between Jak and Chantelle a few weeks ago—you had no idea what, and as with so many things, you had not asked either of them about it directly. Everything around you sounded muffled lately. Your head felt stuffed with things: bad dreams, images, dark memories. There wasn't room for anything more, not even the break between your two closest friends.

You had introduced them tentatively two years ago, worried about upsetting the equilibrium of your friendship bubbles by bringing Chantelle and Jak together, but you need not have worried. Jak was a transplant from Melbourne with Malaysian roots, and Chantelle was a Jamaican Londoner, but her grandmother had Malaysian heritage too. You watched her connect with Jak in a different way when they discovered this small commonality between them. Soon enough, the three of you had your own thing going: huddling together at parties at the end of the night, planning your next meal out, or sharing war stories about bad dates and bad exes. Your small group would spend long sunny days at Jak's place in West London enjoying barbecues in the back garden of their sharehouse, gliding through balmy evenings filled with new faces, dance parties, and sunrise sing-alongs. It wasn't until Jak didn't turn up for your regular Sunday lunch plans a few weeks back that you noticed something was off, when Chantelle made a comment about wanting it to be "just the two of you anyway." You picked through silent moments from them both separately in the days that followed and pieced together that something had gone awry. You worried it was big, that Jak's coming out to you both as nonbinary six months ago was still sticking in Chantelle's mind, causing her to be a bit standoffish. You had known Jak for longer and in a different way, so the news felt right to you, even if you could not have articulated it before. But Chantelle had admitted to you that she needed more time to understand it. She told you it was not the concept that she was having trouble with, but attaching it to Jak was tripping her up. You stepped out from between them, hoping they would find their own way through it. But perhaps you had taken too big a step back. Or now was now, and it was taking everything for you to even step forward for yourself, let alone for anyone else.

"You're alone, then?"

Jak spoke quietly, pulling you gently from your own thoughts. The two of you were the only ones in the cinema lobby. You nodded, not sad but pensive about the whole thing. You leaned on the wooden ledge of the ticket counter and peered curiously down the

steps to your left, leading to the cinema screens. You realized Jak
was saying something else.

". . . so we can't sit in the back, okay? Lazy arse what's-his-face
still needs to clean up, and he's been gone for 'supplies' for about
an hour."

Jak chuckled lightly, awaiting confirmation that you had heard
them, but once again you had zoned out. They came out from behind the booth, brushing bits of nut shells from the ruffles of their
lap and straightening out the crevices of their dungarees. Jak had
rolled the cuffs up evenly to their knees and wore deep green Vans
trainers to finish off the look. They also had a new bruise on their
knee, which you bent down to touch instinctively.

"New skateboard. I'm getting really good, though, trust me."

There was an assuredness about Jak that you admired. The way
they were always trying something new until they found success,
because they believed in making their own happiness, not finding
it in other people. Your fingers were still on Jak's knee, grazing
the dimple between kneecap and calf. The habit of touching them
hadn't quite left you, even though they hadn't lain on your table for
a year or two. Sometimes the boundaries took a while to reestablish
themselves for you, and you carried around the feel of people under your fingertips for weeks afterward.

Jak first came to you as a new client four years ago, complaining
of back pain with no known physical cause. You nodded confidently at them, assuming a mindset you had long since refined.
You would assess the situation, glean from their energy what you
could, and then do the work. It was methodical because it kept
you grounded, helped keep your boundaries firmly in place. You
washed your hands at the tiny sink in Jak's ensuite. They had
drawn the long straw in a sharehouse when they first moved in.

You gestured to the table in the middle of their bedroom, where they obediently lay down, and you placed a warm towel over their bare back. And then your hands took over, kneading and gliding to the rhythm of Jak's muscles. You had expected a quiet hour; Jak's soft-spoken welcome and offer of water hinted as much. But a few minutes in, Jak began dropping in little facts about themselves, tidbits that helped build up a picture of who they were.

"When I was ten, I had nasi lemak *down*, spent months trying to perfect it in my mum's kitchen. Kept bugging my pa to serve it in his restaurant, but he refused—and not because it wasn't good, just that we found out early on that I had a pretty severe coconut allergy, so my brother would taste-test everything I made—and I swear by his taste buds! But my pa did not have that same trust in my bro, and he wouldn't serve anything he hadn't made himself. I did cook some yesterday, though. My housemates say it's the best thing they've ever eaten, if you want some?"

You laughed and said you'd had a big lunch, though you were tempted. Clients were always trying to pull you into their world—some to fill the silence, some with a genuine interest in connecting. Jak turned out to be the latter. At first you thought their words were of the surface-level, small-talk variety, but you noticed how their tone flowed into a mood of sadness as you pressed a shoulder muscle into submission. Something in them was fighting against you, though they appeared to be lying still. You felt it under the skin, a resistance to the steady pressure of your palms. You wondered what it was that had tripped them up; it was palpable in the room.

"How is that? Is the pressure okay?"

You had asked it at the beginning, but you felt the need to ask again.

"It's good."

Was that a sniffle you heard? You imagined tears dropping onto the wooden floor below them, hopping one by one from Jak's face of their own free will. You considered reaching for a tissue but knew that wasn't quite right either. So you carried on. A few more minutes passed in silence before another thing was verbalized.

"I haven't been back to Aus in—God, a long time. Came here for uni and never looked back, ya know?"

"D'you still have family there?"

"For sure, my brother, my parents. It'll take a lot to get me to go back there, though."

"Oh. How come?"

You were responding to the flow of the conversation, the way Jak's words were opening up the frame of their body under your fingers. It felt right to keep talking. Still, you heard Jak release a big puff of air before replying.

"I had this uncle. Came to stay with us one summer. He was just on my case *all* the time about what girls are *supposed* to do and—you know that shit you don't want to hear when you're thirteen?"

"Completely."

"He needed to get his life together. All he did was drink and bark orders at people—mostly at me. It was bullshit. *He* was bullshit."

And then you felt them push back. You thought it was only anger Jak was feeling, at being victim to this uncle's misogyny. *Fuck the patriarchy and all that.* It was what you thought at the time, though it felt ridiculous and too small a reaction to what Jak's body was telling you. It was becoming one big knot of muscle and flesh, and instinctively you fought back, pressing a thumb against the base of their spine and hearing a cry escape the body on the table before Jak slumped back down, immobilized. You lifted your hands up in surrender, feeling like death might have visited you both for one hot, sharp second.

"Jak? Jak! Can you hear me?"

You expected no answer, and none came. You leaned down and had your fears confirmed: Jak had passed out. You played calm and reached into your bag for smelling salts, though your heart was beating as if trying to get out of your chest. It took a minute for Jak to respond to the salts you were waving under their nose, and they gasped for air when they finally did, as if they had almost drowned. When you had returned the salts to your bag and your heart rate went back to normal, you expected to find them sitting, ready for you to leave, but they lay there on the table, face still down, any expression of pain or relief hidden from view.

"We've still got fifteen minutes," Jak said. "Can we keep going?"

You nodded, and then realizing they couldn't see you, you let your hands answer instead. You thought about turning up the music slightly on your phone to help rectify the mood, to quell the anxiety you felt at making them pass out. It had never happened before and not since. People fell asleep a lot, getting so relaxed that they drifted into a gentle, sometimes snore-filled slumber. But passing out from pain, you'd never had that, though you had heard about it from others, the emotional trigger points you could accidentally push without realizing. You wondered if you'd done something wrong. You would retrace your steps later, when you got back home. For now you would count the final minutes, trying to bring the body back into the room, back to a full consciousness, though it was still a little resistant. And then Jak's voice returned.

"He ruined my life that summer, that uncle. He made me feel . . . disgusting. Suddenly I wasn't a kid anymore. I had to work hard to get out of that place, away from anything that reminded me of him. All that shit."

You needed to take a beat, to reclaim your breath that had been swallowed up by Jak's words. You couldn't let it be silent for too long, though. It felt accidentally cruel.

"Did your parents know?"

"No, I couldn't tell them—didn't really know how. It was easier to just go." Your fingers moved on autopilot as they spoke, the conversation trickling on. "I like it here, though. I've got a garden. I can cook whatever I grow. It's cold as a witch's tit in winter, but it feels real. Like, I can grow my own life and find a way to feel good again. Or to just . . . feel."

You listened and affirmed Jak's words with your hand movements, with the transfer of warmth from you to them with each purposeful touch. And then the hour was up.

You knew you would sleep heavy that night, that listening to Jak's story had left you feeling ragged. It would return to you at different moments throughout the following weeks. So when you heard from them again a month later requesting another massage, you agreed without hesitation. Your connection to Jak was palpable; you hadn't been able to shake it, though it felt almost foreign in origin, which made it that much more intriguing. The second session slipped almost seamlessly toward friendship, despite your coming to know their scars and blemishes more intimately than any partner, so Jak had told you. You were fond of them though, because of nothing in particular and everything that was small. Like the way they wore bright colors and whimsical socks with a sort of childlike self-assurance, or the way they pushed their glasses up to the bridge of their nose right before saying something that demanded your full attention. Eventually, Jak suggested you come along to a film at the Prince Charles Cinema where they had just begun to work. With the employee discount, you agreed to see the first two *Godfather* films there. When you arrived just before the double feature began, you inquired about also seeing the third installment of the

trilogy, but Jak pulled a face as if you had muttered something unpleasant. You laughed and couldn't bring yourself to tell them that
you often hated watching anything violent. But you wanted them
to think you were cool and sturdy and as calm as you had seemed
when Jak was exposed and you stood over their body, promising
relief. You ended up watching both films through your fingers, you
in some obvious element of anguish and Jak engulfed in everything
happening on screen. You thought they might have taken pity on
you sitting there frozen with your shoulders locked in a hunch that
you couldn't release. But you learned quickly that you'd never get
permission from Jak to run away from things that made you feel
uneasy; you'd have to give it to yourself. You were aware Chantelle
would have sacked the whole thing off, saving you from discomfort,
as she often did. So you stayed until the end, wanting to feel what it
was like to just sit with the uncomfortable feeling.

Jak had become a mainstay: a nighttime stop after a night out or
an afternoon hang when a client had canceled. They were always
there with at least three packets of strawberry laces and fizzy bot-
tled water. You wondered now, out loud, how they always seemed
to be around at the right time.

"Genuinely, you're always here when I need you."

"Where else am I gonna be?"

They threw it back with ease, and you shrugged, unsure.

"You should be at a restaurant somewhere. Or in a kitschy café,
running the kitchen?"

Jak snorted at your hopefulness, a surprising sound that shook
their shoulders a little. Without looking at you, they went back to
making pen marks on a long scroll of a receipt.

"Nah, can't afford to do that right now. This pays better. But you
know me. I've always got a plan."

"True. So what's the latest?"

"Right now it's just an idea, but I wanna go to culinary school. I'm saving for it, and that feels like a kind of plan." You smiled softly, hoping to transmit some reassurance. You were good at those kinds of smiles. Jak looked up at you just as it spread across your face and then eventually faded. "Isn't it your birthday or something?"

"It is."

"Okay, here ya go."

Jak handed the long receipt to you, along with two packs of strawberry laces pulled from the front pocket of their dungarees, which you took from them excitedly. You held the receipt up against the fluorescent light. Ten free tickets to any film for the next twelve months. You grinned wide, all teeth and gums, unable to hide your glee, clutching the red licorice close to your chest at the same time.

"Ugh! You know my heart."

You watched Jak blush slightly, pushing the glasses hastily to the top of their nose again before clearing their throat.

"Happy birthday, mate. Now then, we gonna watch a baby hang upside down or what?"

You stepped to the side as Jak led you down the stairs to the screen, sensing a flash of a basement, of darkness, and that cold airiness of being underground, close to the earth. Closer to life, somehow.

CHAPTER 10

Kumasi, 1995

Maame Serwaa

Maame Serwaa was not the superstitious sort, though she often felt tuned in to a higher power—she kept her Bible close and meditated over it before bed every night. But there were other things that inhabited her small world and the world of those she was close to. The Sarpong family seemed to attract these other things. She had heard rumors in the neighborhood of a curse that followed them: an accident of ancestry and circumstance causing them to face difficult moments of unexpected loss. She wasn't sure she really believed it; she had her own experience of grief, losing her eldest brother to senseless violence, a military raid on her village gone wrong, some whisperings of her brother's involvement with people trying to revive another revolution against injustice. It happened unexpectedly, and no real reason—not one to justify the death of someone so good—was ever stumbled upon. He had been the hope of the whole family, already chosen for a full scholarship to study in London, to elevate the lives of his aging parents and younger siblings. His death passed the responsibility to Maame Serwaa, and she left school at ten to join the Sarpong household.

If not for Ruth Sarpong, Maame Serwaa would have had no fur-

ther education. Auntie Ruth insisted on her continuing her studies
by giving her English lessons at the house after work, when she
was pregnant with Tina. Once Gloria returned from school, she
was tasked with sitting down with Maame Serwaa in her mother's
absence, to impart whatever lesson Auntie Ruth had prepared for
them that day. Gloria continued this ritual long after her mother
passed. She and Aretha would drop their books at Maame Serwaa's
door, aware that she had become a keen reader during breaks from
her household duties. Eventually, when Maame Serwaa was reaching the end of her teens, under subtle encouragement from Gloria, their father—Uncle Clinton—paid for and permitted Maame
Serwaa a day off each week to study as a seamstress, to learn how
to sew and eventually pocket some money for herself and to send
home to her family in Ntonso.

Maame Serwaa was broken with the rest when Auntie Ruth
passed, and she held baby Tina in high regard after that. Tina's
arrival changed the dynamic of the house too, and Maame Serwaa watched Gloria grow up quickly with the responsibility of an
eldest sibling. She was there when they lost Tina eighteen years
later, when the light from Gloria's eyes seemed to diminish even
further. Maame Serwaa kept her sadness to herself, alone in her
room, unsure she was allowed to feel a part of the family, now that
the most recent connection to Auntie Ruth, as she saw it, was gone.
She wanted to shut herself off from this thing, this shadow of grief
that insisted on chasing the family down. Her own mother had
begged her to return home to the village lest she be touched by it
too. They could not afford to lose another love.

But Maame Serwaa was at home in that big house by then, knew
every crevice, every creak of each door, every sound of the sisters
and baby Bobo as they awoke each morning, as she prepared their
hot water for bathing, as they rushed through breakfast to get to

where they needed to go. After more than twenty years of watching them go through the ebb and flow of growing into themselves and growing with them, she was part of the family now. And she felt it was her duty to watch over them, as she would her own flesh and blood.

It was easy for her to do, to pay attention to the things others might not immediately see. Viktor was one of those things. His presence had bothered Maame Serwaa the first day she had met him. Six months later, he would end Bobby's life, and she was still trying to wrap her head around how it had gotten to that point.

The Sarpong house was often open to visitors: cousins from Accra, aunties from the US, uncles from the UK—they all passed through the house in Manhyia based on loose promises of accommodation from Uncle Clinton, most often when he was away on business. Maame Serwaa did not mind catering for new people; sometimes she even enjoyed it, feeling a new energy in the house, hearing new stories. But Viktor did not make himself a welcome guest. His first visit to the house had come after he dropped Bobby off at the end of his first full week in his new Kumasi job. Bobby was still getting used to the Sarpong home, going from a back room in Accra he was renting from his mother's elder brother, to the spacious, but lived-in expansive compound of the Sarpong's home. He had gotten used to visiting, but staying permanently was still an adjustment. He didn't know anyone else in Kumasi, and so he had made fast friends with Viktor, a fellow Danish army cadet, now stationed in Ghana. Apparently, they had met while Viktor was doing a security check in Bobby's office. He had eagerly offered Bobby a ride home when he heard he was a young father, waving away Bobby's willingness to just take a tro-tro. After they pulled up to the compound in Viktor's car, Bobby asked Viktor to come inside for a drink before he went home, to thank him for his hospitality.

"Auntie, please, can you bring myself and Mr. Hansen a drink?"

Bobby was always so polite, even formal, with Maame Serwaa, and she liked it. She had expected him to be the barking sort, the foreign Ghanaian unfamiliar with his homeland but well acquainted with how to treat the house help badly. His soft countenance, both calm and unassuming, was refreshing, and Maame Serwaa was always lighter on the foot when he was around. She nodded as he showed Viktor to the living room, watching Bobby sink into one of the armchairs awkwardly, while Viktor plonked himself down as if he already lived there. Maame Serwaa scrunched up her nose but kept her comments to herself. When she brought the drinks in, she heard a small part of their conversation.

"I am telling you, man, you *need* to come to this bar near work on Friday. You can blow off steam, get away from family for a bit longer—"

"I moved here to be *closer* to family, Mr. Hansen."

Bobby had answered with a smile, but Maame Serwaa was sure she heard his teeth gritting as he spoke. She knew what his daughter meant to him; everyone did. But this man, Mr. Hansen, he didn't know Bobby yet.

"Please, I've already told you, it's Viktor. You know, my family back in Denmark isn't really like yours—I got out of there as quickly as I could! No kids, sadly. But I'd love to meet your little one?"

Viktor looked around as if Bobby's daughter might materialize immediately upon his request, but Bobby looked at his watch and then shrugged.

"Sorry, she's still sleeping. Won't be up for another hour."

Maame Serwaa caught Bobby's eye then, and he smirked proudly, knowing it meant something that he was aware of Bobo's sleep schedule. He was trying to be the father that he never had. Maame Serwaa felt the pride swell for him as she left the room. But it was only afterward, when Viktor was finally leaving almost an hour later—overstaying his welcome in Maame Serwaa's opinion—that Bobby seemed to briefly share her hesitation about this Danish officer. She crossed the hallway to reenter the kitchen and heard Viktor lean into Bobby in an attempt to speak quietly, though his volume actually remained the same.

"Your house girl, she lives here full time?"

"Maame Serwaa? Yeah, she's been with the family for years now. Why, you looking for some help?"

"Maybe. How old is she?"

"I'm not sure, late twenties at least."

"Ah. Too old."

Viktor had screwed up his face as he said it, as if he smelled something bad. Bobby had given him a look of mild confusion, but Viktor just clapped him on the back and said goodbye loudly and then left the house. In the kitchen, Maame Serwaa rinsed the glass bottles to be taken outside later. She couldn't shake that bothersome feeling about Viktor after that. Something was not right. She hoped to not have him visit again and was glad that Aretha and Gloria hadn't met him. She didn't like the way he made the house feel.

CHAPTER 11

London, Present

Whitney

Your week off was dwindling away behind a Monday spent in bed doom-scrolling and watching episodes of *Moesha* on Netflix. Tuesday had been a rainy day—your plan for a leisurely city walk ruined. You had persevered and found yourself inside Spitalfields Market, your coat soaking as you wiped your face dry in front of a stand selling handmade candles. You ended up doing two loops of the market and buying a new umbrella with a parakeet on it. Later, at home, you pigged out on Ready Salted crisps and drank vodka with a dash of apple juice, falling asleep in the living room after you'd made it to season three of *Sister, Sister* without stopping for a break. You shot up bleary-eyed at four a.m. on Wednesday morning as a car alarm went off outside, followed by angry voices in what sounded like conflict. Your first thought was to text Chantelle, suspecting she wasn't at home and hoping the random hour might jolt you both back to just being okay again. But then you thought better of it. A lot of things didn't command enough of your energy these days. It felt like pieces of you were dropping off the edge of a precipice; you were trying your hardest not to lose hold of the little you had left, but you didn't have enough hands. You shot a text to Jak instead.

You awake?

Always Whit 😊 Y R U?

Too much vodka and neighbors are loud

Standard. U okay?

You about later tonight?

U ignored my question. And yeh am about, finish at 7 2nite

Cool, let's hang. What question?

R U OKAY?

Sorry yeah, I'm bleh I think. Birthday blues. All good though.

K laces, c u later on then.

Lol "Laces"??

Ur obsession w/ strawberry laces has become untenable

You're an idiot. Luv yoooooouuuu

Same same 😊

Afterward you snoozed for another hour, this time in your bedroom, and then dressed slowly to get ready for the day. You listened out for the door, for the return of Chantelle perhaps, wondering where you were going, how you were doing, but nothing. Paris was back, and he had all her time now. You thought that after three years you might not still feel resentment for him, but it only ever left you after he left. You were tired of going over it in your head and turned your attention to spending the day in your childhood home, easing into the presence of Ma Gloria.

It was the first time you hadn't seen her on your actual birthday— she had a long-awaited hospital appointment for some joint pain she was having, and you insisted that she go. She refused to let you accompany her, though. You spoke to her often on the phone, about everyday things. The questions that you used to have about your history now rarely made it into your conversations. You had long since been deterred from announcing your curiosity about life before it was just you and Ma Gloria, when your parents were alive and you were microscopic in your mother's womb. There was nothing wrong with wanting to know how you came to be; you knew that, but Ma Gloria for one reason or another disagreed.

"There is something to be said for facing your front, Bobo."

Now you had trouble looking back at most things. But sitting on the bus to her home, you felt a sense of foreboding following you. You settled at the top deck in front, staring into the road ahead. Soon you had stepped off, rounding a familiar corner on the way to a familiar street. You were sure you could feel Ma Gloria waiting, counting the minutes until you arrived. It always felt like that: like anticipation constantly ran through her veins and she was always trying to share it with you. But it often got lost in translation and came off as anxiety. So when you lifted the letter box flap and let it drop to imitate a knock on the front door, you knew she was already on the other side, reaching for the door handle, ready to receive you. Yet when you had eyes on her, you jumped at her newly cut hair, now merely a close shave on her head, only her eyebrows remaining thick and perfectly shaped. Her glossy, full afro was gone. She was surprised by your own surprised face, until her gaze followed yours and she self-consciously ran a hand over her head.

"It's too much hassle, all this plaiting and styling—I got tired. I have wigs for a reason!"

"Did you . . . do it yourself?"

"Me? Please, you know I don't have patience. Julie did it for me."

She grinned at the last part, referring to her neighbor who moved into the street not too long after you and Ma Gloria. Julie was a Trinidadian woman who had taken up hairdressing at aged sixty, a passion she hadn't had the courage to pursue until her husband passed away. After a year of mourning, her outfits went from blacks and grays to vibrant greens and yellows. She redecorated the house and started a hairdressing course at the local college. Ma Gloria had been championing this transformation, heading over to Julie's for a weekly shandy and a gossip, singing the praises of her once quiet and reclusive neighbor.

"She's really living life now, you know? We're all blessed to do it, but only some of us choose to."

"She sounds happy."

"She is, and she deserves to be. Especially after her husband and all his . . . faults."

Everyone on the street knew something about his faults, and being next door you knew better than most. You heard them through the walls, the screams and thuds that exploded into the early hours of the morning when you were a child of six or seven. You were at a loss for what to do, and would run into Ma Gloria's room, sleep still in your eyes, certain you were having a nightmare. She would reassure you that you were safe, make up something about how Julie and her husband were just fixing things in the house and being loud about it. When you got older, the lie unraveled delicately, when you'd stumble into the kitchen in the mornings before secondary school and find Julie there with Ma Gloria, speaking in hushed tones, nursing warm cups of tea, and avoiding eye contact with you. Sometimes you glimpsed a bruise on her neck or a cut on a bloated lower lip and said nothing; you'd learned that to be quiet meant staying safe. You were only privy to a microcosm of what was happening to Julie, and you knew that. Now Ma Gloria was a guinea pig for Julie's new lease on life.

"It's—"

"Short. Yes, yes, I know."

"I was going to say 'different.'"

You shifted your feet uncomfortably, still sometimes feeling like you were playacting at being an adult in the eyes of the only mother you'd ever known.

"Take your coat off."

She approached you and swiftly tried to remove your jacket before you were ready, so your arms got caught in the material and you were suddenly twisted up inside it. You wanted to snap at her, but you didn't have the energy to deal with the implications of doing so. Instead you let her whisk your jacket away from you and point toward the dining table at the end of the kitchen, a warm plate of jollof rice and roasted chicken waiting for you. You walked over and lowered yourself into a creaky chair, reaching for the bowl of homemade coleslaw and piling it onto the small space still left on your plate. Ma Gloria returned to the table, and you waited for her to recite the same prayer you had heard before every meal of your childhood.

"Heavenly Father, we thank you for this food and pray that it gives us sustenance, that it energizes us, that it clarifies us. Amen."

As a child you'd thought this was what everyone said before eating, until you visited a church friend's house and sat through a ten-minute worship, before dinner was even served, that was somehow interspersed with the Lord's Prayer. When you returned home, you asked Ma Gloria why hers was different.

"We won't be honoring God and the bounty he gives us if we let our food go cold, will we?"

These were the memories you returned to: her accidental humor, the lighthearted ways she imparted life lessons. It seemed effortless, though you suspected it wasn't. You were grateful for what she was to you, for the way your life together began. The story you were told was that Ma Gloria had brought you with her to London when you were only a toddler so that you could have a better life. It had been the final step in leaving her homeland to journey across continents when airplane tickets were more valuable than gold and you were a three-year-old who had never tasted your birth mother's milk on your tongue.

Growing up, you had spent a lot of time quietly worrying about this, about your departure from Ghana, which was almost framed as escape. You had always assumed it had to do with the deaths of your parents, but beyond that, there was just a story of leaving and then arriving under a new sun where safety was supposedly guaranteed. Your own memories of Ghana had failed you, with too many missing parts to ever make a whole, so you took what Ma Gloria told you and filled the gaps with your own imagination. It wasn't much, but you savored it.

Your favorite of the few stories Ma Gloria shared was about your maternal grandmother and her love of soul and R & B. She believed that all her joy and hope was to be trickled down to her three daughters, so that they might have an easier life, filled with opportunity. Your mother was named after Tina Turner, and in fact her sisters' names were also inspired by musical legends: Gloria Gaynor and Aretha Franklin. You came after this with a moniker adopted for a new generation of power through voice in the form of Whitney Houston. Apparently, Tina played "I Wanna Dance with Somebody" nonstop when pregnant with you. She hoped you would continue the tradition of women who carried life like a melody, who brought joy to other people when they needed it most. You used to feel the expectation of what you might become like a burden, preordained to make the sacrifice your mother and Ma Gloria had made for you worth it. But any additional wondering you did about life in Ghana was rarely spoken out loud in front of Ma Gloria anymore. From one moment to the next, she could never be relied on for a straight answer about the past. Or she would burst into angry tears if you pressed too hard. Trying to engage with it always felt like a struggle.

Ma Gloria cleared your plate away and asked how your birthday was and whether business was picking up. She also wanted to know if you'd had any calls from the ladies at her church who she had recommended you to.

"I can think of a few who could do with having hands on them to help get the bitterness out." You often found it amusing when she spoke like that, every now and again causing double entendres to drop from her mouth without her permission. "And why the face now?"

You blinked at her words and saw her eyes on you properly.

"No face, just tired."

"Wow wow, thirty and already tired? Wait until you have children, then you'll know what tired is."

She was smiling but her gaze was steady, purposefully carrying the warning.

"I was a breeze as a child. What do you mean!"

She scoffed in response, shaking her head.

"Hm! You, this mayhem child? You know that when we first arrived, I kept finding you out in the garden when it got dark? I thought I had brought home a wolf."

You burst out laughing. She had never mentioned such a strange thing about you before.

"I used to hide in the garden?"

"No, no. You were fine."

The levity had dropped from her voice suddenly, replaced by a weariness you were overly familiar with. You'd suspected this might happen when you were getting dressed this morning. That asking her something about you as a child, about who you were before, was going to be risky. You had practiced all the things you wanted to ask her in the bathroom mirror anyway, calmly, slipping it into a partially open doorway during conversation.

"Just fine? Apart from acting like a werewolf?"

You were trying to reintroduce humor into the conversation, but she whipped her head back around in your direction, as if you had answered her back.

"You were just a child."

Suddenly, you were more determined than ever. It was like jamming your finger into an old wound, one that had remained untouched for years. Now the slightest amount of pressure caused it to ooze something that looked and felt deeply unpleasant. Ma Gloria made a face, confirming as much. She stood up to open the back door, muttering that there wasn't enough air in the room. You watched her unlock the door and kick it ajar with her foot, even though the sky was overcast and about ready to open up. Then she turned back to you, retaking her seat at the table. You had eaten countless meals there; she always insisted that breakfast, lunch, and dinner needed to be a seated affair. Anything else was disrespectful. She tapped the table with her finger somewhat absentmindedly.

"You know, you were very quiet most of the time. And you were good at hiding, do you remember? It was your favorite game, that hide-and-seek. But yes, you were a good girl. The only thing you ever cried over was when you couldn't find your teddy bear—that cheap thing someone bought from a hospital gift shop. You'd had it since you were a baby, and it was the only thing that soothed you. You never slept through the night without it."

You knew this story of hide-and-seek, of your teddy; but today the words felt pointed, like you needed to pay attention to all of them. You wondered what wasn't being said. Who bought the teddy for you? Did they know you held it close until you turned ten years old and placed it carefully in the back of your wardrobe because you were "too old" to sleep with it? Had you always been good at hiding things, or was that something you learned in Ghana?

"What was the teddy's name again?"

It was not quite the question you had wanted to ask, but being adjacent to the truth felt closer than you'd ever gotten before. Perhaps Ma Gloria was getting soft in her old age.

"You don't remember?"

She threw the question back at you with such ease that you didn't see it coming. She was acting as if the whole thing were entirely yours to handle. But aren't memories shared, even if created from different angles? Hers was a bird's-eye view; yours was obstructed by something too far out of reach.

"I think it was Teddy Milo. Anyway, I was just thinking about it the other day. Getting older does that to you, Ma."

She scoffed again, happy that you seemed to be moving the conversation on.

"You're still my little Bobo, no matter how old you get."

Bobo, that name that you couldn't bear to hear from anyone who wasn't Ma Gloria. An approximation of Abena, your day name—Tuesday-born—that you couldn't pronounce when you were a child; all you could muster was "Bobo," and that's what stuck to you. You didn't understand the depth of the thing until later, how not saying your own name properly meant you might always wonder who you were, in the fullness of everything going on around you.

CHAPTER 12

Kumasi, 1995

Maame Serwaa

Once Bobby had moved to Kumasi permanently, Maame Serwaa noticed how his daughter looked for him everywhere. Bobo searched for her father when she awoke in the morning, when she wanted a witness for a new game she had invented for her dolls and teddies, when she wanted her favorite bedtime story read. Usually these requests were kept for Gloria, and sometimes Aretha if the thing she wanted was to be carried somewhere. But now Bobby was home. It fascinated Maame Serwaa. Once Bobo had located him—her tiny legs toddling out of bed, running across the tiled floors barefoot toward his voice to find him outside, chatting with Kwame in security or with Prince before he took Gloria to work—Bobo hooked herself onto his leg. He looked down at her with love, as if she were a precious thing that he could only ever feel joyful about discovering. He would peel her off his calf gently, swinging her up into his arms, holding her toward the sun like a prize. And Maame Serwaa would wait by the door until he was done whispering whatever a father whispers to their only daughter before they go out and try to provide for her. He would hand Bobo back, and she would sink into Maame Serwaa's arms willingly, having now had her fill of Daddy for the time being. A year earlier, she had recognized him and his weekend arrivals, but they were infrequent enough that he was just a friendly visitor when she was one and two years old. Now that she was a little older, memories were forming, and an undeniable bond had grown between father and daughter.

Today, just as with the rest of the house, Maame Serwaa had not slept. She was standing in her room as the sun rose, washing and dressing quickly, to prepare the nkate nkwan she always did on the Fridays that Uncle Clinton was home. She would make sure the whole house smelled of groundnut by the time she was done, even though she knew this was a different day, a terrible day. But what else could she do? The house carried a stillness she had never felt before, and she had to keep going for everyone, just as she always had, no matter what was happening outside.

Hours later, she entered the living room, bringing a breakfast of egg and bread to Uncle Clinton seated at the dining table with the elder uncle who had just arrived. Maame Serwaa felt a pain in her chest when she saw a flash of Bobby's picture, his passport laid open on the table among papers Uncle was going through. The tears came before she could grab them in her mind, push them back into her head, feeling as if she had no right to cry. Uncle Clinton looked up at her, at first in alarm, and then, as if remembering himself and the reason he had rushed home in the first place, he looked back down at the table and cleared his throat.

"Maame, please call Aretha for me. And . . . wipe your face before Bobo sees you."

She left the room quickly, relieved to be out of sight. She curled around a corner, a few feet from Aretha's room and wept. She did it quietly, holding her grief close to her own chest, cradling it like a newborn, its fragility vibrating throughout her whole body. It was almost unyielding, and she wondered if she might lose control of it unless she found something to ground her. She hesitated outside of Aretha's door for a few seconds, and then turned to the door to the left, pushing it open slightly to check on a still-sleeping Bobo. Something about her soft breathing, the rise and fall of her small chest in her too-big bed, the light sheen of sweat on her brow as she dreamed about whatever it was that children dreamed of, calmed Maame Serwaa, as it always did. This was the thing of her mother—Tina had been the same kind of child, carrying the hopes of the family under her tongue, small snores sometimes escaping her as she imagined things that perhaps Auntie Ruth might have also wanted for her, if she had remained alive. Maame Serwaa had watched over her then too, even though she herself was still just a child.

But those things, Maame Serwaa did not think of too often. Not about the way Auntie Ruth had gone to the hospital healthy and was carried out of it without life. Or the way Tina used to share secrets with Maame Serwaa: that she feared she was to blame for her mother's death, that if she were not here, Auntie Ruth would still be. Maame Serwaa had tried to quell her fears, of course, ignoring the nugget of shame she felt at the same thoughts crossing her mind those first few months that Auntie Ruth was gone and Tina was a baby. It was only as she got older, grew with the sisters and the house, that she realized what true helplessness came with being a child, that the world of adults was strange and lawless, and sometimes you felt like your parents' pain was your own.

Even Bobo was caught up in it, in the pain of those taking care of her. Her name was a testament to it—Gloria called her Bobo, in affection and perhaps as a way to impart autonomy onto her—allowing her to choose her own name, even by accident. But Aretha stuck with Whitney because that was the name her mother had given her, so it was a rule to be followed. Aretha lived her life by similar rules, even when she desperately didn't want to. Gloria often found ways to bend the rules to her whim. So this too became another one of the small wars between the sisters. Maame Serwaa suddenly felt like she had to stop watching Bobo. She had to complete the task Uncle Clinton had given her, because the pain in her chest had returned when she thought of the night before.

The way the music of Bobby's small party had ebbed away as people left the compound with hearty but tipsy goodbyes. The way she sat in the doorway of the outside kitchen, turning the radio down so that she could listen to everyone leaving, waiting to hear that particular beep of Viktor's car to know that he was also leaving. He was always the last one, a signal that the night was really over. But his car horn never came, and she suspected he was still around, chewing Bobby's ear off about some other new venture he wanted Bobby to invest in—he was still technically a Danish officer, but he was always doing something on the side—"Some scheme," as Aretha often said in distaste. Maame Serwaa knew how she felt about the military. It represented everything her father was, and so Aretha revered it.

Maame Serwaa had left the kitchen then, the hour being a bit too late now for visitors to hang around. She could smell the smoke lingering in the air. The fire from the barbecue had been put out, the coals underneath no longer glowing red. She walked toward it for some reason, some other thing pulling her there. The smell or the sounds of the evening, the muffled cry of a bird somewhere driving her on. She should have called for Kwame, his security attention rightly on the road rather than inside the compound itself. She should have called, but she didn't. She hoped the sense of dread rising in her throat was just a fear of the unknown. But then the bird again, a muffled cry, and how strange that it came at night, and she recognized the tone of it but could not identify the bird.

And then before she could round that corner, she heard the sharp break of men's voices, an angry tumble of sounds meshed with the crash of heavy bodies thudding against each other. And then she ran and watched them wrestling, watched Bobby's shirt rip and Viktor crush him against the floor. And Bobby rolling and resurfacing again, gaining the upper hand, a knee on Viktor's groin as he brought down fists on Viktor's face, only landing a few punches before Viktor kicked him off, twisting back to cover his face again. He opened his eyes for a second to look at something, and Maame Serwaa followed his gaze toward the whimpering circle of a body a few feet from him. Bobo. Maame Serwaa went to scoop her up until she heard a piercing sound, a guttural moan that echoed in the compound, that alerted the whole household. There was the creak of the security door being pushed open, and then suddenly Aretha was outside, screaming a big sound Maame Serwaa had never heard from her before. While she was still frozen in a bend, ready to pick Bobo up, Aretha got there first, vanishing the child from the scene faster than Maame Serwaa had ever seen her move. And finally her eyes moved across the ground to Bobby, no longer writhing as he had been but still, hands limp by his sides now, eyes a half-open memory. Nothing was what it had been.

"And where is he now?"

"With the police, of course."

"Arrested? Under the jail? Which one?"

"He is being dealt with."

"No. No, no, no, Daddy. I don't like that. Dealt with? That means he can pay whoever, and then he's free to walk on the streets tomorrow. I can't have it!"

"Who said he will walk free? I said he is being dealt with, Glory. I am taking care of it, okay. It's enough."

Maame Serwaa stood almost to attention in the corner of the room, having been summoned by Uncle Clinton. She watched Gloria pacing back and forth between the dining and living room, seemingly exhausted from her brief exchange with her father, her chale wote slapping angrily against the floor. All the house staff were present—Kwame and Prince stood on the other side of the room, both wearing different, worrisome expressions. Paa Kweku was there too, perched on the edge of a chair in his slacks and shirt as always, trying to emanate a sense of calm. Maame Serwaa recalled how awkward he used to be, bringing flowers, snacks, and notes to the house for Gloria when she was unwell and they were just leaning into their teens. It was odd to see him now, as a man, self-assured and included in this family meeting. The events of yesterday were still unfolding. Twenty-four hours had not yet passed.

"Glory's right. We need to be sure that he pays for this. Law enforcement is not enough."

Everyone turned toward the sound of Aretha's voice. She sat with a straight back at the dining table, away from everyone else, both hands laid calmly on the tablecloth. She had washed her face and returned it to its stoic position since Maame Serwaa had seen her earlier that morning. Then her eyes were bloodshot, the smell of vomit lingering on her breath. She and Gloria only ever agreed on one thing—Bobo—and even then there were tiny arguments. Her support of her sister surprised everyone. Except Uncle Clinton, Maame Serwaa noted.

"Whatever you're suggesting, we are not that kind of family—"

"Then what kind are we? Ones that invite everyone to this house of death? Where even a child is not safe! Did you know Whitney was out there when it happened? That I found her crying next to his dead body? This family, this family . . ."

Aretha rocked slightly on her chair, tapping her fingers on the table, letting her words trail off from the rest of the room and back into herself, like she was trying to meditate upon what it meant to be in the family. Maame Serwaa wanted immediately to go to her, offer her a drink or a kind word. And if not her, then Gloria, even Uncle Clinton, but no one moved. They let Aretha's words hang in the room, and no one plucked any of them off to repeat, which surprised Maame Serwaa, because all of it was true. Truer even than she feared anyone else might know.

"Kwame? What did you see?"

"Sir?"

Kwame's eyes bulged wildly when he realized Uncle Clinton was addressing him.

"I said, what did you see yesterday evening? What was Viktor's countenance like?"

"Eh, count who, sir?"

"His mood! Did he seem funny or what?"

"Oh, no sir. He was the same, you know, always smile, smile in that obroni way. Nothing special."

Kwame rubbed the back of his neck nervously, as if his own actions were under the microscope. Uncle Clinton looked displeased.

"They were singing, sir," Prince piped up then. The room's focus was now on him. "Just before everyone left. They had been drinking, so it was getting loud."

"And then?"

Uncle Clinton asked it calmly, his voice never really changing, modulating only slightly, never raised. But Maame Serwaa saw the vein in his neck bulging, a signature of his stress. She wondered about bringing him tea but felt afraid she would break the room, defying his initial request for her presence. She was aware too that all she wanted was to escape, that perhaps she would be next to be called upon, and she would give anything to not share the thoughts that had been rattling around her head all night. Again, she thought of Bobo, cocking her ear to listen for the faintest whimper, the sound of a little bird.

Prince stumbled over his next words, knowing more was expected from him.

"And then they—everyone else left, sir. I mean, that one, Viktor, he came to ask me to take him home to Nhyiaeso because he'd had too much to drink, but I said no—"

"Ah! But it's only a twenty-minute or so drive!"

Paa Kweku's voice had taken on a thunderous quality for a moment, mimicking both Uncle Clinton and Gloria somehow. Uncle Clinton looked almost as impressed as Maame Serwaa felt. Prince, however, looked affronted, accused even. He faced Paa Kweku confidently.

"I said no because Ma Gloria was not yet home, and I was waiting for her to call me to come and pick her."

Prince spoke slowly, never breaking eye contact with Paa Kweku, and Maame Serwaa saw silent words pass between them, filling the atmosphere with something no one else in the room wanted to touch. Paa Kweku even dropped his shoulders then, as if in surrender.

"There is only one man to blame for this thing. Okay?"

Uncle Clinton looked back and forth between Prince and Paa Kweku, who both nodded, letting whatever was unsaid dissipate into the thickness of the air around them. Maame Serwaa wanted it all to be over then, to remove herself from what was coming next. In this room of men and large voices, their chests bared as if to show strength in the face of something that had rendered one of them—Bobby—so weak, she knew her voice would leave her body as a small thing. She knew that with Gloria and Aretha she could speak up and she would be listened to, that her voice had value, and her perspective was important. But with the men, it was always different. She always felt less. It was only Bobby who had met her eye, who had asked her how she was and stayed to hear the answer. Who requested help with Bobo when he was left alone to bathe her, insisting to Gloria that he was ready, and then calling Maame Serwaa quietly to watch and make sure he was doing it right. He was different in that way, even in his youth, and he called her "Auntie" affectionately, with respect, even though she was not used to commanding it. And he was good. He was young, naive even, but good through and through. The loss of him in the house; it was fresh and stinging, and everything felt sour now.

"Maame. Please, do you know anything?"

The question from Uncle Clinton was expected, but its formula was a surprise. He was not accusing Maame Serwaa, but it felt like he was questioning her character, as though she had already offered something useless and he was reprimanding her for it. Except that his voice was soft and tired, strained from his long flight back home, from the agony of what he had arrived home to, from everything. She tasted bile at the back of her throat, considered letting it come forth to stop the exchange before it got started, but she swallowed it down. She was not a person who ran away.

"I saw them fighting and it was very fast and it was dark so I did not know Bobo was out there until Sister Aretha came and by then it was too late."

She exhaled, her words a fast train to an unknown destination.

"But you did not see what they were fighting about?"

"No, Uncle, I did not see it."

She wondered if she had lied, if what she held back was written on her face, because both Aretha and Gloria were watching her keenly, their eyes searching and curious. Uncle Clinton seemed also to sense something else was at play.

"And Whitney, she was okay?"

Maame Serwaa hesitated again, thinking it through, her fears at the front of her mind but her face trying to remain in one place, in one expression. Because suspicion at this moment in time would not help. And anyway, what could be worse than murder?

"She—she was crying and I think . . . perhaps she came outside looking for her daddy and slipped? I don't know, Uncle, I don't know."

She dropped her head to the ground then as she remembered the moment. Looking up again suddenly felt impossible. And then there was a hand on her shoulder from Gloria.

"Maame, come. Let the men talk."

Aretha also pulled her chair out and followed the other two women out of the room, into the afternoon air and then back into the kitchen. Maame Serwaa felt herself being guided by the two of them, aware that something else was coming, something big.

She had a sense of these things.

CHAPTER 13

London, Present

Whitney

You remained in your childhood home for the rest of the afternoon. Ma Gloria made you both steaming cups of Milo—the hot chocolate malt drink you only ever enjoyed with her—and you relaxed into opposite ends of the sofa, waiting for lunch to settle in your stomach. You had decided not to prod with more questions of your past for now, even if it felt like you only got the chance to do it once a year, on your birthday. Ma Gloria became chatty again.

"So, how is work? Do you still need to practice, or are you now an expert?"

You couldn't help but smile at her words, knowing what she was getting at but deciding she should ask you outright for a massage—she could at least give you that.

"I'm basically an expert, yeah."

She kissed her teeth but allowed the tiniest smirk to find her lips. "Aynh, so when will you bring the expert money then?"

"Soon come, Ma. It's about more than that."

"More than making a living?"

* * *

Eight years prior, you had spent twenty-four months as a masseuse, and you imagined you'd seen every type of body. You had recently left the spa in Kensal Rise, could no longer stomach the over-manicured, privileged masses who passed through its halls on a weekly basis. The women tipped well, but it came with an air of self-congratulations hidden in whatever written message was left with cash at the front desk or spoken casually into the lavender-scented air in the treatment room itself. Many of the white women had similar complaints about their slightly absent but wealthy husbands, the inconvenience of the children they had chosen to have, the general lack of awareness from the "less fortunate" about how difficult it was for these women to maintain their privilege. They were realizing that it wasn't hip to brag about anymore, and even employing "people from other places" didn't carry the same cultural capital. One regular client made a point of always bringing up her Ghanaian nanny with you—somehow learning about your heritage through super sleuthing and probably slipping the newer receptionist a ten-pound note to reveal it—wanting reasons behind some of the things the nanny did that she found bothersome. Like taking time off to attend a funeral in Ghana.

"Is that all you people do? I swear she's been to about five since I hired her. Don't get me wrong, we should all be allowed to mourn and whatnot, but my father-in-law passed not long ago and we just couldn't make it there, so we sent flowers. Maybe it's a cultural thing? The cleaner at Penny's school, Koh-Joe, said that it's a part of the social calendar for you people! He's a funny one. Always has words of wisdom on the days I'm volunteering there. Did I tell you I volunteer—ah, yes, there they are, those magic hands. Whitney, honestly, you're the only thing I look forward to each week."

The men were different. Many were quiet, in and out without a fuss. Still, you held your breath a little longer with them, made sure to leave the door ajar, just in case. You looked them in the eye when they entered the room, trying to take a mental photo of their face, what they were or were not wearing. Their scents began to mix together, even the regular clients. You could differentiate them by voice, but they all had that same aura about them, the same tepid humming of testosterone bubbling and alive. Your job was to keep it at bay. You became a snake charmer. When they were elongated on your table, their full length apparent and measurable, you were in control. Their muscles and nerves were calmed, loosened, soothed under your hands; you pummeled, kneaded, and struck them into submission before they even considered protesting. They left transformed under your gaze; you were no longer just another transactional object to them—you were powerful. They couldn't take from you by force what they really wanted, and now you both knew it.

That first client, Harry, had never returned. Perhaps he knew you wouldn't be fooled a second time, that you stopped being new as soon as he left your treatment room. And that might have been the main problem for you—the work stopped being about connection and more about what you could wield over whomever you deemed unruly.

You handed in your two weeks' notice soon after that light bulb moment, and Ma Gloria suggested you join the physio team at her hospital after a vacancy had become available. She had already talked you up to colleagues—something you were keen to witness firsthand but knew better than to ask for—and you started quickly, passing your three-month probation with flying colors. You felt purposeful again, challenged but enthusiastic. You didn't have that tinny taste in your mouth when someone new walked through the door; you weren't sizing people up like warriors anymore. People were just people. It also didn't hurt that you were only seeing women. You'd been placed with a physio, Nina, whose focus was women's health. And it was Nina who taught you about trauma in action.

You had read about it during your module on chakras—how a childhood response to trauma that begins as a defense mechanism can become a physical and mental pain in adulthood, that repression can become chronic. The night before your exam on the seven main energy points and where you fit into it all, you dreamed of hands. They grew from a body with no face, sprouting from the hips, the neck, the bottom of the feet, the base of the spine. A disembodied voice barked questions at you that you couldn't answer, and then you held a shovel in your own hands, damp soil thick under your fingernails. You dug until the hole was big enough for you, and then you lay down inside the makeshift grave, your palms behind your back, digging into the ground underneath. You woke up in a sweat, in the same position as in the dream. You aced the test but refused to ever learn another thing about it; it wasn't for you.

But Nina disagreed. She thought you had a knack for picking up on people's energies, drawing out the sticky sadness of their traumas, big or small. You didn't understand it—you were just connecting with people again, unpeeling those unspoken things that exist between the invisible layers of human-to-human interaction. You said none of this to Nina, though. You just nodded along, shrugging shyly, unsure if she was giving you praise or delivering bad news.

"You have a way with people, Whitney. I've had quite a few patients disclose . . . well, some difficult things after seeing you. But it's so helpful for their treatment. You know we take a holistic approach here? You're doing some good work, is all I'm saying. . . . What's wrong?"

You imagined your face must have been revealing what you felt on the inside as she spoke—not the pleasing, calming expression you were hoping you had displayed. Terror was hitting you, and you couldn't explain it. The weight of it, the responsibility of the reveal was a bit too much. You were not the trauma-whisperer. Or if you were, that needed to change quick-sharp. You had only just begun to love your job again.

You requested a team transfer, to a new physio. Nina was disappointed but understood your explanation, that you wanted experience in a different department to widen your scope of work and clients. She gave you a glowing reference, and you moved into elder care. It was slower paced and required less energy. Less of you. It worked for a while, until there was no more room for progression, and you decided to take another leap, to step out on your own and finally just work for yourself.

"Is this where you tell me I should aim for wealth because we're royal?"

You considered using air quotes as you responded to Ma Gloria's question about why you weren't earning a higher salary yet, but then you remembered that you valued your life. This was an ongoing conversation. When you were younger, she would reprimand you with the threat of higher responsibility based on your family lineage.

"You must be royal in your thinking, in your doing, even in who you choose to be around, Bobo, eh? Because we're a kingly family, I've told you. Don't ever forget it, in everything."

She would mention it most often when you were a teenager being pulled too close to the streets of London for her liking. She would use it to snap you back to her reality—away from the "road-men" someone in her Women's Group had told her horror stories about—and closer to the tentative ties your family had to the Asante Empire and to the muddy and bloody history of surviving colonialism that ended in rebellion, ensuring the survival of your bloodline.

At school you wanted to look into it more, to dig deep and find something at the roots of who you might be, but it would have had to begin with Ma Gloria, with her willingness to trace the lines out loud, from you, to her, to family in Ghana. Asking her felt like a violence you were committing on her character and memory because of the strong ways she reacted to your curiosity. Now it was as if the violence were visiting you. Which is perhaps why you remained by her side, under the guise of a birthday visit, hoping for something to slip from her. But she was never easy, never as open with you as you knew she could be. Today she just shrugged, like your words about royalty weren't inflammatory, even though her nostrils flared and she closed her eyes a second too long, as if gathering her calm.

"Wealth is not always what is in your bank account, okay? But am I not allowed to hope that you are healthy *and* can afford to one day buy your own place? Then at least I can feel good. I will know you have a second home here."

By then you knew the words were coming and you couldn't stop them, even though there was only the slightest slither of light through this door. But it was something.

"What about the family home in Kumasi? Pastor P mentioned something about it the other day . . ."

You knew you were playing a dangerous game as you watched Ma Gloria's jaw jut out slightly behind clenched teeth. You also knew that by mentioning Pastor P, you had evenly distributed her anger between the two of you, taking some of the heat off you if this backfired.

He and Ma Gloria had been childhood friends, and he had been around for as long as you could remember. He came to London before you and Ma Gloria, to grow the church that had originated in Kumasi, and as soon as you were both settled in north London, Ma Gloria made herself available to help him. You recalled trekking from school hall to school hall on cold and wet Sundays during your childhood—first to Croydon, then Deptford, then Hackney, before the church finally found a permanent home in Bounds Green. Ma Gloria hosted fundraisers for Pastor P, fed him many a dinner when he barely had a place to stay, and helped grow the congregation whenever she met a Ghanaian parent or fellow nurse at work. When you were a preteen, their relationship had been mysterious to you—how they were always together but never really *together*. You assumed that perhaps he had taken some kind of religious vow that meant there were certain desires he couldn't pursue, and she respected that. But he was also the only significant male presence in her life as far as you knew, so the whole thing frustrated you. You wanted more for her.

He was kind to you as a child, albeit from a distance. He would always arrive at the house with a gift for you—a key ring from an airport he'd passed through on his travels to Ghana and the US, visiting different branches of his home church. A snow globe from a museum in Minnesota. An *Ebony* magazine from Chicago that you couldn't get in London. And most famed was a wooden giraffe he'd bought in Makola Market in Accra, with your name etched into the bottom of it. That one still took pride of place on your bedroom windowsill because it had been your favorite animal as a child. Outside a church setting, though, the two of you interacted very little; he would throw you the courtesy "Wo ho te sɛn?" after taking a seat in the living room; Ma Gloria was already in the kitchen preparing tea. You would reply with your minimal Twi "Me ho yɛ, medase." Then you would leave the room, passing

Ma Gloria as she reentered it, and they would continue a conversation they had likely begun during his last visit. You didn't know what they spoke about in the interim. There was a time after you had moved out that you returned home for a surprise visit—and to collect food—and found him relaxing in the living room with his shoes off. Ma Gloria emerged from the bathroom, and you saw shock cross her face for seconds before she asked you in a high-pitched voice what you were doing there.

She was different when he was around too. You saw the way she got lighter on her feet. You always knew he was coming when she was preparing kontomire stew and yam—you couldn't eat it because you had a seafood allergy, but you had seen him wipe his plate clean when it was served to him dozens of times. At church, when the spirit caught her, you watched her dance somehow in his direction, though they never made eye contact, but their rhythm was the same, even as he stayed by the pulpit. You witnessed something you couldn't name. She even laughed differently with him. It wasn't false; it was just another laugh, one that belonged to her and him.

You had been waiting for her to say something about the Kumasi house, give some confirmation that it existed and that the world wouldn't end if you knew about it. But no.

"Will you rub me later? The thing in my back has been playing up."

You were not surprised that she didn't answer your question, only that she didn't even try. She was choosing complete ignorance. You had to get on board or stay mad about it and make your exit. You shook your head, vaguely annoyed.

"I keep telling you to stop trekking with all those 'Ghana must go' bags on the bus, Ma."

"Yes, yes, I know. Will you rub or no?"

You gathered your now empty cups, gave her a mm-hmm, and headed to the kitchen to wash your hands.

CHAPTER 14

Kumasi, 1995

Gloria

It had not even been seven days since Bobby's death, and already the negative chatter about the Sarpongs seemed to be hitting Gloria's ears from every direction. Distant aunties and uncles were calling with concerns about who might get caught in the cross fire next and who could even associate with such a family, such a burden? Meanwhile, there was little care given to how everyone in the house might be feeling. Bobo especially. She had been asking for Bobby all week, and at every question Gloria could only pick her up and hold her until she quieted down. Gloria never did this, always encouraging Bobo to walk with her. She worried that somehow the child, as small as she was, would know that this meant something bad.

Bobby no longer appeared around corners. There was no smoke in the courtyard from some fish he had caught himself—skills he had acquired since childhood, fishing in the cold water of Sluse-holmen. He no longer stomped in with his boots untied, already unfurling any unnecessary clothes so that he could sit in his vest and dress pants after work and cool down listening to Bobo babble into her ears about her day filled with nursery rhymes, "cooking" with Maame Serwaa, and tea with Teddy Milo.

There would never be any more of this, and Gloria could only barely stand to be in the house now. Everything had changed. Even Maame Serwaa, dependable and steadfast, was different. Gloria recalled how distant she had been after Daddy carried out his interrogation of the house staff. Maame Serwaa said very little afterward, but a few days later she whispered to Gloria the thing that she had been holding inside, that had been keeping her up at night and causing dark circles to sit under her eyes. Outwardly she was trying to keep things as they always were, but Gloria had already caught her twice, wiping away sloppy tears in the storeroom, searching for spices and getting caught in a wave of emotion. Both times, Gloria did not make herself known. Everyone should have their time. It had not even been a full week.

Even Daddy remained at home, the longest he had stayed in the house at one time in almost a year. That was not to say he spent any time with them, so that they might grieve together, plan for Bobo's new future even. No, he remained in his office for most of the day behind a closed door; passersby could only hear muffled phone conversations and the ticking of the grandfather clock that sat behind his leather chair. Gloria desperately wanted to know what had become of Viktor, as did everyone else. But Daddy remained tight-lipped about it, even though she was the oldest and she should be told these things first. So, she only imagined what would happen— that Viktor would be sent away for a long time to pay for his crime, perhaps even happen upon a fight in prison, lose his life the same way Bobby had lost his. And then she prayed for forgiveness for having such a thought. But it hung somewhere inside her like a pendulum. It swung back and forth in intensity, and that dark hope never actually dropped. She wouldn't speak these things out loud like Aretha, either. She had been on a tirade for days, bothering Daddy daily with questions about his plans, with irritations about not being able to bury Bobby in Kumasi or celebrate his life in the proper way, with an event. She was told that it was not what we did, that Bobby had not lived a long enough life for there to be a celebration after his death. And that he was his mother's only child, so if she wanted to say goodbye to him in Denmark, then she should be allowed to do that. They should all just focus on the lives that were still here, like Bobo's.

Since then, Gloria had not seen Aretha much. The house was falling apart. And then the aunties and uncles came by, and that same Auntie Vida brought with her whisperings of the story of the Asantehene's niece again. That was when Gloria decided she had had enough. There were some things she just could not abide, including entertaining the idea of the fate of the family being completely out of their hands because of a decision someone else had made more than a hundred years ago.

A young man had just died. A father. A good friend.

He had left behind his last bit of goodness, the last of Gloria's baby sister, the last of Tina. Why wasn't everyone as concerned about preserving that as Gloria was?

"I don't understand what you're saying to me."

"I am going. That is what I'm saying. You will take us with you, away from this place of ghosts and death and whatever other nonsense that insists on following all of us!"

Gloria was exasperated but determined. She couldn't understand why she needed to keep explaining what was very clear to her. That she had to take Bobo and go somewhere else, for now London because at least Paa Kweku would be there. And then, who knows? But the idea had taken hold overnight, and she could not shake it. When Paa Kweku had walked through the gate that morning, carrying fresh coconut for her and Bobo, she took it as a sign from God. The decision must be carried through, and he was the key. She could think of nothing else, and her plan was already mostly thought out. Her nursing experience would help her apply for something in their National Health Service. She would rent a small place for her, Bobo, and Aretha, and they would have a better life. Perhaps Aretha might protest a little, but she was not moving forward. She had graduated with a business degree, but since Bobo was born she had deferred her plans to enter the military. Maybe her interest was not as strong as it once was?

Some part of Gloria suspected that she might be wrong in this assumption, but if it came to it, she would take Bobo alone. She only knew one thing with absolute certainty: they could not remain in that house now. Too much had been lost.

Paa Kweku perched on the edge of one of the living room chairs, watching her with a quizzical look on his face. Gloria wondered why he always did that, why he always seemed to perch these days. Was he allergic to just relaxing? What did he think would happen if he sat correctly?

"Glory, I'm not sure your father would approve. And besides, after what happened between us, I was hoping—"

"I am not speaking about that, about when we . . . This is something else, PK. You know I am right."

He shrugged at her words, running a palm from the back of his neck all the way to his forehead, going against the grain of his own short hair.

"Right now, I don't think I know anything. Chale, I don't understand. I cannot get my head around this thing, that this boy would fight *to the death*. What reason would he have to even do that? It's the first time . . . anyway. I don't know about this new plan of yours."

"The first time, what?"

Gloria plucked the question out of the air because Paa Kweku's face was suddenly closed as he spoke. A shadow felt like it hovered over his brow, and she wanted to pull him into her arms. She hadn't engaged with those feelings all week, but they were still there, burning and alive between them. The physical distance remained, however, and so she could only reach toward him with her words, as if the time they spent together had never happened. In the light of the days that followed, perhaps it had not. He looked into the distance, biting his bottom lip as he conjured the words.

"The first time that I asked God for answers, and I'm realizing . . . maybe there wasn't one. Not the one that I wanted, anyway."

She smiled at him softly, carefully, even as she locked her fingers together in her lap.

"We can't know everything. But there is always a reason, even if it hurts." He looked down at the floor, tipping his head slightly to the side, showing he was listening, processing what she was saying. Suddenly the thing came to her, the thing to help him understand her decision to leave. "Maame Serwaa thinks that the fight had something to do with Bobo."

"What do you mean?"

Paa Kweku's head whipped up, and she saw the veins in his arms bulge slightly as he clenched his fists. She had not even examined how she felt about the theory yet, aware only that it was delicate and difficult to hear if she sat with it alone. This was the best way to consider it, to sit next to Paa Kweku knowing that wherever he was, she was safe. They would all be safe. She got up and moved to the sofa that he was perched on. He watched her sit beside him, leaving some space for him if he chose to sit on the chair properly. As though finally listening to her thoughts, he stood confidently and sank down into the cushion, turning toward her slightly. Their

thighs were reunited, side by side and pressed into each other. And
then he repeated his question.

"Glory, what do you mean?"

"She thinks that something happened with Bobo. That perhaps
Viktor put her in harm's way, and because he had been drinking,
Bobby became angry or . . . I don't know. I wish I had been there.
That I had not been so . . . distracted. She needed me, and I was
not there."

Gloria could not look at Paa Kweku. She knew what she had
said. The warnings she had issued of what was to come, of what had
already passed. He sighed softly beside her.

"He was there, and he was her father. You know, maybe, maybe
he thought he was saving her from something? Maybe if you had
been there, you also might have been in danger and then—"

"At least it would have been for something. She would still have
a father."

"Hey, Glory, you don't know that. Don't say that again, please."

"We cannot take this back, PK. *I cannot.* I promised Tina I would
be here, and I wasn't. I don't need to learn that lesson again."

She turned away from him as she spoke, brushing imaginary
crumbs from her skirt. She heard the faint hoot of the Fanice
man outside, considered running out of the room, out of the
house, through the gates, onto the road, letting dust cloud her
vision for a moment before she found him. She would buy two
for Bobo, keeping one for next week as a treat when she cleaned
up all her toys or sat quietly during this Sunday's service. Although, perhaps that wouldn't happen now. It would be the One
Week for Bobby, the eighth day in the Asante calendar after his
death. His body would be in Europe by then, but the ceremony
would take place without him. Everything now would take place
without him.

"So, you want to run away instead, to assuage your guilt? I mean, not guilt—no, no, Glory, that is not what I meant!"

Paa Kweku stood up to follow her as she headed toward the doorway of the living room. She wondered how he could dare bring that word to her ears, after the part he had played in keeping her from home. She knew that he had planned it that way, that he had waited until the very last moment before his own escape, to dangle the thing she had always wanted in front of her face. She did not think something as stark as Bobby's death was complete punishment for her actions, but she knew that it mattered, that one thing happened, and then the other thing happened, and somehow everyone was suffering. Who would not also want to run away?

"You are my oldest friend, and that's why I am asking you for help. If you don't want to give it because of some small thing that happened between us—"

"Hey, *small*! Okay, okay, Glory. If that is what you want, fine. But if you come to London, I will also be there, d'you understand me now? If that's what you want, what you are ready for, you know I will help you. Chale, you know that."

He stood in front of her, arms folded. They had not made it out of the living room but stood hovering by the open doorway. She could smell him, the shea butter on his skin, the faintest hint of talcum powder that he sometimes applied to his face when he got razor burn. This and so many other little things she knew about him. Could she live with it, to be near him once again, only in a new place where he was the only person she knew? Was it worth the difficulty?

"It is not about whether I am ready or not. It's about Bobo. I have to make sure she is okay. I have to. Wote ase?"

She looked him in the eyes then, though somehow it still hurt her a little to do it. It took him by surprise, and he blinked a few times before replying.

"Of course I understand. But surely she will be better here, in the home that she knows?"

His question was earnest but misguided. She let the tears come, the same ones she had been holding back all week, since the morning after Bobby had died. It was as if the whole thing were only just sinking in. That there was more than just him to mourn now. That nothing was as it had been, and she was supposed to pick up all the pieces. She did not want to leave her home. She did not want to leave the comforts she had known her whole life. The slow crawls of the day as everyone moved easily through the heat. The splashes of laughter that hit the air sometimes from passing hawkers, people heading to work, people just sitting together outside, sharing news and jokes. She did not want to leave the cradle of Maame Serwaa's home care, the way she kept the house running whether Gloria was around or not, the heart she filled with love for family that were not hers by blood. She did not want to leave the gates behind, or the red dust that sometimes found its way onto the hem of her skirt, the taste of fresh fruit whenever she wanted it, or the community she had grown up with.

She did not want to leave. But she had to because she also did not want to stay. There were ghosts, and then there was whatever hung over the house now. She had been haunted for years: first by Mommy, then Tina, and now Bobby. It was no way to live, always looking back in anguish when she thought about the ways her heart had been broken over the years. Aretha was just as broken, just as tired, but she had always planned to leave. Gloria was the one who stayed, who held down the fort. But she refused to pass that burden on to Bobo. She would not grow up with ghosts. She would not grow up looking back. They would start again, even if it hurt to do it.

"This is not the home that any of us know. Not anymore, PK. So, will you help me?"

* * *

Gloria missed the sound of Bobo's voice. She had been too quiet all week. She lifted arms up to anyone coming close, wanting to be carried as if she were a baby again. This was the child who would wriggle away from everyone once she found that her legs could take her to other mischiefs much faster. But since Bobby had died, she did not seem to want her feet to touch the ground, and especially not outside the house. Gloria wanted to pretend she did not feel the way Bobo held her tighter, burying her face in Gloria's chest when they walked to the car, past the spot where Bobby had laid, covered carelessly with that cloth but still visible until they came to take his body away. Bobo had been in her room by then, being soothed to sleep by Maame Serwaa. But still, she knew not to look at that piece of ground, over there. Her behavior only increased Gloria's worry, made her more determined to get Bobo out of the house, out of the country. To save them both.

She just needed to speak with Daddy. As much as she hated to admit it, she could not do it without his support and his connections in London. She would let him believe that she was merely asking for his blessing. That made the most sense, because she knew he had a soft spot for Bobo, just as he had for Tina. They all did. She would use that if she had to, to get what she wanted. What she needed, really. But that required courage, and she was unsure she had much of it left. So she pulled out her cassette tape player. It had belonged to Tina, a present for her eighteenth birthday. There was only ever one tape in there, and Gloria smiled when she clicked the eject button and pulled out the white plastic rectangle to see the black writing and bold capitals that spelled WHITNEY. Gloria pushed it back in, closed the tape player, and put the headphones over her head. The cushion of the headphones didn't fully cover her ears, but they were enough for what she needed to do. She made sure Tina's bedroom door was closed behind her. She didn't do this often, didn't really enter this room unless she had to. Only when required, when she wanted to sit with the memory of Tina. And who knows, this might be one of the last times.

Gloria recalled taking Bobo into Tina's room just after she turned one, just to sit and be there. Then she returned to the room a few weeks later to find Bobby in there too, sitting on the floor, thumbing through Tina's records, Bobo climbing on his back, using him like a tree and laughing. He was deep in concentration and wonder, as if he were only just discovering Tina, just learning about her after she was gone. Gloria supposed that that was true, and she left him alone with Bobo to do that, to commune with his young family.

Gloria felt a flash of pain in her stomach at the memory. She had not come in here to feel sad. She wanted happiness, joy. She wanted to feel like she was dancing with somebody. It was the perfect song, Tina's favorite. Gloria switched it on and swayed to the music, listening to the soft opening of the percussion, moving her hips slightly in time with the beat, in preparation for the explosion that followed, the way the song burst into celebration. Gloria pictured curtains opening, Whitney Houston making her way to the stage, dancing onto it, flicking her long legs in the air and shimmying her shoulders, making room for her voice to expel that captivating quality that it always had, no matter the backing track. Now Gloria was bouncing in time to the beat, jumping around the room, letting her neck get loose, and punching the air as she mouthed along to the words. Channeling everything that was Tina and her and Aretha as children, the way they used to swing and sway to their mother's records when Daddy was away. She wanted to be a child again then, to be free of everything that had happened since they'd grown up, to be free of everything that was about to come. If she could just hold on to these minutes, take the power from them that she needed, everything would be fine. Everyone would be safe. They all might find a way to laugh again, to dance even. Wouldn't that be something if they could? If one day Bobo could feel as free as this, no pain or grief in her rearview mirror, just free. *It wouldn't be too much to ask*, Gloria thought. *It's not too much to want such a thing.*

CHAPTER 15

London, Present

Whitney

Ma Gloria pulled out the foldable table from when you were first training. She was already lying face down with cloth discarded by the time you returned from washing your hands. You couldn't help but smile, having pictured this scene as a foregone conclusion as soon as you closed your front door that morning. Usually Ma Gloria's birthday gifts involved things she could make for you. She would cook you a favorite meal or get something with an Ankara print sewn for you in Ghana, some dress or skirt that always ended up at the back of your closet. Your fashion style had changed since you were a child, but Ma Gloria acted as if she hadn't noticed. Besides, you knew that it was deeper than that. That what she deemed a gift was quality time with you. Her full attention had been seeping away as you'd grown older, so now it was precious and much savored when the opportunity came around again.

You were already kneading her back with your fingers, as if tending to her aches was a muscle memory. You knew the pain that resurfaced in her hip as the weather got colder. The crick on the lower right side of her neck where the creases had doubled since you'd last felt her under your fingertips. The scar on the back of her left thigh that stung sometimes though it was decades-old: an injury acquired when she was the star hundred-meter runner for her high school. During a training session at an abandoned worksite, she had lost her footing and felt an errant shard of metal slice through the back of her leg. Pastor P—Paa Kweku back then—was with her at the time, rushing her toward help. She healed but never ran the same after that. And he was by her side during recovery, fetching her things for each class, carrying her bags, and changing his schedule so it would fit better with hers. They had always been intertwined in some way. You tried sometimes to imagine him as the supplicant in their relationship, as Ma Gloria exercised her younger, bossier attitude in his general direction. But you couldn't really picture them in that mode. It was so different now.

Ma Gloria groaned under the pressure you applied to her slowly softening skin but insisted that you continue in that same vein when you checked on how she was doing.

"It's good for me."

As if pain were a rite of passage. And even if that were true, her muscles being shaped by you, under your softened hands and short nails, still felt taut. They fought against you sometimes, as though she were holding on to something so tightly that one wrong move could either be excruciating or like detangling a spring. You both knew she was keeping a lot of things to herself, under lock and key, in her own room with her own door. Growing up, you spent most nights in your bedroom wondering at the gaps in the beginning of your timeline, the holes that became bigger depending on how closely you stared at the interwoven fabric of her stories. But as you got older, you discovered a new way to uncover things, in people and life, through the proverbial touch.

*   *   *

The first time you unlocked something within Ma Gloria that you weren't expecting, you were nineteen, still a masseuse-in-training. She was tentatively laying on your table, telling you to go slow and not push too hard. You pressed and prodded at her while pausing to look at the open book you had on a table beside you, her body a map and you only at the beginning of your journey.

"Do you think you'll go back to Ghana, at some point?"

The words flitted from your mouth into the air, your attempt to fill the silence while you read the next part of the book, trying to retrace your steps, certain that you'd missed one.

"What for? Everyone I love is here."

"But what about grandpa? Auntie Aretha said he misses you."

Back then Auntie Aretha used to call often from Denmark, asking about school marks and job prospects when you were too young to have proper answers for her. But you enjoyed listening to her clipped notes over the phone, imagining her bundled up in a Copenhagen coffee shop, telling you stories about what it meant to grow up in the heat of the tropics and still find comfort in the cold. Just like Ma Gloria, she never gave you specifics about the past, but she mentioned your grandfather from time to time. He was still in Ghana, somewhere. You never quite got the location down; it was always time to get off the call after that. You were considering this as you looked down at your hand on Ma Gloria's puckered thigh: youth juxtaposed with time. You felt the skin with the flat of your palm and tried to stretch it out, watching her time travel under your touch. She was quiet for a long time before responding to your message from Auntie Aretha.

"That doesn't sound like your grandfather."

Then you felt her back go up a little, a tenseness that you later associated with any mention of the place she used to call home. And you too, you used to know it as such, somehow. So you admitted then what you'd been humming around for years, what you knew she didn't want for you. But she couldn't control all of your desires.

"I've been thinking of going there, to Ghana. Auntie and I talked about it and—"

You stopped yourself short when you mentioned Auntie Aretha for a second time, knowing already that it was a step too far. Your words quickly became weaponry that you hadn't had enough practice with.

"And what do you need to go there for? We left that place for a reason. There are other countries to visit, Bobo."

Ma Gloria propped herself up as she said it, ready to turn over so you could receive the fullness of her stern look. But you were still a little naive then, the fuel of your teens propelling you forward no matter what stood in the way, including the one woman whose approval you constantly craved.

"You talk about it like there's a war raging there or something. There isn't. And it's my heritage. Why shouldn't I go?"

"Okay, and why should you?"

You had no answer of course, though you were certain of it when you had last spoken to Auntie Aretha. She'd hinted at new discoveries of yourself, that the trip was a rite of passage, that everyone should have a chance to go back, no matter what came before. So you prepared to repeat this to Ma Gloria, to make her understand that it was okay that you were searching for a connection to your familial home. But when it came to it, your intentions came to nothing in the face of her desperate anger at the suggestion of defying the one wish she had explicitly asked of you.

"I want . . . I want to know where I came from. Everyone is doing it—it's part of the Black British experience, Ma—"

She kissed her teeth so loudly you heard it in the back of your own throat. She was sitting up now, legs swinging from the edge of the table, looking up at you as you stood in front of her, your hands oily, confused. She knew she didn't need to also stand to get her point across.

"Do you not already know enough about where you come from, that you have to return and see for yourself?" You bowed your head, unsure how to respond without receiving a further scolding. "I didn't raise you to be like everyone else, did I?" You shook your head obediently. "Then why must you act like them? Unless you think I am wrong about this one too?" You gave another physical no. There was no room for hesitation when responding to such a question. "Then what do you need to go there and confirm?"

She didn't wait for another answer. She slipped herself off the table, wrapping her cloth around her and leaving the room. You heard her in the distance, sniffling, wiping away unexplained tears. You stood there alone for a few minutes, wondering where you had gone wrong, knowing that you wouldn't get on a plane without her blessing; you couldn't. After that you stopped inquiring, choosing instead to live out the remainder of your twenties within London mistakes and tiny traumas that built up over time.

Days into your thirties, you were revisiting all the conversations you had had with Ma Gloria about the topic of home, and all the ones you had kept inside. Now you were older and more sure of your questions and the answers you were looking for. And you were more in control, because she was back on your table, letting you work her muscles, work out the stress, open her up a little more. It was the first of many carefully curated steps. Your tread needed to be lighter this time.

"A friend is getting married in Accra, did I tell you? Anyway, I'm thinking I might go."

You had never lied so brazenly to Ma Gloria before, and it wasn't even a full lie. You did know someone who was going to Accra to get married, a friend of Chantelle's actually. But you weren't invited, and Chantelle had no plans to go. You felt the familiar feeling of Ma Gloria's muscles tensing against your fingers after you spoke, but you didn't react. You would play it cool for as long as possible.

"No, you didn't say. That's nice for them."

"Well, if I do go, would you suggest some places to visit? I don't want to be a complete tourist if I can help it."

You would use levity to move things forward if you had to. Her silence became an extended moment in the room, and you almost defaulted to putting on music to alleviate the tension. But you stopped yourself just in time.

"You know I don't like to get involved in these things."

"But why, Ma? You know all this stuff about the place that I don't, and you . . . you won't share. I'm starting to take it personally."

You chuckled emphatically as you said it, a false instinct while your stomach was in your throat and you pushed the words out, anxiety gripping you from the inside at what you were forcing into the open. On the outside you held a steady calm in the room, continuing your work on her muscles. You stepped to the side to work on her calves, waiting for her response.

"This isn't relaxing, Bobo." Her refusal to engage irritated you, and you had to stop your hands for a few seconds to gather your next thoughts. Before you could verbalize anything else, she spoke again. "You know I will never stop you going wherever you want to go. I just want to be kept out of it."

Her body seemed to unclench once the words had come out, as if she had said all that needed to be said. Usually this was true, but today her dismissals made you angry.

"How can I keep you out of it when you're the only one with answers?"

"Ah, so this is an interrogation now?"

She wasn't yelling, but her voice felt bigger, uncorked, with a sharp edge around it that used to strike fear into you as a child. Now it stoked the flames of your fury.

"I'm only asking questions about my life, Ma. What's wrong with that?"

"No. This is also *my* life you're questioning. Have I not shared enough of it with you?"

"You haven't shared anything! Not about Tina, not about my father—I have no memories of him, *nothing*!"

You were both stunned by your outburst, by the way your voice reached an octave you had sworn never to reach in her presence again. The only other time was when you were a teenager, about thirteen or so, sullen after she refused to let you go to a friend's sleepover because she had never met their parents. Your screaming then had led to two days of silence from her, with a frosty atmosphere every time you crossed paths. The disappointment in her eyes whenever she looked your way was almost too much to bear. Now that same look was aimed at you as you backed into the wall, as far from the table as possible. She slowly sat up topless, staring at you in disbelief, before remembering herself, stepping to the floor and reclaiming her cloth from the sofa.

For a long time as a child, you had assumed that the feeling of not being whole was because of your parents, a space that couldn't be filled because you had no memories of them. But it was only now, standing toe to toe with Ma Gloria, that you began to suspect you were missing something else, something more significant. Ma Gloria continued to stare at you, the moment still fraught with angry energy.

"Not everything needs to be shared. Leave this alone, okay?"

"Why can't you give me a straight answer, for once?"

Your voice was already getting smaller, breaking, losing its vigor.

"The answer to which question exactly? What do you desperately want to know that is worth ruining both of our days for?"

And then you felt silence finally wrap itself around your tongue, clamping your mouth shut at the height of a moment of revelation, as always. Only now Ma Gloria looked ready for it, prepared to fight you further—or at least up to a point. You saw her poised, and then watched her face slip into relief when no more words came out of you. Her shoulders fell and she resealed the cloth around her body, then suggested you have some tea before you went back to the flat. Nothing had happened. You were both safe.

When you left, it was dark outside. Your head felt like cotton wool, and you remembered that you never came home and gained clarity. You had been foolish to expect it today. You took the first bus that came and sat downstairs by the window, watching the city lights edge toward you and then fade into the background. Eventually you reached Central London, the twinkling shop lights beckoning you further. You picked up a *Metro* newspaper from the seat beside you, just to feel like you were holding on to something. The contents didn't matter. A wave of sadness from the day hit you before you finally stepped off the bus. You could get lost here if you wanted to, drifting between the eager shoppers, the smell of fresh crepes and smoky nuts from street vendors, the sweeter scents of a London evening in spring. You walked on autopilot toward the noise of people, going against the flow of the crowd to make it to that familiar corner. You looked to your right at the neon lights of Leicester Square, and then sent off a text to signify your arrival.

CHAPTER 16

Kumasi, 1995

Aretha

All Aretha wanted was answers, even if everyone else in the house pretended that it didn't matter anymore, that whatever Viktor had coming to him was in God's hands now. Aretha was not prepared to take that chance. She had to be sure that that man paid for what he had done. But she suspected that it would not come to pass, not on Ghanaian soil, anyway. She knew from enough of her cadet friends who were now in the military that the foreign officers living in Ghana had certain privileges. Not quite diplomatic immunity, but something similar, something that held more freedoms. This was why she had spent the last three days rising earlier than usual, leaving everyone in their beds, stealing away from making preparations for Bobby's One Week, to catch three tro-tros and walk the last bit of the journey to the courthouse where Viktor's trial would be taking place. It had already been fast-tracked. *The judicial system favors even the ones killing us*, Aretha thought when she arrived that third morning. She took her usual place and perched on the courthouse steps, ready to wait out the day. She opened her bag and pulled out a short, fat banana and a small tub of cashews, taking a bite of the first and throwing in a few cashews as a chaser, chewing both together, and slowly filling her stomach for the morning.

She had been starving that first day; she hadn't thought to bring food on the journey at all. She had only woken up with a simple purpose: fix this thing. In the house she felt useless. She needed to be doing something practical, helpful. The Sergeant would not let her help him make calls, and she could not bear to greet guests in her current state. Smiling in the face of the terror that was keeping her awake? No, she refused. But soon she realized there was no news from the Sergeant about Viktor, and she became afraid that he had not dealt with it as he had promised. In fact, perhaps he was avoiding it altogether. He had a good relationship with the Danish government. He had been the military attaché to their Ghanaian embassy for a long time; he would not rock the boat in such a way as to ruin his own career, no matter how much power he held now. Aretha could no longer trust that he would do the right thing, and that thought crushed her. It was the first time her faith in him had chipped away a little, and she thought that perhaps he was not infallible after all. So she let her youth lead her to the next decision: to take things into her own hands, just to make sure Viktor got what he deserved. She would be there to testify on behalf of the family if it was needed. She would be there to look him in the eye and let him know that she knew exactly who he was and what he had done in cold blood. She would be there, and if she got in trouble for it, well, then for once it would be worth breaking the rules.

So she traveled to the courthouse every morning and stayed there until the sun was setting, waiting for Viktor's case to be called. A friend in a judge's office had let her know that it would be any day now. On the third day, she jumped from the final tro-tro, finished her breakfast alone, and said a silent thank-you to Maame Serwaa for the fuel. Maame Serwaa had knocked on Aretha's door late the night before, brought her a bag of food and snacks, and made her fresh bofrot to have after lunch. Aretha looked at her suspiciously at first, as she took the food from her, smelling the donuts with a smile, but Maame Serwaa said nothing. She only gave Aretha a kind look and then left the room again before she could even express her gratitude. Aretha made a note to buy Maame Serwaa something, a new dress for church, or maybe a Mills & Boon book if she could find one; Aretha knew she loved those.

Aretha heard the sound of voices coming from inside the court-house, and she moved toward the open doors of the courtroom, trying to stay out of sight and hoping to squeeze in the back. The security guard recognized her but said nothing, simply nodding her toward the back of the room before the judge arrived. Now she just had to wait.

She should have already been making her way home before Gloria or the Sergeant started looking for her. But Aretha could not move. She remained at the back of the courtroom, slumped in her seat. Viktor was exonerated so speedily that if she had blinked, she might have missed it. Not quite cleared; he was being extradited to Denmark to face judgment there, but she already knew that with the lawyer he had, he would have a clean record by the time he landed on the other side. No one would know what he had done, what he had taken from them all. And she wondered how she could have been so stupid as to expect anything else. The judge's hands were tied; it was a military matter that they would deal with themselves. She had to let him go, let him be dealt with by his own people. But Aretha knew he wouldn't be dealt with—he would return to a new-old life and go about his business. She had not seen remorse on his face when he was walked into the courtroom by an officer. He was stoic, the least animated she had ever seen him. She wished to never lay eyes on him again, but she still burnt holes into the back of his head throughout the entire trial—all fifteen minutes of it.

What a waste, she thought. She had fixed nothing and was not even called on. Just an extra thing in a room that no one needed. An hour had already passed since then, the sky was starting to turn orange. Soon it would be evening and getting back on the tro-tro would not be as safe as it was coming. She knew the Sergeant would have already been told of the outcome, called on the phone to be informed officially. Perhaps he was sitting in his office now, staring at papers, wondering how to deliver the news to the rest of the house, to his remaining daughters and granddaughter. He likely wished for any other job but that one. Maybe he too was as angry as Aretha, maybe it would fuel him to appeal the decision, or to find out Viktor's whereabouts in Denmark, finally take matters into his own hands. Would that not be something? Aretha was sitting up now, alert, with a new direction in mind. Nothing would bring Bobby back, or Tina. Or Mommy, for that matter. But that didn't mean she should sit still and accept things as they were.

She left the courthouse finally, and that same security guard greeted her with a questioning look on his face. She asked him if there was a telephone she could use, and then she called Prince and asked that he come and pick her up.

"Has everyone in this house lost their heads, or what is it?"

The Sergeant was standing behind his desk. He had launched himself up to standing to address both his daughters, who were requesting time with him for different reasons. Aretha had only just arrived as he was in the middle of what appeared to be an argument with Gloria. Aretha had taken it as a good sign, that perhaps a dressing down of Gloria meant he would adhere to *her* requests a little easier. He had a habit of going with Gloria's decisions; she made them seem like they were his. So if he disagreed, it must be serious.

"Daddy, what are we supposed to do when you have to leave again for work? D'you think I can hold off everyone then? They are only now staying away because you are here. I'm afraid to leave Maame Serwaa by herself with Bobo, before that Auntie Vida or someone on her mission comes to "cure" Bobo? What then, Daddy? We have to leave!"

Gloria looked desperate, her eyes wet from recent tears, staring at the Sergeant with conviction. Aretha realized she needed some of that same courage to make her own statement. She stood in the doorway, watching as the Sergeant surveyed them both.

"Aretha!" She jumped at the sound of her name, wondering if she had already confessed her thoughts without knowing. "Where have you been? Bobby's mother has been on the telephone *three times* today looking for you. As if I am your houseboy to be taking messages. So? Where were you?"

Aretha started to open her mouth, to tell it straight even if her insides were trembling. But Gloria jumped in.

"Father! Please, don't ignore me."

She walked to his side of the desk suddenly and planted herself opposite him, in front of his broad frame, looking him in the eye to show she was serious. Aretha decided to stay quiet for this one, interested now in whatever it was Gloria was requesting. The Sergeant furrowed his brow, a look they had all received as children—it only needed to happen once for everyone to fall in line. But he had also inadvertently been the creator of these defiant, self-possessed women. Some of his absences had left them to fend for themselves, to take care of each other. And his presence had been framed by book recommendations, conversations about what was in the paper and what was going on in the world. Now they knew themselves better than he knew them, and every time he came home, he learned that lesson again. He looked at Gloria as if this were all floating around his mind then, and Aretha knew that eventually he would give her what she wanted, whatever it was. Gloria always knew what was best for everyone, apparently.

"Okay, Glory. So you want to . . . what? Take my granddaughter out of the country because you're afraid that one of the elders will do some voodoo on her?"

"That's not it. Please don't make fun."

"Do I look like a clown? It's what you just said to me."

Aretha watched the Sergeant express the faintest flicker of a smile.

"This is about Bobo's future. *Our* future. You know what it will be like for her if she remains here. That talk of a curse? Daddy, it's not a joke. It doesn't matter if you or I believe it. It will follow her. Just as it has followed us."

Gloria turned to Aretha then, reaching an arm toward her, including her suddenly in the reasoning for some kind of trip. Aretha wanted to protest, but there was nothing Gloria had said that she could deny. Gloria turned back to the Sergeant. He was sitting back in his chair, but he held his hands up slightly in question.

"Why London of all places? We don't have much family there."

"I know."

"Hmm. And Paa Kweku, he will be there also?"

"Yes, Daddy."

Gloria's voice dropped at that point, and for a moment Aretha remembered them both as children, chasing the chickens onto the road, throwing them wrapped up balls of sweet bread to eat, and then receiving a telling off from the elderly neighbor because she said it was bad for their diets. Gloria had been solemn then, just as she was now, shy even in her regret at hurting the flightless birds.

Aretha swallowed hard, a lump of grief threatening to dry her throat. She had to say something.

"Glory? London, really?"

Aretha had not considered it a real possibility until the Sergeant took a seat and was obviously thinking it over. Gloria turned to her, as though Aretha had only just entered the room.

"It will be good for all of us. I know it."

Aretha froze in shock for a moment before coming back to herself and storming up to Gloria.

"Us who? Me? I'm not going!"

Aretha was ready to fight until she heard the rumble of the Sergeant's laughter behind them. It was steady and thick, like a babbling brook in full flow.

"So the two of you have not even agreed on this yet? Glory, I expected more." Then he closed a leather-bound folder on his desk as if the matter were done. "Please, I have work to do."

He pointed them both toward the door, but neither moved. Aretha worried that the standoff would drain her adrenaline before she said what *she* had wanted to say, but then Gloria walked to the door and pushed it closed. She turned back to the room.

"We are not done yet. Aretha, I know you can understand wanting to go somewhere else right now?"

Aretha could only nod, catching herself before she was able to speak up. She needed a minute to think through her words, to consider everything that was at stake. To finally have her say.

CHAPTER 17

London, Present

Whitney

"This place is not the one, Whit."

"What's wrong with it?"

"The plastic menus, for a start."

"Really? I kinda like it."

"Well."

You shrugged with a smile at Jak's disdain for your chosen meeting place, sipping at an Aperol spritz that was a bit too light on the prosecco. If you closed your eyes, you could imagine you were sitting under a blue sky, not hunched over a booth on the first floor of a twenty-four-hour pancake restaurant that overlooked Leicester Square, the day already stretched into evening as Instagramming tourists surrounded you. Still, you liked the decor and the soft, vanilla-like atmosphere. It felt like a neutral place to be, somewhere to clear your mind and start the day over again, even as it was ending. Jak had texted to say they'd gotten stuck on a bus diversion on their way back from a meeting they had also been late for. They had arrived an hour after you, flustered and wet from a sudden downpour that you'd managed to escape. You wanted to ask about the meeting, but then you held back. You would let Jak get settled into the conversation first.

"How you going? Shaken the birthday blues yet?"

"Not really, but maybe this is who I am now. Or I'm still recovering from the Tuck Shop." You smiled as if it were a joke. "Anyway, how are you?"

Jak shook off their coat and shoved it beside them in a damp heap.

"Mostly wet, but alright. I meant to say, sorry I couldn't make it out to the Tuck Shop the other night."

"Oh, mate, don't worry about it. I know you've had to pick up extra shifts. It's cool."

Jak made a face you didn't quite understand and took a sip from the Oreo milkshake you'd ordered for them.

"Yeah, that. And also . . . I just didn't wanna make it awkward with Chantelle. 'Cause we're still . . . whatever, and there should only be good vibes on your birthday, so . . . yeah. Sorry I couldn't make it. I wanted to."

You slid your tongue along the top row of your teeth, unsure what to say. You hadn't given it much thought, that the disagreement between Chantelle and Jak had kept going and was spilling out now into other things. You had not assumed it was resolved; you had just stopped thinking about it. Jak avoided your eyes for a moment, using a napkin to wipe away the endless condensation forming on the sides of the tall glass that held their milkshake. You found yourself clambering for the right words to say. Each new minor inconvenience seemed to be catching you out, tying your tongue up into anxious knots. You looked past Jak. There was a family sitting at the table next to yours: a mum, a dad, and two toddler-age children who were screaming bloody murder and trying to steal each other's pancakes. The mum tried to satiate them with juice while her husband sat beside her quietly, reading the menu with the same amount of concentration required for Russian literature. She glanced down at her wedding band as if in reflex, and you accidentally caught her eye, giving her a friendly smile in the process, one of the many you handed out from time to time. She smiled back and shook her head in amusement, as if to say, "Motherhood!" As if you would know exactly what that meant. You turned back to Jak.

"Where were you before? You said you had a meeting?"

You couldn't say what made it sound so brisk, only that your question felt a little like retaliation, like sudden irritation at being a casualty of Jak and Chantelle's silent war.

"Just this group I go to sometimes. To talk and stuff."

"Oh. Like a therapy thing?"

"I guess, sometimes it can be like that? My own therapy sessions always feel a bit more intense, though. This group is more about support and stuff. I'm not really explaining it, am I?" You shook your head, and Jak chuckled nervously. "Look, it's for trans and nonbinary folks. But it's also just people getting together, chatting, finding community, ya know? We talk about all kinds of things. Like tonight I dropped in on a big convo about identity, which I'm annoyed I missed the beginning of. But anyways."

Jak sucked on their straw, visibly bothered by the recollection. Or maybe they were just bothered by the whole conversation, by having to explain it to you, hesitant because maybe you'd judge them for it or ask stupid questions or make them feel othered. Make them feel like what's happening with Chantelle is happening with you too. But Jak deserved for you to be vocal about that. Your friendship hadn't changed, even if your conversations about your lives had. That was okay, and you needed to be okay to talk about it—to let Jak know that it was always going to be okay between you. And that really, your feelings about it shouldn't matter. You loved them.

"I'm really happy for you, that you have that. People who know how it feels, I mean. Do you—do you feel like you know who you are now? Like, do you feel more certain?"

You had hoped your words would be more eloquent, less clunky than they sounded when they came out. Jak half shrugged and then tapped the table to a steady rhythm, thinking through a response.

"A lot of the time now, I feel like I do, but then there are new things I discover about myself, and I'm like—oh, this is cool, I didn't know I would like that as much as I did! So, it's like, it's never just about one thing. *I'm* not just one thing, ya know?"

"Yeah, I guess not. But . . . what if you're not *anything*?"

"As in . . . ?"

"Like generally, a lot of the time it seems like everyone knows something about themselves, some reason why they are the way they are. They find some connection to their heritage or their identity and experience, and something slots into place, even if it's small. But what if there is just . . . nothing? Like, that connection doesn't seem to exist for you? Who are you then, d'you know?"

You wanted the words to tumble out of you and form some kind of meaning on the table, rearrange the letters and give you answers to the questions you were asking that didn't really make sense. At least not according to Jak's face.

"C'mon, Whit, you know who you are—at least *I've* always felt that way about you."

You felt sadness swipe across you suddenly. You wanted to order another drink and disappear the feeling, but it also didn't feel right to do that. You tried to elaborate.

"I've just had questions for so long about what happened before we came to London when I was a kid, and—I've just got gaps. Like, no memories, just black holes of time where my favorite books might have been or my favorite toy or even my dad's voice. I don't have any of that stuff, and it's . . . it's bugging me, Jak."

You ran your hand over your head briefly, aware that you might have disturbed the perfect direction your afro had been taking all day. Jak leaned back, and you watched them calculating which thing was right to say: what you needed to hear versus what you wanted.

"You remember when we first met, right? And I told you about that uncle, what he did?"

"Of course."

You tried to stop your face wincing at the memory, hoping your response was calm and even, but Jak wasn't really looking at you then. Their line of vision went past you for a moment.

"Well, I'd never told anyone that before. Like, you were the *first*, mate. And that's why I called you again. I felt like you might have magic hands or something! And it made me realize how much I'd been holding in, and the physical pain it was causing me. Like, that childhood shit was making me crook. And you fixed that. *You*, Whit. I think you're more connected to yourself than you think."

You didn't know what to say, but you felt that stab to your gut that was starting to become familiar. As if someone had punched you hard enough to take your breath but not to do any lasting damage. A question danced across your mind.

"But why did you tell *me*?"

"Why not you?"

The reply came quickly, and you blinked as if the words had caught you in the eye. You rubbed them, hoping to find clarity again.

"But I was a stranger. I'm not a therapist. What if I made it worse? You just trusted me. I just, I don't get what made you tell me then, in that moment."

You realized that you had always wanted to ask Jak this and had never known how to. It was a question that you could never really get off your mind. You worried that Jak would be bothered by it, that they had shared this extremely tender, painful thing, and you could only wonder why, rather than just be grateful that you didn't ruin everything for them.

"I guess I just felt like I could, like you would get it. I don't know, Whit, there was just something about you. And anyway, I was right, wasn't I?"

Jak smiled warmly and raised their eyebrows in a comical way that always made you cringe-laugh. You chuckled but felt their words settle into your chest. You already knew you would dissect them later, try and figure out what that *something about you* was exactly, that thing Jak saw and you did not. Some other secret part of yourself, perhaps? Another puzzle piece to find.

Soon you had both finished your drinks, the family with the screaming children had left, and there were only a handful of people now remaining. Through the window looking down onto the square, you could see that the crowds were more sporadic but also more energetic. The groups on a night out were only just beginning their adventures, jumping through the puddles that looked like rainbows after an hour of rain on black tarmac. Even the casino and the fast-food stands looked enticing, almost magical if you had enough hope to take with you into the night ahead. The sound of Jak zipping up their coat ripped you from your own thoughts, and you looked up at them dazed.

"I've gotta get up super early tomorrow, so can we head out?"

They asked it gently, as if you looked as fragile as you suddenly felt, which was worrying. You obeyed and stood up yourself, pulling on your coat and grabbing your bag as you followed them to the door, not even looking back to see if you'd left anything on the table. It didn't feel like it mattered. Outside, the smell of rain hung about your head, and you both walked silently to the Tube station, saying your goodbyes at the top of the steps before entering to avoid the transiting crowds inside as you joined different Tube lines.

"Text me when you get home, yeah?"

Jak hugged you before you could answer the question you always asked each other before traveling home. You held on a little longer, so unlike you but there was something you needed from Jak that wasn't available through words just then. When you finally pulled apart, you exchanged soft smiles and Jak gave you a squeeze on the arm.

"Later Laces—don't forget to text me!"

They poked out a tongue after assigning you the nickname you definitely hadn't agreed upon, and you grinned in spite of yourself. They disappeared down the steps, and you waited a beat, breathing in the cold air and the smell of Peking duck wafting from the restaurants nearby, nestled neatly into the bustling narrow lanes branching off Chinatown. You watched a mother rush past with a stroller, the baby inside holding a doll with a vice grip as city lights flashed across its face. You thought again of Teddy Milo, of the childhood bear you suddenly wished you were in possession of. It would be something to physically hold on to, so that you could finally feel grounded again. Now all you felt between your fingers was air.

You half woke the next day to the sound of birds cawing too loudly. You smelled red wine in the air. You couldn't recall opening the bottle when you got home, only the mug in your hand, sitting on your bed staring at your laptop screen, gulping mouthfuls in an effort to forget something you only half remembered. Now you were still stuck in the why of it all—why your tongue was dry ash and why the smell of roasted plantain wouldn't leave your nostrils, as if something had been unlocked. No one else was home, but that smell, that smoked edge of something bulky and hot, seemed to be filling your lungs, punctuating your senses, your personhood. It felt as though you were still half in a dream, that you had returned to the place you stumbled across while high in the Tuck Shop. A vision seemed to be moving toward you, and you saw red: a blush of it on the walls, the doors, your own fingers. How had all of it, all that red, come out of you? The granules of the moment slipped through your mind as you fought with it, trying to regain consciousness, to force yourself to actually open your eyes. When you finally did, you felt a familiar ache dragging you back into the dark, toward a resurfaced pain that was frozen in youth, childishly poking you but never really revealing itself.

Jak's words still rattled around your brain, about you being the first person they disclosed their assault to, that they were ready to tell because you were there. You felt your throat trying to close suddenly, to force an intake of breath, just before a sob escaped. It shocked you, the rapid change in mood, the rush of emotion. A wail followed, practically beating its way out of your chest like a trapped bird, escaping so violently that it sent the pigeons on the roof outside fleeing. Now that your eyes were fully open, you looked down at your body and saw that you were drenched in sweat. You must have been stressed even in your sleep, your nightmares tossing you from one end of the bed to the other. The covers had been tangled around your legs when you first felt the morning light hit your eyelids, twisted ropes holding you down for a few terror-stricken seconds before you freed yourself.

You sloped off the bed as if your bones had disintegrated. Tears climbed furiously down your face. You wondered briefly if something terrifying had happened when you'd blacked out, and now your body was just reacting. You pulled all your clothes off, suddenly wanting to be free of them. You needed to shower or bathe or bleach it all away. Something that could cleanse you. You stood up quickly, as if driven by a force outside yourself. You made it to the bathroom, naked and shivering. There was a chill in the flat. Chantelle had left all the windows open again, to take her pick of where to smoke. You considered it a selfish act, and the thought entered your mind viciously, leaving a stark taste in your mouth before disappearing again. You reached behind the shower screen and turned the hot tap on, watching the steam rise quickly around you. Maybe you could disappear. You stepped in and let the shower rinse and wash with its streams and droplets. But it didn't bring the immediate calm you were hoping for. You closed your eyes, and the hot feeling returned again, all smoke and earth, the muffle of voices and your body trying to get away from itself. You had hoped that under the cover of the bathroom waterfall you could find safety. But the splash on your skin suddenly felt like someone else's sweat, and you were trapped again in a small space with nowhere to go. There was almost a comfort in it, in feeling suffocated.

You felt your fingertips wrinkle under the water, some other internal alarm going off and telling you to step out of the shower, pull your fluffy robe toward you, the one forever hanging on the back of the bathroom door. You did as you were told, forgoing a towel entirely because there was no point. You could drip all over the flat and watch the puddles dry in your wake, comforted that there were still traces of you that could be evidenced, seen with your own eyes. You returned to your bedroom and threw on some joggers and a jumper, trying to pull yourself out of the funk.

That was when you looked at the time, held safely in the form of the clock that lived on your bedside table. Ma Gloria had given it to you for your eighteenth birthday. It was carved into the shape of a bird, painted with a rainbow of colors. The bird had its head turned toward the tail, an egg hanging from the beak. The clock face was in the center of the bird's chest, and you wondered about the unreliability of the heart.

You considered doing something meaningful with your last day off. Instead you moved toward the chair in the corner of the room and picked up your laptop, searching for a distraction in a new limited TV series. You heard the slam of the door a few minutes later and Chantelle trudging through heavily, first into the kitchen, then her own room. She sounded angry. Months earlier, you might have checked she was okay, but these days your love language was hesitation, and you both suffered from all the inaction between you. It was an hour or so later that you heard a knock on your door. You invited her in, and you moved your laptop to the side, assuming she would come in and sit on the bed with you. Instead she opened the door only a little and stayed there.

"Did you buy more milk?"

It wasn't the question you had expected, and you couldn't remember the last time you'd been food shopping, not this week anyway.

"No, was I supposed to?"

She huffed in response, almost rolling her eyes before thinking better of it.

"Literally on Tuesday, I texted you to grab milk because I was running late." You looked back at her blankly because the previous days had already rolled into one. "I don't know what your problem is at the moment, Whit, but I can't help you if you don't talk to me, yeah?"

"Because I didn't buy milk?"

You hadn't meant to sound facetious, but you couldn't help it. It felt like she was blaming you for how weird things were between the two of you.

"You know what? Never mind."

Her head disappeared, and it was like she had slapped you in the face. You felt an explosion coming and leaped off the bed to follow her into the kitchen.

"How are you mad at me right now? And why are you wearing a scarf inside?" The first question was your anger, but the second made you both crack a smile, briefly. You couldn't even fight with too much conviction. She didn't reply and instead plonked herself on the sofa and grabbed the remote, the television blaring into action. You always left it on too loud. You sat beside her, taking the remote from her to turn it down, and she didn't resist. She just stared into space, in the direction of the TV but not actually watching it. "Something's going on with you too. Did you and the French boy have a fight?"

Chantelle's face crinkled.

"Sort of. It was stupid, and it's put me in a bad mood, that's all. Sorry."

"Well, what can we do to get you out of it? Disney film? Take-away? Wine? I'm easy."

She didn't respond, and you were growing tired. You couldn't force her to say more if she didn't want to, and Chantelle was hard to be around when she and Paris fought. You wondered if she knew that. You began to turn away from her and get back up, but she caught your attention again.

"Wait. What else is going on with you?"

You raised your eyebrows in genuine surprise. When was the last time she had asked? You couldn't remember.

"Nothing much. Went to Ma's yesterday, and I saw Jak. Anyway, it was fine." She stared at you as if trying to read your mind, to find where the lie ended and the truth began. You felt heat rising up your neck. She didn't say anything for a long time, so you countered. "What were you guys fighting about then?"

Chantelle swallowed down a breath and then cringed as if that action physically hurt her. Your eyes went to the scarf again. You were worried, and you didn't hide it this time. She tried to swallow once more before responding.

"It was dumb. He literally just got to London, and already he's going back home. I asked him, I said what are you rushing back for, some girl? And he just laughed. Didn't even deny it, so I . . ." She let silence hit her words momentarily. Then she threw on a semi-convincing smile and shrugged at you. "You know what I'm like, big words and a quick temper. I shouldn't have said anything."

"Yeah, well, he also shouldn't be laughing at you. You deserve better than that."

"It's fine. He's just being a boy. It's whatever. We agreed to an open thing, so this is part of it. I know you don't get it."

You frowned at her dismissiveness.

"You're right, I don't. I thought you guys were working on the whole monogamy thing before?"

"We were."

"So how is this supposed to help that? Like, didn't he have problems being honest with you last year?"

"Yeah, and this is supposed to make that better because if we're seeing other people, we tell each other about it."

"But you just said he might be seeing someone that you didn't know about. So he's still lying to you."

Your words sounded like attacks because that's what they were. You felt untethered, and the only thing around you to roughly grab hold of was Chantelle. You knew it wasn't fair, that your upset with life was separate from your judgment of her relationship, but now it was all mixed together in an ugly soup, and you were in the thick of it. Chantelle shook her head at you, as if you were a spoiled child throwing a tantrum. She began to smile then, moving her head from side to side, and then an audible snort escaped her, and she made no attempts to hide it. She said nothing more, still chuckling as she stood up to head back to her room. You felt a snap to your irritation.

"Why are we laughing?"

She whipped round at your question like she had been waiting for it.

"You're one to talk."

"Am I?"

You suspected that Chantelle knew something about you that you hadn't told her. Her face told you that she did, and that's what was worrying you now.

"*You* lied to me. About you and the Bard—that eejit—getting back together. For months, Whit. Months."

She was hurt. All over her face was pain, and finally you were starting to understand why. And then she leaned on the door frame as if standing was suddenly too much. You didn't know what to do, what truth to tell, or whether to just stick with the lie. Wasn't the lie always a little bit easier anyway?

"We weren't really together, though. He was just hanging around, and I didn't know how to tell him no."

It was ironic, your choice of words. The taste of them, the way they slid up your throat and out of your eyes. You felt your cheeks damp, unsure of what was going on. Chantelle looked at you, alarmed suddenly. She was by your side now, arm around your shoulder and guiding you back to the sofa. Her face was still pulled down into sadness, but she looked at you anyway.

"You coulda just told me. Like, you're my best friend. I know I gave you shit about him sometimes, but—"

"A lot of the time."

"Sometimes deserved. But then you got all sneaky with him, and you just cut me out. Like I'd done something bad to you."

Chantelle leaned back into the sofa, a gentle hand on your thigh, not fully rested and as if she might take it back at any moment. You wanted nothing more than to go back to your room, but you felt stuck. It was fine as long as she didn't find out the thing about the Bard, the bad thing he had actually done. She wouldn't be able to look at you again after that. You tried saying something closer to the truth, even if it wasn't the whole thing.

"I didn't know it was coming out like that, I was just a bit . . . embarrassed?"

"It just felt like, bad mind, ya know? We don't let *men* come between us, or we didn't before. Then suddenly you were all quiet and distant, and I felt like anything I said you'd take wrong, so then maybe I couldn't tell you stuff either, and . . . now I don't know how to talk to you. Like, for real."

"I don't know what to say."

You knew that there was a way to explain away her frustrations, to explain the space that had grown between you, if only you could tell her what had happened. But how to make the words with your mouth? How to explain the moment comfort turned into a curse, the moment you were both changed irreparably and entirely familiar with that change? That you felt a very present and seething rage toward the Bard, as well as curtains of shame at ever feeling like you might love him. This wasn't something to be said in a sentence, to be used as a bargaining chip in a friendship you held dear but had let slip from your periphery in the few months since you became lost. So you really did not know what to say.

Chantelle's voice became smaller then, and you resisted the urge to lift her chin up, help her project like she usually did.

"Maybe, maybe you felt like you couldn't come to me, and I get that after me and Jak sorta fell off—"

"Chan, I don't even really know what happened with you two.

Like, you never told me. So how could I talk to you about stuff when you won't talk to *me*?"

You were twisting things back onto her because the light on you was becoming unbearable. Maybe this could be smoothed over in a different way, where you did not need to reveal anything more. You turned your whole body toward her now, running a small finger along the edge of the sheer scarf she still wore.

"But you're talking to Jak more, innit? I just feel . . . shut out of everything. Like, we live together, and I've honestly got no clue what's going on with you. It hurts."

Chantelle wiped away tears with her thumb and ran a hand down her hair, long black waves staying in perfect place even when she was distraught. You loved this woman in a way that told you she was kin, and with that familial attachment, you had inserted a distance that you were used to with family. You were beginning now to regret the steps you had taken to get here. Not that you were wrong completely, but perhaps misguided.

"You're right. I've been missing, and I'm . . . sorry for it. And I wanna know what's going on with you too."

Chantelle smiled in response, a genuine one this time, not of ridicule but acknowledgment. You looked up at the kitchen counter, surveying the car keys she had dropped there, aware that Chantelle did not own a car. But Paris did. This time she followed your gaze and then looked down at the floor.

"I'm an open book. What you wanna know?"

Her voice had gotten very quiet. You paused for a moment. You could see that she was opening a door again, one you had not had access to in months. Your fingers moved as if independent of you, toward the scarf around her neck. But she didn't flinch, didn't stop you, so you untied it and pulled it gently loose. It unfurled and floated down to the sofa. The red marks around her throat were visible now, and although you had suspected it, seeing them fresh like this still sent your stomach plummeting. She was still looking toward the floor. You watched her tears roll, and then your own followed suit. You pulled her to you finally, and she sank into it, into an embrace that was long overdue.

You stayed like that with each other. The debris of the week settling where it may, neither of you close to rebuilding anything except what this moment was making.

CHAPTER 18

Kumasi, 1995

Maame Serwaa

It was the shouting that woke her. It was always the shouting, or at least the memory of it. Maame Serwaa's mind playing tricks, trying to give her another chance to run faster, get there sooner, before any lives were taken, before they were ruined. She shot up from the chair she had dozed off in, now that her bed was no longer a peaceful place. She jumped to the doorway, trying to hear the thing that had pulled her from a dream, and immediately ran toward the commotion when she heard Aretha shout, "Heeeey!"

Aretha was standing in the doorway of Uncle Clinton's office, her hands raised in the air dramatically, palms open as if pleading.

"You cannot be the boss of my life! Not anymore, Glory. No more, eh?"

Aretha had brought her hands down to her hips now, as if about to pose. Then she looked up at Maame Serwaa, suddenly infuriated as she pointed at her, while turning back to the office.

"And what will you do without Maame to take care of Whitney? Unless you want to take me so I can be your nanny? And you do know that these pastor salaries cannot provide for you—Paa

Kweku will not be worth much more over there. Ah! Daddy, you have to say no to this foolish idea, abeg."

Aretha seemed desperate and upset, two things Maame Serwaa had rarely witnessed in her. She watched Gloria walk out of the office casually, brushing past Aretha.

"This is the first you have heard of this, so I'll ignore your disrespect this time. But that is it, little sister. If you keep speaking as a child, then I will address you as such."

Gloria was measured in her speaking and turned her back on Aretha, which only fanned the flames of her sister's anger. Maame Serwaa was sure this was Gloria's intention, and true to form, Aretha flew at Gloria with such speed that Maame Serwaa was afraid she might not catch her, but she got there just in time, grabbing Aretha's wrist, pulling her backward to avoid their bodies colliding.

"You do not run my life! I have plans for my future, even if you do not!"

Aretha spat the words out and then wriggled free from Maame Serwaa's grasp before storming away. Gloria had been trying to wear a hard scowl, but now she stood frozen to the spot, her hand cupped to her mouth moments before letting out sobs that were only slightly muffled behind her fingers. The sounds morphed into wailing, as if a trapped animal were crying for its life. Maame Serwaa wrapped her arms around Gloria, hoping to quiet the sound, to stop the way it was cracking open her own chest.

The fighting had stopped, and suddenly the house experienced movement again. Maame Serwaa was supposed to get everything ready, and as she waited for plans to be confirmed, she was not sure where to start. Gloria's idea was to leave Kumasi with Bobo, and she insisted it would only be for a short time, a year or two until the talk died down, but Maame Serwaa knew better than that. Everyone did, but it helped to keep the pretense up, to act as if they were going on a long holiday, nothing more.

Aretha would not be going with them. Some hours after the fight, she had received a phone call. Afterward she said nothing. She went quietly to her room for the rest of the evening. The next morning, Maame Serwaa prepared her hot water and knocked on her door, but Aretha was not inside. She panicked until she found Aretha outside, still in her nightdress, sitting on one of the balconies, looking out into the middle distance.

"Sister, wo ho ye?"

Aretha nodded to say she was okay as Maame Serwaa moved to stand beside her, following her line of sight, the blood orange of the sunrise splashing a golden color onto both their faces.

"You know, I haven't prayed in a long time. I had stopped believing that God was . . . for me. And then last night—a real prayer was answered. Before I even prayed for it—can you imagine?"

Aretha was softened somehow, her voice at ease, no longer carrying the short, sharpened angst it had held all week. Maame Serwaa wanted to tell her that; perhaps she hadn't noticed.

"God is for all of us, especially in these times."

Aretha laughed lightly, as if Maame Serwaa had said something silly, but then she turned to her.

"In a few weeks I will go to Denmark. Auntie Penny has asked for one of us to come for Bobby's funeral. He told her I was the sister he never had, so she said that makes me her daughter too. So I am going. I have to."

She stared at Maame Serwaa as she said it, waiting for her to respond in kind with something helpful.

"That is a good thing, for one of us—one of *you* to be there."

"This has to be God because, Maame, that Viktor, that *devil*, that is where he will also be. So I will find him, and I will fix this for all of us. I promise." The intensity in Aretha's eyes was hard to look away from, despite the chill now running down Maame Serwaa's spine. "You cannot repeat this to Glory—or to anyone. Understand?"

Aretha had taken hold of Maame Serwaa's wrist, just as Maame Serwaa had done to her the night before, stopping a physical altercation between the sisters. Now she felt the grip as a warning, Aretha's fingers getting tighter, waiting for her to confirm the command.

"Yes, sister, I understand."

The house was heavy with all the things it was holding, and Maame Serwaa knew this was the last time it would feel this way. Uncle Clinton had asked for something special to be prepared for his last Friday in the house before he traveled to Germany for a new work assignment. Tomorrow would be Bobby's One Week—his mother's uncle and older brother had made all the arrangements in her absence. Gloria, Aretha, and Uncle Clinton would attend. Maame Serwaa would stay home with Bobo, planning to do her own prayer, say her goodbyes with the other house staff, with Kwame and Prince. Bobby had meant something to everyone. He was too young for there to be any celebration, and the truth of it hung over all their heads now.

Maame Serwaa brought in the food, one tray at a time. Three large bowls of fufu and light soup were placed on the table. Then Maame Serwaa left and returned with Bobo's high chair, placing it next to Gloria as it always was. Bobo was playing a game with her dolls on the floor, and Maame Serwaa scooped her up without a word, fastening her gently into the high chair before she could protest. Then she came back again with a bowl of warm soapy water, going first to Uncle Clinton, then Gloria and then Aretha. When all hands were clean, she nodded in the general direction of the table and turned to leave.

"Maame, wait." Gloria's voice thudded into the room unexpectedly, and Maame Serwaa turned back around. "Come and eat with us. Daddy, it's okay?"

Gloria looked at Uncle Clinton, and Maame Serwaa realized it was not for permission but assurance. He nodded, and Gloria looked back at Maame Serwaa with satisfaction. Maame Serwaa had been looking forward to a moment alone, with her thoughts and her food, but she did not eat with the family often, and she feared it might be one of the last times they were all together. Plus, this week was unlike any they had had before, a time Maame Serwaa hoped would never be repeated. So she brought her own food and sat down in one of the empty seats, previously assigned to Tina. The other empty seat was for Auntie Ruth, and no one ever sat there.

"Gloria, I have spoken to your Uncle Derek. The family he had staying in the house in Golders Green, they are purchasing their own home soon, so it will be free for you and Bobo after that time. In perhaps three months or so."

Uncle Clinton quickly threw in a mouthful of food after speaking, somehow ensuring none of the soup dripped down his fingers.

"Oh. Three months? That's a long time."

Irritation had returned to Gloria's voice, and Maame Serwaa caught Aretha's eye as they both waited for Uncle Clinton's reply. He dropped his head for a moment, as if to calm himself. Then he spoke to Gloria directly, his eyes piercing from across the table.

"Your uncle is doing me this favor because he knows I need my daughter and granddaughter in a safe home. If we had to wait three *years* for that, trust me, we would wait. Hmm! You thought this would be easy, eh?"

He shook his head, baffled by her insolence. Gloria hung her head, but still, to Maame Serwaa's shock, she had more to say.

"I am grateful, Daddy, I am. I was only trying to be fast in my preparations, to apply for the hospital jobs now, but if we won't go for a few months, then—"

"It will take that long for us to arrange Whitney's passport anyway."

Gloria opened her mouth to respond again, but this time Aretha jumped in. "I have a question. Who will take care of Whitney, if you are out all hours working in hospitals and this and that other job, to survive in that place?"

There was genuine concern on Aretha's face as she asked it, Maame Serwaa could see that, but Gloria would take it as an interrogation. These were the times that Maame Serwaa was thankful briefly that they were only house sisters, that she did not need to vie for Uncle Clinton's attention in the same way that they did. Nor did she carry the burden of loss in the same way as them. Every day that passed, she understood better why Gloria was leaving, how perhaps it was her only chance to escape the place for good. She had put her family first, education and work second. Her own romantic life did not exist, and Maame Serwaa no longer wondered why. She had seen Paa Kweku and Gloria together enough now to know that they belonged to each other and were unlikely to accept anyone else. Was there a happiness in there somewhere, between them? She was not sure. Nor could she be sure that Aretha's wants and desires could ever be truly met if she too stayed in the house. Maame Serwaa could not speak on it too much; she had her suspicions, and she also felt warmth toward Aretha as the middle sister, the easily forgotten, left to forge her own path. Aretha had watched Gloria's life and desired nothing like it for herself—her departure from the house was almost an inevitability.

"You think I have not thought that through? There are more

prospects for me there as a nurse, you know that. Who do you think was paying for Bobo's clothes and food but Bobby, myself, and Daddy? At least there, I can build something for her, something Tina and Bobby would have wanted. If you come, Aretha, you can help me do that for all of us, hmm? School is finished, you can just join."

Gloria looked at Aretha imploringly.

"Auntie Penny has invited me to Copenhagen. One of us should be there when they bury Bobby. If you had sense, you would come with me and drop this ridiculous London plan."

"Or you could just come to London once everything is done. I lie?"

Gloria asked it to the table, challenging Aretha again. Maame Serwaa continued to eat, looking deeply into her bowl, not wanting to accidentally let slip anything about Aretha's real plans. She would not be dragged into this one—she could separate herself from the family when she needed to, even if her worry for both sisters was reaching boiling point.

"I told you, I don't want to be in London. And you haven't answered about Whitney. Who will take care of her? And if you send her away, to one of those places with just obronis and farms, Glory, ɛrensi da!"

"Enough!" Uncle Clinton banged a heavy fist on the table, causing everyone to flinch. Bobo immediately began to cry, her face and fingers messy with noodles. Gloria turned to her automatically and began to wipe her fingers with a tissue Maame Serwaa had pulled from the end of the table and handed to her. Then Gloria stood and lifted Bobo out of the chair, so that she could perch on Gloria's lap. Bobo's cries became sniffles. "Has there not been enough fighting in this house for one week? Eh? This is a time of mourning. A time for quiet, to reflect on a young man's life, before all of you depart from here . . . potentially for good."

Uncle Clinton's voice cracked again, under duress, under the pain of his daughters, of his lost wife and youngest child, his orphaned granddaughter. He hung his head for a moment, sure there would be more answering back, but nothing came then from Aretha and Gloria. The mood was not lifted, but it was changed.

Soon after, Maame Serwaa cleared the plates, washed them outside, and put away all the cooking utensils. Everyone retreated to their corner of the house, and she walked out to the front. Kwame kept a chair for her when she was mostly done for the day, and they would talk for a while, until the evening became that darkest blue and Kwame requested a coffee to become alert again for the night watch ahead. This time she had come out with the coffee ready, and he thanked her with his gap-toothed smile and easy nod. She liked him in a simple way, and she knew she should consider that more in the coming weeks.

In a few days, she would go to Kejetia Market with Gloria to find new suitcases for her and Bobo. She would also find one for Aretha, knowing she won't have thought about it properly yet. They would also visit the tailor to make some new dresses for Bobo—Bobby had given her three different Ankara cloths as a birthday present, brought back from Ntonso on Maame Serwaa's last visit home. Maame Serwaa had taken hours to pick the right patterns, repeating Bobby's request to herself for "Big, bright colors for my baby girl." She had taken them home to her mother in the village, airing them out in the morning to remove the musty smell from the place they were stored in at the weaver's workshop. She made sure to fold them well, so they looked freshly laundered, and piled them into a pretty bag she had been given by Gloria years before.

Bobby had been ecstatic, overpaying her for the cloth, insisting she keep the rest of the money for something nice for herself.

"Auntie, will you also help me find someone to make her dresses from these? Ones that she can point to and say—this one is from Daddy?"

Bobby had made the request proudly, confident in Maame Serwaa's support in helping him become the best father he could. She had nodded emphatically, squeezed his hand with reassurance, excited already at the designs for Bobo that he was going to love.

And this was what she was now looking forward to the most: measuring Bobo for her first proper dress. Keeping her promise to Bobby, even if he wouldn't get to see it with his own eyes. Still, this way Maame Serwaa would rest a little easier knowing Bobo had everything she needed before they moved to London: some small part of home.

CHAPTER 19

London, Present

Whitney

You had finally found sleep after an evening of binge-watching rom-coms with Chantelle, both of you huddled under three blankets, empty share-size packets of popcorn and crisps littered about the sofa. You didn't talk much more, only about what was happening on the screen. Silence finally felt comfortable. No one mentioned Paris, the agreement already made that he had taken up enough space between the two of you.

But the next morning you were wrenched from sleep by the sound of the flat buzzer crashing into your restless dreams with its intruding bark. You knew Chantelle needed a much louder sound to be pulled from her slumber, so you jumped out of bed, wrapping your robe around you quickly to answer it. Ma Gloria's voice greeted you with exaggerated cheer over the intercom phone. You pressed the button to let her in and waited. You heard the squelch of her wellies before you saw her as you opened your front door. She looked drenched from the rain, with only a hood to protect her head. But her face was differently anxious, and she rushed into the flat before you had a chance to usher her in. She slipped her boots off easily at the door.

"Tea?"

She threw the word at you as she made it hastily to your kitchen, as if you had been expecting her and she hadn't just woken you up. You hadn't returned her calls last night and she had panicked, so she decided to pop by this morning. This was what she told you as she reentered the living room after making two cups of tea, and you laughed because why was she talking like that? "Pop by" was something you heard your white English friends' parents say, not your Ma Gloria. Perhaps she had picked it up from one of the neighbors or from someone new at church. You wondered what other new things she had brought into your home. Glancing at the clock on the wall, which said nine thirty a.m., you questioned whether you should feel embarrassed about not yet being dressed. Usually you were an early riser, but it was your week off. Well, the end of it. You prepared yourself to give this justification out loud, but Ma Gloria was paying no attention to your attire, which meant something was *really* wrong.

"The meter is doing the *dzz dzz* thing again. You'll fix it for me?"

She was referring to the prepay electric meter she insisted on keeping, even though she had officially bought the house from the landlord ten years ago and was now free to remove the meter entirely if she wanted. But she was very slow to change her routine. You had been suggesting getting rid of it for years, and she replied as she always did when you offered to do something different at home: "What for?" You fought the urge to repeat that question back to her now.

"Okay."

"About our talk. I've lost sleep thinking about it."

Ma Gloria looked around the room as she spoke to you. She often chose to sit on the purple armchair whenever she visited your place—a super-soft second-hand gift from Chantelle's grandmother—but now she sat beside you on the new peach sofa, which had been purchased during the January sales. The old leather couch was in a dump somewhere. Her body warmth brought you a familiar comfort. You crossed your legs as a small breeze from a still-open window hit your bare thigh, causing you to untie and then pull the belt of your dressing gown tighter. She shifted closer to you, reaching for your hand. You cleared your throat to say something, to acknowledge the moment somehow, but she dropped your hand suddenly and stood up, changing the mood in the room again.

"Did something happen?"

You assumed it was so, that something big had motivated her to travel all the way to you, finding you in this most unmade state. You put your hand to your head absentmindedly and found your headscarf was still wrapped tightly. You sighed in relief that at least your hair wasn't in ruins. When you looked up again, Ma Gloria was standing over you, looking down as if you were kneeling at her feet. She didn't seem to know what to do with her body, where the words she wanted to say would best sit in the room, perhaps believing that how well they landed depended on her location. You tapped the empty sofa space beside you, making your face a little more open, hoping to calm her. It usually worked. She hesitated and then sat back down, and you felt your chest heave like something horrible was about to enter the room.

"I am going to tell you something that you have been asking for. You are older now, and you deserve to know. So." You nodded slowly, feeling your heart rate already climbing. "But after I tell you, that's it, okay? I can't—I won't say it again."

You felt her addressing the room rather than you. She leaned back into the sofa, no longer trying to reach for your hand, which was now hidden away against your chest, under your folded arms. "Your father. He didn't pass from an illness. He was killed."

"I don't . . . what?"

It was as if she had slapped you, and the sound of it was still re-verberating in your ears. You stared at her, waiting for more. She looked down at her hands and paused for such a long time you thought she had said everything she was going to say. But then she continued.

"He was murdered by a friend—someone he thought was a friend, anyway. And I haven't told you before because . . . I didn't want you to carry that throughout your life. It wouldn't have been fair."

Her words came out rehearsed, almost without tone, and you wondered how many times she had practiced it before making it to your front door.

"I don't understand."

Your mouth felt dry. You wanted to drink the tea in front of you, but your hands weren't moving, nor your arms.

"I'm sorry, I'm not explaining it well. I decided—*we*, the family, decided that I should bring you here to London, to keep you safe because you—you were there when Bobby's life was taken. You wit-nessed it all. And it was affecting you."

"Oh."

You said it quietly, the only reference you could make to this new revelation. Of course you had no recollection of the thing she was talking about. The memory wasn't there.

"But how did it happen? Was it an accident?"

"Just a fight. A silly thing that men think to do because they cannot use their words. Even though . . . well."

You frowned at how she was still trying to hold some parts back from you. You could tell.

"Ma, you said you wanted me to know, so tell me the whole thing. Please?"

She stared at you as if about to reprimand you, forgetting that she had come to *you* to finally give over something, answer at least one of your questions. You were aware that you hadn't been prepared for the answer, not in the least, and it was hitting you awkwardly, catching in your throat to even say the word. But you couldn't help yourself in trying to keep the window open before she closed it again and you learned nothing else. Who knows when she might let you in again?

"I was only going to say that Bobby, he didn't fight. He wasn't like that, so it made no sense. I wasn't even there to see it myself, so I can't say why, but *that* obroni, he was a stranger to everyone, and we couldn't have known what he was capable of, and . . . anyway, it is well. He has since passed. But your Auntie Aretha and your father, they were very close, so I think it was most difficult for her at the time. I mean, to explain, eh? Why she hasn't always been around. Anyway, now you know it."

You could tell she wanted to dust her hands off, to be done with her task for the day. You still couldn't really move but needed some way to keep her there, just a little longer. To let you sit with the bombshell, with her there for a few more minutes. Didn't she owe you that? And that window, you could already feel that it was closing.

"But why? Why tell me this now?"

It was a risky question. The answer could be nothing or everything. You were not convinced that she had been moved merely by your last encounter. She looked confused suddenly.

"Ah! But you've been asking me questions all this time—now you don't want to know the answer?"

"Of course I want to know! I'm just wondering why now? That's all."

She stared at you, as if she had offered you a kidney and you were requesting the heart and lungs as well. Maybe you were. There was a long moment of silence, and you suspected that perhaps there wasn't any more for her to say. That feeling in your chest that was constraining your breathing was merely your own anxiety, you processing all that you had heard, trying to find some sense and order in it. The load had been heavy, much heavier than you had anticipated.

And then she raised herself up from her seat beside you on the sofa, pausing in a squat before standing fully, as if the weight of the conversation were still on her shoulders. When you looked up at her, she suddenly looked older, more tired than you had ever seen her. Her cropped hair made her look youthful in one light, but her expression was all frown and worry. She picked up your two half-drunk cups of tea, carried them to the kitchen, and left them in the sink, unwashed. Then she turned back to you and sat down in the other armchair, the purple one, her usual place.

"I'm not well, Bobo."

Part 2

CHAPTER 20

London, 1996

Gloria

When Gloria arrived in London, she was consumed by how cold it was. Paa Kweku had tried his best to prepare her for it, telling her to wear two or three wraps over her clothes, and arranging for a heavy coat to be sent to her in Kumasi before she and Bobo took that plane journey. They had been hopeful Gloria would arrive while the sun still shone, during the summer months. But the wait for the passports had been longer than even Daddy had anticipated, and it was six months before she found herself disembarking from that airplane, enduring multiple hours of her stomach never quite settling. She found herself facing cold winds, gray skies, and pale, weather-beaten faces. If not for the tight, warm grip of Bobo's hand in hers, she might have turned back, found some way to return to the plane and forget this silly plan of a new life. She even wondered, in those first few months, what on earth she was doing. Still, three months passed before Gloria felt the sun creeping out from behind the clouds, and people whispered that this was the first light of a British spring. Although it wasn't the hot heat that made her skin glow as it did back home, it felt like something good was coming. At least, that was what Gloria was hoping for.

She had already gotten used to the chilly nights, to the sounds of drunk people shouting at each other late at night outside Golders Green station, and to the tinkle and gruff motor sounds from the milkman making deliveries early in the morning. She even tried to get used to the neighbor who refused to take care of his garden and, she suspected, the rest of his home. She only caught glimpses of him when she left the house with Bobo to visit the supermarket, his curtains twitching as she walked past, his face only a flash of something sinister. But then she found Bobo outside in the garden again—the third time in as many weeks—this time talking to what looked like a family of rats. Gloria buried her scream deep down in her throat so as not to scare Bobo, but she locked the back door securely every day afterward until Uncle Derek came by to "have a word" with the neighbor. Eventually, the council was called. The neighbor's home was overrun with things living and dead; the filth had piled up and was now reaching over into Gloria's new home. He was evicted soon after, and Gloria stayed away from her own curtains that day, the guilt of it weighing on her as she pressed a finger into her Bible, trying to summon forgiveness and reason from its pages. She was only stirred some weeks later by the sound of a van pulling up outside. Gloria watched as a colorfully dressed woman of about her age climbed out of the passenger seat carrying two lamps, quickly followed by a tall man carrying two boxes balanced on top of each other. The woman fumbled with a key before opening the front door of the neighboring house. Gloria stayed by the window watching them in the morning light, unloading box after box into the house—the woman picking up all the loose items, her husband (Gloria assumed) doing most of the heavy lifting. At some point, the woman turned and waved at Gloria through the window, and Gloria found herself waving back, smiling at the only other Black woman she had seen on their street since moving in.

These were the things that kept her busy, watching the street and watching Bobo as she waited for university transcripts to come through so that she could properly begin to look for work. Eventually Paa Kweku began coming by. He was staying with a cousin in Lewisham and never complained about the number of buses he had to take to reach Gloria on the other side of London, though she knew it was plenty. It was him who coaxed her out of the comfort of the small home she was creating. They rode the bus together, the three of them—to the bigger shops in Brent Cross, the stalls in Finsbury Park, and then to visit distant aunties and uncles, cousins and second cousins of Gloria and Paa Kweku's parents in Tottenham and Peckham and Deptford. Initially eager to fulfill her duties of visitation as the eldest daughter, Gloria found herself hesitant as she faced more questions about her journey to London with Bobo in tow. She became afraid of that family connection, of something else following her from Kumasi to London. Now she was standoffish with them, reluctant to visit with Paa Kweku, not answering the phone when they called. What if they had heard about the circumstances around Bobby's death? What had they been told about Tina's passing, about Mommy, about the things Auntie Vida had stirred up with her big talk? Gloria made this journey to get away from all that, to keep Bobo away from it. She would avoid any spark of connection with her hometown then if she had to; Bobo was more important than all of that. She didn't care that her new attitude bothered Paa Kweku.

"Glory, I'm trying to build a church community here. I thought you came to help me."

They were heading back home after a visit to an elder in Edmonton, and Gloria was already planning how to get out of all future visits, so she dismissed his words.

"I came to make a life for *us*." She pointed at Bobo, who was standing quietly by the bus stop, staring into space in a way that had begun to make Gloria a little worried. "You also being here—it's a help. But you are the pastor, not me."

She shrugged, not meaning it with any malice, but Paa Kweku looked annoyed.

"London is a lonely place, trust me. My first few months here? Hey! I was my only friend. It wasn't until someone told Auntie K I was here that I found other Ghanaians. But I did not come to run a church of one."

Gloria rolled her eyes at his dramatics.

"And so am I this one you're referring to? Why are you so obtuse, PK?"

"You think I don't understand why you are being this way with them? Where this new rudeness for your elders has come from? I'm not a fool. I am just saying—"

"You don't want me to be alone, I get it. But I am not alone, am I, Bobo?"

Gloria crouched down so that her face was eye level with Bobo's, regaining her attention so that the child looked at her and smiled as Gloria pulled faces to make her laugh. Gloria heard Paa Kweku sigh above her, but he said nothing more. When they returned home, Paa Kweku still came in to eat, chopping vegetables and cooking rice while Gloria headed upstairs to put Bobo to bed.

She tried hard not to think about the other thing then—that perhaps they could be a family, that it already felt like they were. She remembered with painful clarity the last time she had trusted that feeling, what she had missed when her eyes were only on Paa Kweku, even if just for a night. She needed now to stay focused, to build a life that was good. She needed to stop thinking about the past and face her front, once and for all.

CHAPTER 21

London, Present

Whitney

There had been a momentary feeling of relief. After you and Chantelle had cried together on the sofa and you had discovered the truth about who Paris really was, you were sure something had shifted for you both, and you could move forward. But then Ma Gloria visited. And in the days that followed, Chantelle told you that she was thinking about going away for a while, maybe visiting family in Jamaica. She hadn't thought it all the way through.

"I just need to be somewhere else, to do something else. Find *me* again, I think."

Her words were pleading, and all you could do was nod. You considered telling her about Ma Gloria in that moment, about her health and all the things you didn't know yet and all the things you were worried about. You hadn't even begun to process what she had told you about how your father died. But you told Chantelle nothing, decided it was best to wait, that she was already carrying a lot. Instead, you slipped out to meet up with Jak, and on a canal walk from Camden Town to Paddington, everything about Ma Gloria fell from your mouth. Jak listened, and then their own concerns spilled out, about *their* mother and some tests she was

going for. It was the first time Jak had really expressed a desire to
be back in Australia, even if it wasn't for a nice thing. You were both
quiet afterward, but the silence was affirming somehow. You were
grateful for the camaraderie in the concerns you and Jak shared,
and it temporarily soothed your maddening thoughts. When you
returned home, the sun had been down for a few hours, and there
was no sign of Chantelle. But the following day you woke up to a
text message.

> Helping with some salon paperwork until late tonight but will pick up
> milk on the way home. I think I need more than a holiday; I think I need
> to move out. Sorry Whit. Chan x

You could think of nothing to say in reply, so you sent an "X."
Two weeks later, she was on a cheap flight to Kingston, Jamaica, to
visit her grandmother for a while. It was the best thing for her, you
knew that. But you struggled with the way you missed Chantelle as
soon as she was gone.

You tried to face your front and pay attention to Ma Gloria.
She was finally letting you ask about her treatments, about what
was creeping through her veins and trying to destroy her from the
inside. She said you were being dramatic when you described your
fears to her.

"We've been through bigger challenges. This is a thing so many
people have survived. Why should I be any different?"

But she *was* different, and that was the point. She chose not to see
it that way and acted sometimes as if she were invincible. You had
to bully her into letting you come to the hospital appointments, to
sit in on the consultations. You insisted that you wanted to know
everything that was happening, and after a day of blood tests and
scans, you finally had a full picture, and now you felt numb. You

wanted to be strong for her, but she cradled you in her arms as if it were happening to you.

"Psalm 46, verses 1 and 2: God is our refuge and strength, an ever-present help in trouble. Therefore we will not fear, though the earth is transformed and the mountains are toppled into the depths of the seas."

Perhaps she had meant it to be reassuring, but it sounded to you as though she had all but given up. She was the mountain toppling, and who were you to control the sea? You stayed with her in the house that night, though she protested. You lay down in your childhood bedroom and cried. You felt small and stupid. You blamed yourself, that you hadn't picked up on it before, hadn't found some way to cure her. You would search for help wherever you could get it, even in prayer.

"I just wanted to check in. See how you are doing?"

Pastor P spoke to you in a familiar way, as if you were his own child. A closeness had returned that you hadn't felt with him in a while. You had entered his office reluctantly, showing up to Holy Grace Church once service was over to pick up Ma Gloria and take her to the next hospital appointment. You were happy to be her aid, to pay for a taxi and accompany her if it meant she would actually make it there, give herself the best chance of getting better. Some members of the congregation were still chatting in the main hall when you arrived, and Pastor P waved you over while Ma Gloria disappeared to use the bathroom. Now he looked at you from across the desk, his office freshly cleaned and filled with the smell of pine, mixing with his lavender aftershave. You noted that his eyes were a little bloodshot, even though he wore a freshly pressed suit and shining shoes—his Sunday best. It was the first time you wondered how he might be feeling about everything, about Ma Gloria.

"I'm fine, thank you, Pastor."

You wanted the exchange to be brief, noncommittal. You were afraid he was expecting to see you at the next service; you hadn't attended in years, and Ma had even stopped mentioning it to you, except to tell you she was always praying for you.

"And you don't need anything? Either of you?"

"Not at the moment, but I will let you know if we do. Sorry, we should get going, I don't want Ma to miss her appointment. It took ages to get—"

"Yes, yes, of course. We have prayed very well today, so maybe you can also pray again for her at home. Yes?"

He looked so expectantly at you that you just nodded, noting the salt and pepper on his temple, the dot of it on his cheeks, exposed by his close shave. His eyes crinkled into a smile, and you felt bad, wondering if you would keep your loose promise. As you stood to make your exit, your eyes fell on a colorful bird-shaped pin on Pastor P's lapel. The bird was looking back at its own tail with an egg in its mouth. He followed your gaze and a genuine smile appeared on his face for the first time since you'd arrived.

"A gift from Glory—Ma Gloria—when we had the twentieth anniversary for Holy Grace here in London. You must know this proverb of Sankofa? It's one of her favorites." You half nodded and then shook your head. You recognized the image of the bird; it looked just like the wooden clock that Ma Gloria had gifted you years ago, the one Chantelle would always take from your bed-side table and bring into the living room after a night out because the colors "soothed her" apparently. But you hadn't realized there might be meaning behind it. "Ah! I was sure Glory would have told you. Se wo were fi na wosan kofa a yenkyi: it is not taboo to go back and fetch what you have forgotten."

He was beaming as he said it, as the fond memory washed over him, but you stared back blankly, not quite getting it.

"I don't think I understand."

He looked at you and chuckled as if you were a child not quite getting the lesson. At least, that's how you felt under his gaze.

"We need to know our past in order to look to the future."

The irony wasn't lost on you, that Ma Gloria held dear something related to acknowledging her history. When you met her outside, you said nothing. There was not much you had to say, anyway.

You became used to your childhood bedroom again. You stayed there with increasing frequency after learning of Ma Gloria's diagnosis. Visits to the hospital were illuminating, but one day in particular left you feeling blinded by it. You tried to sleep when Ma Gloria did, but she was turning in much earlier than you these days, and you spent several hours staring at the whipped-cream-swirl patterns in the ceiling, unchanged since you and Ma Gloria had first moved into the house. Eventually you wrapped yourself in one of the robes you had left behind when you had moved out six years ago; it was still hanging on the back of your bedroom door as if you had never left. You headed downstairs to the kitchen, taking with you some books you'd bought recently, hoping to do something better with your busy mind than just stare at your phone. Closing the kitchen door behind you and switching on the kettle, you sent a message, and Jak arrived exactly thirty minutes later. They buzzed your phone to let them in, neither of you wanting to disturb Ma Gloria's slumber by flapping the letter box. Jak immediately made a beeline for the kitchen as if they had been there before, putting down the two plastic bags they were carrying, containing what looked like multiple cupcakes. Jak did a lap of the kitchen, pulling out the drawers, eyeing the gas top and the small oven, somehow locating a mixing bowl and a whisk, into which they poured the contents of a smaller bag they had brought with them. You sat at the table sipping your tea, not wanting to interrupt whatever was now brewing in the kitchen. Ma Gloria was a keen baker, always taking a pie, pastry, or cake to a church function. She saved the best ones for you, though.

You listened to the steady rhythm Jak was making with the hand whisk, unsure of what was being created and not really caring. You wanted to offer them tea but thought better of it; they seemed to be in some kind of trance. And the silence was nice, being with someone without having to really be present.

"You're not gonna try the cakes?" Jak finished the mixing, and now they were looking at you, leaning against the kitchen counter and smiling softly. Before you could answer they put the plastic bags on the table in front of you carefully, rolling the edges down until the covered trays of cupcakes were fully revealed. "This one is lemon, berry, and white chocolate. This one is red velvet chocolate chip, with a citrus icing that I haven't put on it yet."

Jak removed one of each cupcake and placed them in front of you, as if you were a competition judge.

"So, this is a bad time to tell you I don't like cake, right?"

Your attempt at a joke was ignored. Jak chose instead to grab a paper towel from the roll in the middle of the table. They placed it in your left hand and put one of the cupcakes in your right.

"You'll like my cakes."

You took a bite and found they were correct. The cupcake was gone before you could even utter a "thank you." You suddenly realized you hadn't eaten since breakfast.

"Wow. How did I not know you baked?"

"You never asked."

"And who are all these cakes for?"

"Oh, a bridal shower. Just a little catering gig I've got going. Extra cash and all that."

"No wonder you don't sleep." Jak grinned and pushed the second cupcake toward you eagerly, and then brought the mixture of icing over to the table, a piping bag appearing as if from nowhere, ready to be filled. "Can I?"

You hoped you were asking in your sweetest voice, and Jak looked you up and down doubtfully before handing the bag over to you.

"Here. Use the spoon to fill it, and then you can do a practice one on your cake, if you don't eat it first."

Jak stuck their tongue out at you, and you fake-guffawed back. You tried to delicately fill the bag with the icing, but soon splotches of it were all over the table, and Jak just watched you struggle, laughing as you did it. You flicked a stray bit of icing at them, which hit their cheek with a comical *pfft* sound. You both burst into laughter and then immediately fell into whispered chuckles, aware that it was getting late in the evening. Afterward you both returned to a calm quiet.

"How she going?"

Jak threw out the question you'd been hoping to avoid all night. They took the almost full piping bag from you, wiped the excess icing away neatly with another paper towel, and expertly twisted the opening closed. You stood up and walked over to the sink to wash your hands, running a finger under the cold stream, waiting for it to heat up.

"She's not great. I think . . . I think she's known for a while. Not sure what to do with that, to be honest."

By the time you took your clean hands back to the table, Jak had already iced half of their cupcakes with rosettes that now looked too pretty to eat. They passed the bag back to you.

"Squeeze softly for a second, and make sure it's at an angle—

yeah just like that. Careful it's not too close to the edge though. Yeah, you got it."

Jak looked pleased with your work, and you felt their approval rise in your chest. You hadn't realized how much you'd needed a win, even a small one like that.

"She won't talk about it with me, not really. We went to the hospital today, and—I asked all the questions because she was just quiet. Like, if she buries her head in the sand, maybe it'll go away, which is just fucked."

"She's probably just scared."

Jak finished piping the cakes as they spoke, and you felt yourself get rigid.

"I'm fucking scared too! She's all I've got left, and I'm not gonna waste time pretending shit isn't happening!"

"Ssh! You'll wake her up."

Jak had a serious look on their face, but you wanted to scream back, suddenly not caring if Ma Gloria woke up, if the whole street woke up. You wanted to rage, smash all the cupcakes, and break all the dishes and wreck the house. Maybe if you made enough of a mess, enough noise, you could undo this thing. But now Jak was on your side of the table, their arms wrapped around you, their body shaking against yours. It took some time to realize that it was you who was shaking, *your* body making you both rumble, *your* sobs wetting your face. And your hands clutching the end of the table as if you meant to crush it between your fingers. You rode the wave of your tears for a while before they subsided.

Later, Jak had made you a second cup of black tea and an herbal tea for them. They flicked through the books you had brought downstairs and read the back cover of one titled *You Are Your Best Thing*.

"Let's see. Tarana Burke says, 'We often carry our trauma in similar ways, but the roads that led us to the trauma are all so different. We must pay attention to that road. That road is our humanity.' Yikes, this is not bedtime reading, Whit."

"I've only just started it. Well, I meant to start it." Jak nodded at your haphazard reply, holding on to the book and passing it from one hand to the other lightly, like they were thinking something over. You felt the sudden urge to interject. "It's from a client—that's why. I mean—a client recommended it as a good read."

Jak put the book back down again but let a hand sit on top of it.

"Have you read *Not That Bad*? That's a good one too, a collection of essays." Jak paused for a moment, watching your face before continuing. "Essays by trauma and sexual assault survivors. But it's also about living in a culture where you feel unsafe, dealing with it every day."

Their hesitation suddenly made sense to you.

"Shit, I'm an idiot. I shouldn't have left the book out. Let's talk about something else."

You reached for it, but Jak slid it away from your eager hand.

"Why *are* you reading this? It's not really for work, is it?"

Jak held the book up again to assist their questioning, and you had a flash of the Tuck Shop, your throat suddenly dry, your voice hoarse. You gulped down some of your lukewarm tea.

"I just gravitated toward it the other day. There was this book fair on in King's Cross, and I just thought . . . God, it's stupid."

"Better say it then."

"I wanted to read about people who've been through the worst thing. See how they came out the other side. Then maybe I can cope better with what's happening with my ma. It's a weird thing to do, I know."

Jak shrugged. "Sometimes when things feel chaotic, you wanna try anything to feel a bit normal again. Even if it feels unconventional, and ya know . . ." Jak took a moment, and you breathed a sigh quietly, happy they didn't think you were completely losing it. "Well, I was gonna say, Chantelle was getting into tarot, and I don't know much about it, but she said it grounded her when her nan had that scare a few years back."

You hadn't talked about Chantelle for a while. But hearing her name, recognizing the fondness that Jak clearly still held for her, melted something inside you a little. You suspected Jak didn't want to talk anymore about it, though, given they had stopped looking at you and were packing their things away. You noted the small recommendation they had imparted on Chantelle's behalf and tried to move on to other things.

You brought some extra bedding from the airing cupboard down to the living room and said goodnight to Jak, though you could both see the sun beginning to creep through the gap in the curtain. You hoped you would hear Ma Gloria wake early as she usually did, in time to tell her Jak was there so she wouldn't get the fright of her life.

At some point after crawling into bed, you fell into a dream where someone was reaching toward you. Their long fingers on your arm, your thigh, against the tips of your own fingers. You felt a warmth and familiarity that quickly became sinister, the Bard's face emerging from the darkness suddenly, wrapping himself around you like a snake. You lurched awake, gasping for air, with knots in your stomach and no one else in sight.

CHAPTER 22

Copenhagen, 1996

Aretha

Aretha was learning that she liked the cold in Denmark. It could freeze her bones if she stood outside for too long, but once she stepped down into a shop, bar, or restaurant, the warmth of the fire might be waiting, the steam from a hot cup of something ready to soothe the coldest of patrons. So by the time summer arrived, she felt a double joy at seeing the sun, at walking outside without a jacket. Some days she let herself enjoy the city of Copenhagen as it was, forgetting her motivation to travel there in the first place. To say goodbye to Bobby. To find Viktor. What she would do when she found him, she was not sure. She could not give it too much thought, not until she had located him.

She enlisted the help of a new friend, Sofia—an African American woman from Chicago who had traveled to Copenhagen for a one-year study-abroad opportunity and to use her new journalism degree to find her Danish father. In the midst of her search and trying to learn Danish, she met Aretha in the same language school. Aretha was already excelling faster than most in the class, and she was intrigued by Sofia, the only other brown face among the white students. Sofia offered to buy her a coffee.

"I need serious help with this stuff, and you're basically as good as the teacher. So, help a sister out? You scratch my back, and I'll scratch yours?"

Aretha had never heard this idiom before, and she laughed, confused.

"You want help with your Danish and a . . . back scratch?"

Sofia's laughter was an explosion of sound, all joy without the filter, and Aretha was immediately smitten. They had a deal. In return for tutoring, Sofia would help her track down a white Danish military officer with some ties to Ghana. Aretha was ready with an invented story about how he was an ex of her sister's whom Aretha wanted to confront over a betrayal, but Sofia never asked for an explanation.

"I got you."

And that was that. Sofia's command of the local language was improved because of Aretha, and Aretha's social circle in Copenhagen was expanded because of Sofia, her affable nature, and her ability to gather the lost and lonely until a community formed. Three months later, Aretha had almost forgotten her request, so enthralled was she in this new life of food and art and language, and her new job in the Ghanaian Embassy as an executive assistant. So Aretha was surprised one evening when Sofia met her outside her office building, revealing news she had been holding on to all day. She had found Viktor.

He was living in a rundown building on the outskirts of the city, in an apartment with three other men. He seemed to be doing odd jobs around Freetown Christiania: cleaning and security mostly. Aretha felt the weight of this knowledge on her shoulders again, and the cloud of what had brought her to Copenhagen in the first place seemed to return. As did her obsession. She visited his apartment building as soon as she could, waiting a few feet from the entrance for someone to exit so that she could sneak in. She took the groaning elevator up to the seventh floor, his apartment number memorized. It was the middle of the day on a Saturday. He might not be home, but perhaps she could find a way to break in, have a look around, find some weakness of his to exploit? She laughed at herself for a moment, standing outside his door. She was not a super sleuth, and she was watching too many detective shows with Sofia. This wasn't like her at all. She needed a plan and an opportunity. A real one.

Aretha had hoped that hearing Viktor had fallen from grace would have satisfied her, that it would have been enough. But it wasn't bringing Bobby back. It wasn't reducing any of their pain. And it definitely wasn't the justice she had been looking for.

But she was good at being patient. So she kept abreast of his movements. And she dipped back into the life she was building, becoming closer with Sofia with each new week, heading into something beyond what Aretha had previously thought she could ever have with another woman. And she knew that she couldn't return home again. Not when there was still unfinished business, and she now had this other life, this other part of her that she was allowed to explore. So she stayed.

CHAPTER 23

London, Present

Whitney

You felt as though you had been watching things tick along since your thirtieth birthday. The calendar told you that was six months ago. Your moments no longer felt linear, though time still dragged with slow steps when you wanted it to move much faster, or it broke into an anxious run when you would have given anything for it to stop completely. And you were trying to be in the house more, getting reacquainted with the color of the walls, the hum of the fridge in the kitchen, the rattle of the front door when someone closed it too hard.

You had been awake since the early hours, waiting for another difficult day to begin. You stretched fully and got up from the armchair in the living room, shuffling through the doorway and into the kitchen in search of coffee. The tile was cold on your bare feet as you stood by the electric kettle waiting for the gentle click once it had boiled. After filling your cup—black, two sugars—you reentered the living room to sit back in the big chair facing the window. You could watch the sun come up that way, watch the day unfold. There were photographs of Auntie Aretha and your parents, pictures you had found in an old photo album scattered across the coffee table behind you.

Ma Gloria was gone, and you were alone.

Chantelle was still in Kingston when she heard the news about Ma Gloria and had jumped on the first flight back to London. She returned with a glowing tan, a new sense of purpose, and open arms for your grief. Her arrival had summoned a downpour, and you met her at the door of your new-old home, the rain behind her perfectly framing what had been some of the worst days of your life. Chantelle had come with a small suitcase and stayed with you for a week, cooking, cleaning, making calls that needed to be made. Jak dipped in and out between jobs, and you remained in a gray haze. A month later, Chantelle and Jak wore the colors of your family's black and red funeral cloth as a show of love and solidarity. You hoped to blur away the whole week, to fade into the background of mauve that formed the groups of people around you. You only felt a connection when you looked up and saw Chantelle and Jak, helping you keep a small grip on reality.

You were told that your grandfather was too elderly to make the plane journey from Ghana, so as Ma Gloria's closest blood relative in London, you had to take part in customs you had only recently become familiar with. You were dreading the viewing of the body; you hadn't wanted to see any part of Ma Gloria there, in a final resting pose, in her favorite dress for the last time, a sleeping beauty pinpricked by the thing you had been terrified of for months. Chantelle stood with you when it was time, walking you over slowly to the open casket of mahogany; it needed to be solid to carry the most precious person in your life. You tried to remember what Ma Gloria had told you, that you needed to look ahead, to not turn back. So you didn't close your eyes, you kept them open and looked at her lying there. Your first thought was that she might be cold, winter already bringing a fresh chill in the air. Your mind twisted on you, and you asked Chantelle where Ma Gloria's coat was, as if she would know. As if what you were asking made complete sense. She told you she'd help you look for it later if you wanted. You smiled back at her in your grief, unable to capture what you wanted to convey, which at that time was simply abject despair. Still, Chantelle and Jak stayed by your side the next day, from the service at Holy Grace to the celebration of life in a newly renovated community hall near the church. Both friends alternated toilet breaks, making sure you were never alone, that you got something to eat. Pastor P hovered nearby, carrying out his own form of protection by ensuring you weren't crowded by the rest of Ma Gloria's church family and other aunties and uncles you'd never met before. At one point, you laughed to yourself, and Chantelle looked worried that you were finally losing it. So you held her hand to reassure her and whispered the thing you were pondering over; that Ma Gloria had organized her own funeral, had set things in motion long before she passed, designating Pastor P to carry out her exact specifications so you didn't have to.

"This one will be the last burden I carry for you. It is well."

It was this memory, this recollection of one of your last conversations with Ma Gloria, that made you push back your chair, leave the head table, and propel yourself toward the doors of the hall. You caught a glimpse of Jak as you rushed past, seated on one of the guest tables. They watched but seemed to know not to follow you. Outside you tried to gulp in mouthfuls of air between sobs. Your hand on your chest trying to slow your own heart rate, you smelled almond and salt water, the odd mixture pinging your memory from long ago. You recognized Auntie Aretha before any words were exchanged between you.

"Whitney? Wow, look at you."

Her voice was softer than you remembered from your many phone calls, or perhaps it was just the nature of the day that was inviting gentleness toward you. She was taller than Ma Gloria—which wasn't difficult—but they shared a face. A crooked eyebrow, prominent cheekbones, a broad nose, and square teeth rarely exposed—Auntie's smiles were just as withheld as Ma Gloria's. She wore the family funeral cloth, of course, as if it were made for her, her curves visible but modest, her makeup nonexistent, but her skin shining anyway, as if she had arrived from somewhere far better than Bounds Green.

"Hello, Auntie."

She took you in too, a moment of searching each other's faces—her for the past, you for your future. The embrace came naturally, pulling toward each other, your tears starting up again, hers unknown to you because your head was buried in her neck. The softness of her skin was the same as Ma Gloria's, and you almost buckled at the knees, knowing then how much you had missed it, that you would never be in the presence of Ma Gloria again. Auntie Aretha took a step back, looking you up and down, brushing away your tears with a manicured thumb.

"Come, let's talk, eh?"

She spoke with certainty: another difference between the sisters. You followed her back into the community hall building, watching her gesture to someone for two chairs at the back of the room. A man you didn't recognize brought them over, and she sat with you to the side, in the carpeted reception area. The music in the main hall was getting louder. It was starting to sound like a party, and you weren't ready for that.

"I wanted to be here yesterday, but my flight got canceled. I'm sorry."

Auntie Aretha bowed her head in regret, and you fought the urge to comfort her, unsure of what that would even look like.

"You're here now."

"And how are you? Really?"

A question you'd been asked so many times, you should have already had an answer prepared. Yet still, nothing.

"I . . ."

You looked at her, hoping she would fill in the silence, make sense where there was none. She looked away as another thought seemed to cross her mind.

"I am sorry it's been so long too, and that *this* is how we are meeting. It's funny, I was preparing for you both to come and visit, finally. Glory wanted to surprise you, or maybe she was making the plan knowing that . . . anyway. We got to see each other after all."

A sad smile and then more silence between you. But you didn't want to leave where you were; you felt safe in her presence, even in the absence of words. And then, there were your questions.

"How is Denmark, auntie?"

"It's good. It's a good life there. You would like it, I think."

"I've always wondered why you chose to be there and Ma Gloria here, but then she—she told me about my father. About what really happened to him. And how close you both were, so maybe . . . Is that why?"

Auntie Aretha's face didn't change, but her fingers jumped in her lap slightly, spooked on her behalf.

"Well, we were good friends, but he was more like my brother, you know? Because we were close in age. I went for his funeral and just . . . never left."

"You wanted to feel closer to him, over there? I get that." Auntie

Aretha nodded, her eyes already a little glazed, pensive. She was opening up now, in ways Ma Gloria never seemed to feel she could with you. "What was he like?"

You hadn't known you would ask until the words were in the air, hovering over you both. She smiled then, big and wide. A beautiful thing to see.

"He was very kind, intelligent, so, so stubborn—we had that in common! And he was caring, just like your mother, Tina. But most of all, *you* were the love of his life. He would have done anything for you. We all would have."

"I wish I remembered him."

"Hmm."

She was holding something back, but she had also given you much more than you'd ever had before. You wanted to keep going, to continue sitting with her like this. To feel this closeness that was developed before you even had conscious memories of it. She was the last bit of you, of Ma Gloria, of your mother. That was how it felt.

"Auntie, will you stay with me, at the house? Just . . . for a while?"

You were an open wound again, pleading for a reprieve from the ache of it. And she saw that.

"Bobo, I'm here for as long as you need me."

Not long after Ma Gloria's funeral, Jak took a trip back to Melbourne. It had been planned quickly after learning their mother's health had taken a turn and she now needed to undergo some kind of surgery. You received a phone call from Jak a few days into their trip, after the success of their mother's operation.

"I could really use your hands right now." You stuttered a reply, unsure how to take Jak's words. "Sorry, I just meant—your masseuse hands, like before. They calmed me down, ya know?"

You flexed your fingers absentmindedly. At that point you hadn't touched another person since before Ma Gloria's funeral. Almost three months. A long time for you.

"What's happening right now? Is your mum okay?"

It was late afternoon for you but hours past midnight for Jak. Their sleeping habits hadn't improved much in Melbourne.

"Yeah, she's good. She's asleep. My bro's gone back to the hotel 'cause there's four of them, ya know. Pa set up my bedroom, but I made up something about the old mattress fucking up my back, that the sofa was better, so it was no stress. But I went in there to grab something tonight, and it's all kinda . . . hit me. How fucked up things were back then and how fucking *sick* of myself I was, sick of that room and by extension this house too. And . . . God, I forgot how much I just didn't wanna be here anymore, after what that rapey piece of shit did to me. I . . . didn't wanna live. I just feel so sad for that version of me, for how unbearable life felt back then . . ."

You listened to Jak's voice take on a croaking edge, until the words became whispers and you could imagine the flow of tears they were trying to stem. You didn't respond initially, couldn't really. It was the first time you had heard Jak use that word: "rape." It hit you like a slap in the face, a painful awakening, and then it rattled around your head for the rest of the day. It wasn't that you weren't already certain that that's what had happened to them, but it still felt like a shock to hear it out loud, as if someone had told you it had happened to you.

"What can I do? How can I help right now?"

There was dead air on the other end of the phone, and you thought you might have been cut off, until you heard another sniff.

"Nothing. Just this. It's good to talk about it. And I keep tryna remember what my therapist said, that I'm in control. And it isn't happening *right now*. Course, in reality, it's fucking hard to remember."

"But you're living it too. You're in the present, you grew up, and now you're in control."

". . . I'm in control."

You'd talked about it before, remembering that you were in the driver's seat whenever it felt like things were spinning out. For Jak, it was the memories that haunted them at times of high stress. For you, it was Ma Gloria and all the missing pieces that seemed to go with her. There wasn't much more to say because you couldn't be there to wrap your arms around Jak, tell them you could face it together. And you didn't even know if that was true. You were about to say your goodbyes when they spoke again.

"Thanks, Whit, for talking things out with me. I know you get where I'm coming from."

You had furrowed your brow, though not completely sure why. Most things were driving you to confusion in the wake of your loss, so you didn't say much more except your goodbyes, promising to call Jak later in the week.

Two months later, you sat down with Auntie Aretha in Ma Gloria's bedroom and searched for solace in Ma Gloria's things. She had requested that whatever could be donated, should be. This included any and all clothes (except her kente cloths, which would go to you), her books (mostly inspirational and authored by various pastors and reverends), and any furniture or wall pictures (three Bible verses written in fancy font in front of varying sunsets) that you didn't want to keep. Auntie Aretha had already gone through Ma Gloria's wardrobes; her clothes and shoes were already separated into "donate" and "bin" piles. Her nurse's uniforms were on the "bin" pile, but you moved them off, to their own place, unsure

what to do with them just then. And there was a cardigan that Ma
Gloria always wore that you were keeping. Auntie Aretha insisted
she didn't want anything herself, that she had her memories. You
wished you could be less sentimental too.

After working methodically throughout the day, and with Auntie Aretha's militant organizational skills, by the time it was dark
outside, all that remained of Ma Gloria's bedroom were black bags,
cardboard boxes, and the faded cream of her now exposed walls.
Her Bible—the gold-embossed one you had bought for her fiftieth
birthday—remained on the bedside table. Auntie Aretha crossed
the room to pick it up from its place, putting it into your hands as
you sat on the now-naked mattress.

"I'm making tea *with* the tin milk, Glory style. You stay here."

She waved you away before you could protest and disappeared
from the room. The Bible still felt the same, of course. Heavy
leather as its jacket, the pages almost tissue paper thin to touch
but colorful with highlights, things Ma Gloria felt it was important
to remember. You thumbed through the pages delicately, bringing
them closer to your face, the scent like a faint knowing, a reminder
of what was or might have been. As you ran through the pages in
quick succession, you watched something drop from between them
onto the floor. A folded newspaper sheet, an old one. Its color was
sandy, the headlines typed in a thick font but still grainy. It was one
sheet of paper only, about letter size, torn from the rest of whatever
that edition was. The top corner read "1996." You wished that you
could understand the rest of it, but the words were written in a
language you didn't speak. Something Nordic, was your best guess,
but you couldn't be sure. There was nothing clear about why Ma
Gloria had kept this paper with two articles split across the page.
One side seemed to be reviewing some kind of event, given the
image of a group of Black people in elaborate costumes of feathers

and headgear. The other article was three short paragraphs underneath a head and shoulders picture of a young white man, side by side with a sketch of a knife. You glazed over the text underneath, unsure whether he was the perpetrator or the victim. It wasn't clear, but you felt unhappy looking at his face. And then at the bottom of the page, in a small blank space, you read Ma Gloria's handwriting.

~~For the wages of sin is death, but~~ the gift of God is eternal life in Christ Jesus our Lord.

It didn't clarify anything further, so you put the article away, closing the Bible and leaving it in your bag of things to keep. You tried to get on with the evening, to drink tea with Auntie Aretha and tidy up some more, but the newspaper cutting remained, your mind trying to decode the language. It was only when you were brushing your teeth for bed that the man in the picture came back to you with more clarity, and the reason for that nagging feeling finally settled. He looked just like the Bard.

You had not let yourself cry over what he had done to you in a long time, but now the stab of the memory took the wind out of you. Immediately you stripped down, stepping into the shower as if to cleanse yourself of it, as if it had only just happened.

Afterward you put on new sleepwear, climbed into bed and wrapped the quilt around you, making a safe cocoon.

CHAPTER 24

London, 1996

Gloria

It would be a small party for Bobo's fourth birthday, but a party nonetheless. Gloria had decided that six children were more than enough. Bobo had begun going to a babysitter—Auntie Maggie—a few times a week. She was the mother of Freda, a nurse whom Gloria worked with and the only other brown face that Gloria saw on her first hospital shift. She gravitated toward Freda without realizing she had done so until they were mid-conversation. Freda had a Nigerian father and a white English mother, as well as three small children and a fair-weather husband. She was quick to tell Gloria her life story and then dole out advice, whether Gloria asked for it or not. Parts of her countenance were reminiscent of Aretha, but somehow they became fast friends. Freda's mother took care of her children and two others, so adding in Bobo would not make too big a difference, Freda assured Gloria. Still, Gloria insisted on meeting Auntie Maggie first, inviting her over for a cup of tea and cake, giving her a rundown of Bobo's waking and sleeping patterns and general well-being, before she was ready to leave Bobo in her care.

The arrangement allowed Gloria to pick up extra shifts when she needed to, adding a little more money to the pot she was trying

to build. Daddy was sending her a monthly stipend, but it only
went so far after bills and food. It was not pride; Gloria just felt it
unsustainable to continue relying on him to take care of her and
Bobo when he was supposed to be heading toward retirement, even
though he insisted he would work until his body would no longer
allow him to. And if she were asking for things, hoping really, she
would have taken Aretha's staunchly delivered advice, pelted at her
over the phone from Copenhagen.

"Just tell PK he needs to marry you and be done with it, Glory.
It's been long enough."

Gloria had gasped slightly at the suggestion but recovered
quickly before Aretha could pick that apart too.

"If you could see things here, it is him who needs *me*. I'm not
going to beg for that one. You know me better, Aretha, eh?"

"But you went to London to give Whitney a better life, no? If
not because he was also there, then why?"

Aretha seemed to really be asking, and Gloria realized that they
had never truly gotten on the same page about the move.

"Don't you think if I had wanted to marry him, we would have
done that back home? It's not everything you need a man for.
Hmm! I would have thought *you* would understand that better than
anyone."

She hadn't needed to say it like that. She could have been kinder,
softer, but she missed her sister and she was still irritated that she
had ended up in this new life without Aretha. But Gloria knew
Aretha well, and when she got an idea in her head, she followed
it through no matter what. She was the same with her anger at
times; she could hold on to it much longer than anyone might
need to. Gloria pretended not to notice the way Aretha pushed her
away after Mabel got married, and she realized too late what damage she might have caused, even by accident. She had mistakenly

thought that helping one of Aretha's closest friends was the right thing to do, but the pain in Aretha's eyes at the wedding told her otherwise. Perhaps Gloria had been looking for forgiveness ever since? Maybe that was why she wanted Aretha in London so badly, to prove that she was sorry, that they were the only ones left and so they needed to reconcile, for Bobo's sake. And for hers. It was a selfish desire, she knew that too. Which was why she hadn't asked Aretha about returning to Ghana, hadn't questioned the fact that she was still in Copenhagen. Because even in her voice, Gloria finally heard the freedom Aretha felt there, the way she no longer clipped her words when she spoke, even in frustration. Something had changed for her too in the last year. Something good had happened.

"Okay. And what about Whitney, doesn't she need a father figure?"

"She has a father, Aretha. What are you saying?"

"Had."

"What?"

"She *had* a father. Bobby is not here anymore. Now she only has you."

The drip of sadness in Aretha's voice caught Gloria off guard.

"She has you too, if you would come to visit."

Then there was silence on the phone for too long to assume that Aretha was just gathering her thoughts. She gave a big sigh before she finally spoke.

"I'm not done here. I need more time."

Gloria knew that should have been the end of the conversation, that they had unspoken rules to not pry further than was necessary. But she was lonely, and still, even if they disagreed, she preferred that they keep talking. So she pushed forward, despite her better judgment.

"It's okay here, you know? You can be . . . free and make friends with who you want and just be happy. It's why I wanted you to come with me. I thought it would be good for you. For all of us."

Gloria thought she heard Aretha smile, heard her take in the message, and felt the love Gloria had for her. This is what she hoped anyway.

"Mete aseɛ, okay? I have to go. Send my love to Whitney."

Gloria hadn't gotten to ask her about visiting for Bobo's birthday. She already knew the answer, so she let the call drop.

Now she was in Kwik Save searching for sausage rolls, cupcakes, and other sweet things—these were Freda's recommendations for the party. Gloria had been planning to make jollof, kelewele, and bofrot, but when she mentioned it excitedly to Freda, she made a face that Gloria didn't like.

"My kids won't eat that, love. I don't really cook that stuff, and I think the other mums won't know what to do with it."

"Other mums?"

"Oh, I just invited a few of Daniel's little friends—he's just started at school, so at least there'll be more kids to celebrate Whitney's birthday—six of 'em isn't really a party, is it? Anyway, just get some sausage rolls and those party rings—biscuits, love—and you'll be alright."

Gloria was grateful for the help, but it rattled her a little bit that she wasn't more in control yet, that she did not even have the last say over who gets to celebrate Bobo's birthday. Back home she would have been running the show, making sure all the cousins, aunties, and uncles were present with their children, that there was enough food to fill everyone up and for them to take home for two or three days of meals at least. She would have opened the doors to the court- yard wide so that people could go between the buildings as Highlife music flowed throughout the house. There would have been buckets of ice with Supermalt, Fanta, and bottles of water everywhere, for people to take as they saw fit. She would have put Bobo in one of the dresses she had gone with Maame Serwaa to get made, from the cloth Bobby brought home: the blue and purple one with a splash of yellow here and there. She would have spoken to the Fanice man the week before, paid him twice as much to stay at the house for a few hours, so that the children could enjoy ice cream all afternoon, because it was Bobo's birthday after all. And then she would have sat outside chatting to Paa Kweku, laughing with Bobby, gossiping to Maame Serwaa as they watched Aretha play airplane with Bobo— throwing her small frame up into the air and catching her with full hands—the only time Aretha seemed filled with unfettered joy in the house. It would have been a real celebration.

Gloria looked down at her basket of goods and felt a sadness sweep over her, but she would not allow it to stay. She blinked it away behind withheld tears and began to unload her red and white items onto the conveyor belt.

When she returned home and fed Bobo her dinner, she decided that she would still bring the jollof and the bofrot because Bobo loved Gloria's food. Her thoughts were interrupted by Paa Kweku ringing the doorbell. When Gloria opened the door to him, she felt her stomach plummet in a way it had not done for months. Paa Kweku was dressed in a deep blue suit, white open-collared shirt, and new shoes. He smelled like sawdust and red wine, and she was not sure how he had acquired such a scent, but she imagined herself briefly doused in it. She waved him into the house as if she had not noticed his clothes and how handsome he looked in them, and he walked in easily after her, carrying a gift for Bobo. And then he turned with a confused expression.

"You're not ready?"

"I already told you I'm not going. I need to get ready for Bobo's party tomorrow—"

"You need to also have your life. You can take one evening off, Glory. And look, even me tonight, I'm not a pastor; I'm just PK. It's only the naming ceremony party, not even the whole thing. You need to meet more people. When I'm busy with new church members, then who will you spend time with?"

Gloria made a face but stayed quiet a moment, thinking her words through carefully.

"Right now I'm the only member of your church, and it's been six months, PK. I'm not worried about you getting busy. Besides, I will meet the other mothers tomorrow that Freda will bring to Bobo's party."

He looked at her in mild shock, as though she had tried to hit him and he had only just dodged it. Then he crossed his arms and leaned against the wall, staring at her. It was the look he gave when he was trying to work something out, and a wry smile followed that she recognized from a year earlier when there was much less space between them—and fewer clothes too. She closed her eyes and tried to think of something else.

"Glory, what's going on? You're afraid of something."

"I just need to go at my own pace, that's all."

"I think you should call your new friend Freda. You can bring her, huh? I think it's a good idea." He walked past her as he spoke and headed to the living room. Bobo was on the floor, coloring pens and paper in both hands working on her latest masterpiece. Paa Kweku knelt down beside her. "Bobo, do you want to go to Auntie Maggie's house?"

She nodded as if they had rehearsed it, still furiously scribbling into what was already an angry tangle of colorful circles.

"Ah! Now you've put the idea in her head, she will be upset if we don't go."

Gloria only pretended to be annoyed. She knew that if he had given her a choice, she would have sent him away by now. She stood in the doorway as he walked back over to her. He stopped only a few inches from her face, and again she resisted the urge to wrap her arms around him.

"Call your friend."

Paa Kweku had already lifted the phone receiver to her, the coiled wire pulling from the base of the phone in the hallway. She snatched it from him and began to dial.

CHAPTER 25

London, Present

Whitney

Jak was looking at paint samples. They tapped the table in slight annoyance, forcing you back into the room, to answer their question about your new therapist, Denise.

"I don't know. She's alright so far, I think."

"But you're getting on with her?"

You had agreed to provide the tea if Jak helped you pick out colors for the kitchen. Since sorting through Ma Gloria's things and starting therapy, the weeks had tumbled by and you threw yourself into more change. In a way, it made you feel like you were finally moving forward. But Jak didn't like to rush. They pushed the sample book to the side to focus on their own queries. You noted that it was really too early for questions. You stirred both teas; yours was a caramel color that they called "tea-dipped"; theirs was a dark purple, a berry blend you'd picked up from Ally Pally Market. You took your seat on one of the old wooden chairs Ma Gloria had shipped from Ghana. You heard them creak every time either of you shifted your weight slightly.

"She's fine. She's nice. A bit confrontational sometimes, but—"

"And you're easy-breezy, yeah? You just don't know each other well enough yet, that's all. It's only been a few weeks."

"It's been *six* weeks. And isn't it *her* job to get to know *me*?"

You hadn't taken on any client appointments in a while, but you felt your fingers craving the work again, to make someone else feel right, even if just for an hour. You had begun to notice how your hands would not keep steady; there was a mild shake that would impede your ability to work if you didn't deal with it. Add to that the things keeping you up at night, causing you to be exhausted in the day, slow to move, and unstable in your motor functions. It was Auntie Aretha who suggested you look for a therapist, someone to support you in your grief. You worried that it meant your time with Auntie Aretha was coming to an end, that she was handing you off to a professional so that she could return to her life in Copenhagen. Jak said you were being ridiculous, that she was just looking out for you, that therapy might help.

"It *is* her job as the therapist, but she can't get to know you if you don't let her."

Jak took a gulp of their tea and then looked down at their phone, tossing out the words and hoping they landed in the right place.

"I'm trying."

Your voice had become small, and you didn't know why. Jak seemed distracted, but then they pressed a button on the side of their phone so that the screen went black, and they placed it face down on the table.

"I know you're trying. Of course you are."

They were looking at you fully now, sincerity as their only companion. You looked around the kitchen, uncomfortable with the sudden eye contact. Ma Gloria had kept talking about one day knocking down the half wall to make the kitchen bigger, to open it up more. She always planned to get around to it, eventually. You felt your stomach squeeze itself at the thought.

"What if—what if it can't be fixed?"

"What can't?"

"All of it. What if I'm just going there to talk myself into oblivion?"

Jak put on their thinking face.

"Do you *want* to talk yourself into oblivion?"

"No. No, I don't."

"Then you won't."

They said it assuredly, as if it were a foregone conclusion. Then they pointed to a yellowish paint sample and told you to choose that one, to brighten up the room and give you a clean slate. You just wanted to sell the place, that was all. Auntie Aretha had agreed and was helping you get the process started. You hoped a coat of paint would do more than just clean the slate. As you and Jak drank tea, you shared some cake, as had become your weekly tradition. Your jeans weren't impressed, but it was something you looked forward to. Today was a defrosted remnant of the days when Ma Gloria would bake five or six cakes for church and freeze one for the two of you to eat at your leisure. You weren't sure it was still okay, but you heated it in the oven, and it somehow retained a fluffy interior that was all her. Jak devoured a slice and complimented you on your efforts. You didn't correct them. Instead you asked if they could stay a little longer, but Jak had errands to run. And a date. It caught you off guard; they hadn't mentioned dating in a while, always too busy doing five or six different jobs at a time. Though now you realized it, you had made an assumption. Why wouldn't they be dating?

"Gotta do it. Gonna take them out for their birthday, ya know?"

"Oh, and who exactly is this new friend?"

You felt excited for them, ignoring the twinge of unease at the thought of Jak being around less.

"Well, they're pretty cool, I think. Bit of a neat freak, really good at getting people relaxed. But they've had a tough year, so this birthday is extra special."

Jak was standing as they spoke, their coat already on, looking down at you. You'd had this hangout so many times that you no longer showed them to the door. They continued to stare with an expectant look on their face before it finally dawned on you.

"No."

"Come on, Laces! It won't be like last year, no *oontz oontz* or mystery pills—just us and some good food. You can dress up before the whole day is done!"

"Dress up for who? Why are you like this?"

Jak smirked, put their phone in their pocket, and tapped a finger against the paint sample they'd picked out earlier.

"This is definitely the one. You need some light in your life, Whit. Be ready for six!"

They strode toward the front door and were on the other side of it before you could protest any further.

You dressed up for dinner. You wore a short-sleeved top under your denim jacket that was cropped just above your belly button, and a skirt that swished at your ankles, finishing off the look with bright-white high-tops that you knew Jak would say something about. Jak was always worrying about your sneakers staying white. They didn't feel they could be trusted with a brand-new pair of anything, what with all the skateboarding, climbing, and spills in the kitchen.

"You're gonna scuff those, and then you'll blame me for making you leave the house."

As you both headed toward the bus stop you chuckled, rolling your eyes to confirm you'd been waiting for the comment.

"Why would I blame you? And I won't scuff them."

"We'll see, won't we?"

Jak grinned and tipped their head to the side like a puppy dog, causing their glasses to slide ever so slightly off-center. You reached out to readjust them, and Jak flinched. You snapped your hand back on instinct, and something different flitted across their face, disappearing again before you could name it. You drew your previously extended hand back into your body, folding your arms tightly, and causing the denim of your jacket to crease into your biceps uncomfortably.

"Your glasses look funny."

You didn't want to ask why Jak didn't want you to touch them, so your words came out a little spiky.

"Oh."

Jak readjusted the glasses and then bent to refold the cuffs of their dark blue jeans. They stood back up quickly, straightening out their pink and yellow shirt and then tapping their pockets for their phone as you reached the bus stop. You turned to look at the peeling remnants of what used to be the bus timetable, harking back to a different time. Jak read the code written above it out loud before typing it into their phone to see when the next bus would arrive. It would take longer than the Tube, but you both had an affinity for this mode of transport, for taking the time to make the journey, surveying the city as you rolled through it. The bus came a few minutes later and you got on, immediately heading upstairs to sit at the front. Silence had asserted itself between you, and suddenly you missed the quiet chatter and jokes that Jak threw at you when you were feeling less talkative, which was most of the time these days. But now that *they* were quiet, you weren't sure you were equipped to handle it.

"Are you okay?" They looked away from you, out of the window to their right and into the distance of a setting sun. A few seconds passed before Jak shrugged slightly. You went to nudge them with your shoulder but thought better of it, keeping the slight distance between you instead as you shared a two-seater. "We don't have to do this if you're not in the mood anymore."

You heard your words and felt yourself transported back to the year before, to feeling at points like Chantelle was dragging you along for your birthday fun. You thought about her constantly. You didn't talk as much now that you weren't flatmates. You faced forward because Jak hadn't responded and you felt your peace ebb away a little, at the thought that you barely had the gumption to keep yourself together. You would be of no help to Jak if they were choosing now to fall apart.

"Sorry, tough session today. They don't tell you how going back to that stuff is . . . it's sticky, ya know? Like, it sticks *to* you. Just put me in a bad mood. It'll pass."

You nodded, thinking carefully about your next words.

The last time you'd spoken about Jak's therapy, they had used the phrase "Trauma with a capital 'T,'" and you remembered drawing your head back slightly, the word feeling as stark as its meaning. You were visiting Jak for once—unable to spend long periods of time in the house with too many places where memories were cradled. Jak said they were happy to see you out and about, and they insisted you sit in the garden on a rare day when the sun was out. Their flatmates were at work; they weren't flexible workers like the two of you. You asked how Jak was. So many of your conversations had been about how you were doing that you were already sick of the sound of your own voice. They replied with honesty after seeing their therapist that morning.

"Sometimes it feels like someone's taken over my body. Like, I'm not in the driver's seat; I'm just watching shit happen. Maybe I fight to take back control, but sometimes . . . I just don't."

You had squeezed your eyes shut and dropped your chin down to your chest because it made sense in ways you couldn't begin to explain. You wanted to say something reassuring, something that might soothe them, but nothing came to you. Instead you both listened to the sounds of birds that had landed on the top of the fence at the edge of the garden. You felt the soft-hard fabric of the deck chairs underneath you—a secondhand gift from the next-door neighbor. Jak had long since kicked off their flip-flops, and now they were running their bare feet along the warm grass beneath them.

"Why do you do it? Going back to that place, I mean. Doesn't it make it hard to live in the present?"

Jak scoffed at your question and then straightened up their face just as quickly.

"It's not always like that. Not every week. But sometimes I *need* to go back to it, to work through stuff that's happening now. It's not a linear process, Whit."

"But when you remember what happened to you, doesn't it just make you hate everyone and everything?"

You couldn't say where that question came from, only that you felt its truth deep in your bones. Jak looked up at you then, the two of you suddenly on the same wavelength.

"Sometimes."

Now, on the bus, you thought of all the questions you could have asked Jak in their garden, all the things that had entered your mind since you'd started your own therapy.

"I'm the queen of flaking, as you know—so if you wanna sack this thing off, we totally can."

You said it with a bit more energy, hoping Jak would understand your intent, to let them off the hook, even if you were already feeling disappointed. It was the first time you'd wanted to dress up in months.

"Nope, no way. I am one hundred percent committed to celebrating your birthday this year. I still feel bad I wasn't around for the last one."

"You were around, just not the night before—which is fine because I probably wouldn't have remembered anyway."

You smirked, hoping the joke would lighten the mood. Jak was finally looking back at you too, and they returned your smile in a half-hearted sort of way.

By the time you got off the bus, you were back to a comfortable silence, walking side by side through Brick Lane, turning a corner as Jak led the way. They opened the door to the restaurant, and you walked ahead, stopping a few feet inside. The interior was decorated by someone obsessed with greenhouses and pink flamingos, which was right up your alley. You looked around, taking in the handfuls of people scattered around, and you wondered for a moment if you were really ready to rejoin the world. Then you felt your breath catch when you spotted Chantelle sitting alone at a table toward the back of the restaurant. She wore a bright green dress and was sipping something pink and fizzy. She immediately pushed the drink away from her when she saw you. Jak skipped past you and made a beeline for the table before you could say anything. You followed, and Chantelle stood hastily to greet you as you approached. You shared an awkward kiss on each cheek and then sat down.

You wanted to stare at her, take in her Jean Paul Gaultier scent, tell her you liked her dress, find out how she was. But you were stuck looking down at the table, trying to gather the strength to just be okay tonight, despite your insides attempting to twist in on themselves because you hadn't seen each other in so long. Not since the week of Ma Gloria's funeral.

"You look great, hun. Thirty-one suits you."

Chantelle had turned herself toward you, giving you the once-over approvingly.

"Thanks. I've been on the rum and tears diet."

She looked surprised and then slowly began to chuckle, trying to figure out how serious you were. Jak leaned back in their chair and grinned.

"Told you to prepare yourself."

You saw them exchange a knowing look, and it struck you that they had been talking to each other without you. Clearly you were the main topic of conversation: the sad, grieving friend whom people worried about. You couldn't decide what you hated more—being left out of it or being the person they talked about.

"It was a joke!"

It came out of you a little too loud and rushed, and Chantelle raised that one eyebrow in surprise, before shooting you a fake smile—there were some things you still knew about her. Jak seemed to sense a moment of tension coming and clapped their hands together loudly.

"We need drinks!"

The waiter seemed to have heard Jak's bellowing and responded to the request, quickly taking your drink orders and bringing full glasses to the table a few minutes later. After the waiter had taken your food orders, you wondered where Jak and Chantelle were at with things, whether the truce they seemed to have made after Ma Gloria had died was still in place. They appeared polite at best, which disappointed you on an unexpected level. You leaned over to say something to Chantelle, hoping to redo your hello in a proper way with eye contact, but then you heard Jak clear their throat to regain your attention.

"I wanna make a toast—"

"Oh, we're fancy people now?"

The words came from you like an outburst, something from a time before when the three of you were comfortable together. Chantelle and Jak both smirked and briefly exchanged an awkward look.

"Yeah, Laces, we fancy. Now back to my toast? So about this time last year, the two of you were at some club that has since been shut down, that I—thankfully in hindsight—missed out on—"

"Rest in peace, Tuck Shop!"

You couldn't control your mouth anymore, due in large part to your nerves, you realized. It had been a long time since you were outside your area, at least a week since you'd last left the house. Chantelle was looking at you like she knew. You just grinned back at her, and she responded by kissing her index and middle fingers, and then holding them above her head dramatically. You both started laughing.

"Listen, you can stay hungry making jokes if you like, but we're not eating until my toast is done." Jak wore their best stern look and exaggerated it toward you and Chantelle. You both tried to straighten your faces before Jak continued. "Anyway, you're one of my favorite people, Whit, and in the face of an absolute shitter of a time, you've remained . . . effervescent! I'm happy to know you and to celebrate your *thirty-one years of life*!"

Jak ended by yelling so loudly that both you and Chantelle screwed up your faces, and a few people from the surrounding tables turned around in shock.

"Jesus! I don't think the kitchen staff heard you!"

Jak looked thrilled at your comment and then waved to some unseen person on the other side of the restaurant. Immediately you heard the quaint piano music from the speakers change to Stevie Wonder's *Happy Birthday* as a large chocolate cake with sparklers made its way over to you in the hands of one of the wait staff. Chantelle began to clap and sing along loudly to the song, to which Jak quickly added their own voice, as did a few of the other restaurant patrons. You felt blood rush to your face, your heart quickening without permission, and nausea building in the pit of your stomach. You fought the urge to crawl under the table. You used to like being the center of attention when the occasion warranted it. But this year felt different; you were overwhelmed and searching for the nearest exit. You felt out of balance, even though you were with two people who meant a lot to you. You just couldn't get there, couldn't feel it in the way you were supposed to.

You focused on how your body actually felt instead, like Denise had taught you. You felt the cold stone floor under your feet, the edge of the table against your thigh. You focused on the smells in the room, someone cutting into a steak nearby, a hint of sage and something sweet lingering in the air. You closed your eyes for a few more seconds, feeling your heart rate begin to slow down. You thought you might be smiling when you reopened your eyes, because Jak was smiling back at you. The singing had stopped. It took you a few seconds to realize that Chantelle's hand was on your shoulder, saying something about blowing out the candles.

"Do they *go* out?"

You drew your head back a little when you noticed how close the two sparkler candles were to your face. Chantelle laughed as she replied, "Make a wish and I'll magic them away."

You obeyed and closed your eyes again, wishing what you'd been reciting for months now. It never came true, but that wasn't the point. You could still wish it. You reopened your eyes as Chantelle licked her thumb and index fingers and then put both candles out before the spark made contact with the cake. You felt Jak beside you, gesturing to the waiter who'd brought the cake over to take a picture on the phone he'd been given.

"Wait, wait, you gotta get my good side."

You laughed as Jak twisted themselves to be at an angle, and Chantelle moved in closer to you on the other side. The two of them flanked you protectively.

You watched the cake being whisked away back to the kitchen just after you cut into it—red velvet with chocolate chips. Jak had made it special for you.

"I don't understand. Are we not eating that?"

You pointed, looking longingly at the door labeled STAFF that the waiter had just disappeared behind, cake in hand.

"Full disclosure, Laces? I thought you might bail before we got to the mains, so I got them to do the cake early, just in case. We'll have it for dessert, though. No worries!"

Jak wasn't looking at you as they spoke, perhaps afraid you'd be offended by what sounded like an accurate description of your recent actions. Even when stepping into the restaurant, you had calculated how far you'd get in thirty seconds if you just bolted in the other direction. These days, you were a flight risk. Before you could attempt to reassure Jak, the waiter returned with your mains in hand. You all waited in polite silence for the plates to be placed in front of you.

"So . . . why do you keep calling her 'Laces' by the way?"

Chantelle made air quotes with one hand, and then pointed at Jak with her fork in a mock-accusatory manner.

"Just a little in-joke." Chantelle waited for more. "Every time Whit came by the cinema, she'd get through, like, four or five packs of strawberry laces before we were halfway through the film."

You poked a playful tongue out at Jak in response, but seeing Chantelle's blank face, you suddenly felt embarrassed at the flat landing of Jak's words. You tried to dismiss it, to diminish its importance.

"Five is an exaggeration."

"Hmm, but you did *wax* the ones in those bowls at the Tuck Shop last year, to be fair."

Chantelle's comment caught you off guard, a reminder of what she had seen, of what you'd never really talked about.

"Yeah, well, that'll teach me to take pills from strangers."

"Oh yeah, that redhead, forgot about her! Rah, that was so unlike *you*, Whit."

Chantelle's volume decreased as she said your name, and for a moment the three of you were struck by silence again.

"Haven't touched the stuff since. Don't worry. Scout's honor—well, Brownies."

You pressed two fingers against your chest as if signifying an invisible badge, and you heard Jak scoff beside you.

"No way did you go to Brownies!"

Jak gawked as you took a big bite out of your burger, trying to chomp and look affronted at the same time. You started to retort, but your mouth was too full, so Chantelle interjected for you.

"Nah, she did. I've seen the pictures. What were your skills again? Sewing and starting a fire? Useful stuff."

"The sequined pyro—that's what we should call you, Whit! Kind of a shit superhero though."

"You know she's still got the badges, yeah?"

"I think you've achieved a bit more in your life. You could let those go, surely?"

You watched Chantelle and Jak going back and forth as they took the piss out of you, each getting louder with their quips. You had to defend yourself.

"Bits memorabilia!"

Your mouth full of food only caused them both to burst into more laughter. Chantelle threw a napkin your way with a chuckle as some bits of brioche bun flew from your mouth onto the table. You'd missed this, the three of you together, time stopping in good humor, as it always had. You finished swallowing quickly before the conversation could be derailed again.

"How's it been so long since we've done this? For real?"

You looked at them both, hoping the shakiness in your last two words was enough to push the truth out. Even you might tell the truth tonight. Maybe. Chantelle just looked down at her pasta, poking the edges in an absent-minded way. You turned to Jak for more, and watched their face go through the motions of a decision. The table was quiet for a few more seconds.

"I never wanted to make problems for you. But someone needed to tell him about himself."

Jak was speaking to Chantelle, and neither of them were looking at you. A moment passed between them before Chantelle calmly placed her fork down on the plate. You half expected her to stand and walk out of the restaurant, but she didn't.

"I know. I get it. It just made things . . . harder. But that wasn't your fault. I'm sorry if it seemed like—"

"No, I get it. I understood it then, as well. Just sucked a bit. But anyway, he's gone now, right? For good?"

Jak's eyes were opened wide, earnest and eager for the answer they wanted. Chantelle nodded, but she seemed sad about it. You stayed quiet, aware you could have asked for clarification, to insert yourself in the middle of a thing that didn't completely involve you. But you were learning slowly about not torturing yourself with questions that didn't require an immediate answer. Instead you watched Chantelle's face change, saw the pain seem to deepen slightly as she pushed out her next words.

"It's mad, I know it is, but sometimes I still wonder if some of it—how he was—is my fault. I know that's fucked, I know, but . . . I wonder about it."

Both you and Jak were suddenly protesting loudly, your words clashing into one big sound of disagreement. Chantelle's eyes were welling up, but nothing was dropping yet. You handed her a napkin, wanting to wipe the memory away in the process.

"Look. It's hard to get out from under someone like that. But you didn't make him that way. You just got the brunt of it."

You saw Chantelle's back straighten in response to Jak's words, like she wanted to disagree but didn't really know how.

"You're not with him anymore, Chan. That's the best thing you coulda done."

You knew it was okay to speak then, to say what you would have liked to hear, or what you thought she needed to hear. Jak placed their hand on Chantelle's arm lightly, using a fresh paper napkin to wipe her cheek where a tear had only just escaped. She sniffed, her shoulders relaxing a little as a small chuckle made its way from the back of her throat, just loud enough for the two of you to hear.

"He was such a dickhead, wasn't he?"

She said it with a tentative smile, watching for responses from you and Jak.

"He was the absolute worst. From that first date, I wanted you to bin 'im."

You weren't holding back anymore, and Jak shook their head and clicked their teeth in chorus.

"Remember that bank holiday weekend you all ended up staying at mine, and he was so aggy because no one wanted to share a bottle of wine with him? That for me was like—this dude ain't it."

"He hated *every*one, I'm telling you!"

Chantelle chimed in, a look of surprise and slight amusement on her face, as if she were talking about someone she'd always disliked.

"Oh my God, and how he made you cut his steak? Naaah!"

You threw back your head in laughter, and the three of you began to cackle. Soon enough you couldn't stop, your collective cracking up now turning a few heads around you. You felt a cramp in your side, but the laughter continued to stream out of you, joining with theirs in a medley of dark humor and broken memories. You felt Chantelle's hand clutch your wrist, trying to steady herself, the tears continuing to roll, this time with giggles in tow. It was only the appearance of the waiter that forced you all to try and compose yourselves. You said yes to more cocktails and a mocktail for Jak, and an extra side order of calamari for the table. Chantelle was still dabbing her eyes as the waiter retreated, and you leaned back on your chair for a few moments, satiated. Something small had shifted again between the three of you, making room for more of the truth.

CHAPTER 26

Copenhagen, 1996

Aretha

The one-year anniversary of Bobby's death loomed, and Aretha did her best to swim through it. She was still staying with Bobby's mother, Auntie Penny, as she had been since arriving in Copenhagen almost a year ago. She was aware of the comfort she brought to Auntie Penny, the reminders of Bobby that she carried with her, but she also knew it couldn't last forever. During breakfast, Auntie Penny told Aretha of her plans to move back to Ghana, that there was nothing left for her in Denmark now. Aretha saw how weary she had become, her only child gone from the world. She tried to comfort her with stories of Bobby and, tentatively, with little anecdotes about Whitney. Auntie Penny often didn't react when her grandchild was mentioned, or she dismissed the comment as immaterial. Aretha's patience was constantly tested by this, knowing from her conversations with Bobby how much his mother blamed Tina's pregnancy on his decision to leave Copenhagen, to travel back to his mother's homeland, even when she expressly forbade it. Far be it from Aretha to get into anyone else's family business, but she was realizing that they were all connected now, that Bobby was family *because* of Whitney, whether Auntie Penny liked it or not.

Aretha would never stop reminding her of that, would never stop reaching out even if she was the only one left in Bobby's hometown when all was said and done.

Now she was considering what she would do once Auntie Penny left. She might have to seriously consider taking up Sofia's offer to move into her studio apartment. Sofia was almost done with her studies and had no reason to stay in Copenhagen. Except for Aretha, of course. But she was unsure about involving Sofia in her future plans, given how uncertain she felt about them herself. And she had just heard news from Maame Serwaa back home that they were doing a small service for Bobby, that perhaps Aretha might return to join in?

If Aretha gave it too much thought, it still hurt as if it had happened yesterday. She also did not like to think too much of home, of what she might be missing, even though there were many things in her new life that she loved. But her family felt scattered. Everyone was everywhere else, and what part had she played in that? Had she made it better, or had she watched as more things fell apart, just as she stood over Bobby, watching his life end? What was that all for? She hadn't fixed anything in coming to Copenhagen, and she felt ashamed of it, of what she had not done. She thought then of Whitney, of the birthday she would celebrate without any of the people meant to protect her besides Gloria. As the day rolled on, Aretha's mood plummeted, and this was not lost on Sofia. She suggested they go out, experience some of Copenhagen's more cultural exploits. She had heard that there was an "Images of Africa" festival going on, and they *had* to be there. Aretha agreed, grateful for the distraction from her aimless feelings.

They rode their bikes out of Amagerbro, through Freetown Christiania—where Aretha couldn't help but slow down, look around, and see who she could spot—and onward to Indre By. As they locked up their bikes, Aretha took note of those around her, the bustle of people, the black and brown faces she saw more of as they got closer to the market stalls and event spaces. She overheard conversations between visiting artists and writers, some definitely Ghanaian, one mentioning the Congo and South Africa; all had been invited to take part in the festival and report back home about it. Aretha relaxed into the atmosphere and the warmth of Sofia beside her, commenting on everything she was seeing, the mixture of people.

"Never seen this many Black people since I got here. It's kinda beautiful, isn't it?"

Sofia's voice took on a wistful quality, and Aretha squeezed her hand in response, softly and without letting go. They walked on, stopping at different stands, and as Aretha took in her surroundings, her eyes landed on a familiar face. Viktor.

He was standing in front of a food truck, finishing the contents of a plastic cup, scrunching it up with his fingers and throwing it on the ground. He looked the same, though his cheeks were flushed red in a way that indicated he had been drinking, enjoying the festival, taking in the spoils of Copenhagen's new designation as the Cultural Capital of Europe. But he also wore a T-shirt with "IOA Tour Guide" written on the front, confirming his employment at the festival. Aretha hoped that meant he was no longer an officer in the military, that perhaps he had been stripped of the title and there was some justice after all.

She moved toward him instinctively, trying to get closer and then stopping in her tracks when he waved a group of people over to him. She twisted her face away then, afraid he might recognize her, though she knew it was unlikely.

"I got you this. Thought you'd like it?" The sound of Sofia's voice made her jump, and Aretha turned quickly to see Sofia place a small box in her hands. "Sorry. Didn't mean to scare you." Sofia pushed a braid behind her ear, smiling softly, waiting for Aretha's reaction. She tried to return the smile and ignore the anxiety bubbling in her stomach. She put her arm on Sofia's elbow intimately and leaned into her.

"No, you didn't. I was just distracted, taking it all in. What is it?"

Sofia cocked her head to the side. "Well, if you open it, you'll find out." Aretha frowned but obeyed. She lifted the small cardboard lid easily and pulled out the gift. It was red with a small white cross at the top. She stared at it, unsure of what to say. Sofia watched her, waiting for words, and then she chuckled. "It's a Swiss Army Knife, because you know, you had wanted to go into the army, and I know we're not in Switzerland and—well it's not even a Nordic country really, but . . . it was just a joke. A stupid one—I can take it back—"

Aretha raised her hand out of reach, spinning away from Sofia's attempt to grab the knife.

"No way. I love it. I mean, it's an expensive joke though, right?"

Aretha held it securely in her hands so there was no chance of Sofia taking it back, even in jest.

"Nah, you're worth it. And . . . now you'll have something to remember me by."

Sofia shrugged, trying to look noncommittal even though her stark blue eyes glistened and made Aretha want to say yes to whatever she suggested. Aretha felt laughter in her throat and stepped toward Sofia and hugged her, the two of them sharing heat under the blue sky, the gentle breeze cooling everyone's skin for seconds at a time. As Aretha held her, she couldn't help but get Viktor in her sights again, leading his tour group into a gallery across the road, away from all the market stalls. Aretha tried not to overthink the moment, the chance she might have. She pulled away from the embrace.

"I think the other part of the festival might be in there—can we go in?"

She pointed to the gallery and Sofia shrugged and turned back toward the food stalls. Aretha had been counting on this.

"How about . . . you go in there and look at some art, and I'll stay out here and try to eat my way through the market, and we meet up when you're done?"

Sofia put on her most winning smile, confirming her disinterest in anything to do with galleries, which she had told Aretha during their first interaction. Aretha made like she was mildly disappointed and then nodded in agreement, squeezing Sofia's fingers before they parted ways.

Aretha crossed the road, pushing open the glass doors and feeling a different kind of heat on her neck when she heard Viktor's voice booming from one of the other gallery rooms. She walked slowly past the other visitors, following the sound of his voice and perching by the door, at the back of the tour group. He pointed to the different pieces of art from various African countries and talked in English about them at length to his compatriots, as if he knew the artists personally. She heard him talk about his time in "Africa" as if he had not solely been stationed in Ghana. He discussed the authenticity of the art around him, whether it was a true "image of Africa," as this section of the festival suggested. He waxed lyrical about Africa not being a place he was likely to return to; it had his heart, but his soul had wanted to come back home. Aretha couldn't help but smirk; she should have assumed that he would not miss an opportunity to show off his worldly knowledge, to let everyone know that he was not like the other *obronis*; he understood the "third world" in a way they did not, having lived there for a handful of years. He was still very much a blowhard.

She stepped away after that, training her eyes on the exit instead, listening for his next steps. She waited patiently, standing in front of a large abstract painting but always looking toward the room he was in. After a few minutes he emerged, following his group of now adoring fans, directing them toward a photographic image by a Congolese artist in the corner. He stood on a step in front of the image so that he could tower above his audience and arrogantly project his voice. He spent another ten minutes talking, and then he left the crowd to cross the room. Aretha quickly turned her back to him, and she heard him ask an attendant for directions to the bathroom. He swung around and headed down a corridor away from the main gallery space. Aretha watched him disappear around a corner.

She hesitated, taking in the room for a moment. She looked toward the front of the gallery. Through the window and across the road, her eyes found Sofia easily. She was still in the market, by a different food stall. She took a bite of her smørrebrød and nodded happily at the vendor in approval. Aretha sighed, and a feeling of calm finally washed over her. She had been trying to shake the dark feelings all week, and it was Sofia who had pulled her out of it. Finding Viktor had been a fortunate coincidence, but maybe this was Aretha's only chance to do what she came to do, once and for all? She couldn't help but think of what her sisters might say; Gloria was always telling her to finish what she started, and Tina was the dreamer, always wanting the sweetest version of life, without much stress. The irony. But Aretha was thinking of Bobby today, and he would have looked her dead in the eye and told her to do everything in her power to protect the ones she loved, just as he tried to do.

So Aretha took a step forward, clutching her new gift between steady fingers.

CHAPTER 27

London, Present

Whitney

You headed to a second location after the restaurant—to a bar playing eighties and nineties hits. Chantelle had suggested it, though you and Jak had been apprehensive. You hadn't really been out properly in almost a year. But Chantelle admitted she had missed dancing with you in just as long.

"Let's do it."

You tried saying it with confidence so that she wouldn't sense your hesitancy. The three of you made your way there as a group, walking the ten-minute distance to the Overground and going one stop to Dalston. There was a silence that sat between you that was new and comfortable. You'd never been one for joining groups; you had always considered yourself better one-on-one. Better connecting at the root of someone, making physical contact without the burden of other bodies to distract you. Perhaps you thought too much of people in this way, as a compilation of skin, bone, muscle, and effort. Sometimes it was the only thing you understood about them, though, the only sense you found in a day: controlling the narrative of a painful knot in someone's thigh or the stubborn scar tissue of an old high school injury. Memories of Ma Gloria still hit you in waves. It was to be expected, apparently, grief gestating, being birthed by your movement forward but never quite detaching itself, always there and in need of your attention. It's the reason you said yes to coming out, to being celebrated and trying to smile fully. You wanted to remember life as it had been, despite all the new things you'd discovered; the darker things that were coming to light. You wanted just one night off, to feel good.

Soon you found yourself in an abandoned car park, and the three of you followed the thumping bass sounds to your final destination. The entry stamp on the back of your hand was still drying as you entered the bar, which was once a shipping container, and squeezed into the last available booth. You removed your coat as Tevin Campbell's "Can We Talk" played in the background. Chantelle immediately headed to the bar for drinks, and Jak made a beeline toward the loos. You were alone again. You closed your eyes to take in the room properly. The smell of hookah wafted in from a blocked-off corner to the left. The air carried to your nostrils the sickly sweetness of a strawberry with a smoky musk around the edges. Your mouth watered suddenly, expecting the tang of a strawberry lace between your teeth and tongue, the rubbery texture disintegrating between your incisors, the syrupy liquid coating your tongue and throat while you chewed. It had restorative properties. You were sure of it. You also realized that Jak was right; your addiction to licorice was bordering on unhealthy. You wondered whether there was something in that, something about it bringing you comfort as a child.

The thought was a pinprick to your subconscious, and you felt the result break from you in new droplets of sweat on your forehead. You feared a repeat of your last birthday—the same darkness, the same ocean of music enveloping your senses, the same swathe of bodies around you that individually might have brought comfort.

Even now, as you surveyed the crowd, it was still possible to feel that familiar ache that informed you that you needed to have your hands on something again. You were sure that if you kept your eyes closed and put your hands out in front of you, the world would make a lot more sense. Physically feeling your way through things felt more logical than the emotional work you were attempting in therapy.

When you spoke in that room to Denise, it was like slowly picking apart the smaller details of things you remembered about your childhood and trying to make the correct space and shape for all the things you had no memory of. The spotlight was on you only, and the therapist was merely the electrician, on hand to fix the bulb if it ever went out. You weren't used to it at first—being able to ask questions without fear of offending or hurting the other person in your quest for a clearer truth about yourself. But now you were comfortable offering up an opinion on your own life, thinking out loud, trying to make sense of all the things Ma Gloria held back until the very end of her life. You still felt waves of sickness thinking about all the new parts of yourself that you could no longer share with her.

You took a long gulp of the drink now in front of you, placed down gently by Chantelle. You looked around and found her standing a few feet away, chatting to someone and bopping to the music at the same time. She still knew people everywhere she went.

"You missed her?"

You turned toward the voice, to Jak seated next to you again, flicking their tongue around the straw to their kombucha. You couldn't tell if they were trying to grasp it or just pass the time waiting for you to answer the question.

"I miss them both. Her and Ma Gloria."

You answered absentmindedly and heard the clink of Jak's glass hitting the table as they placed it back down.

"Chantelle's still here."

"Is she?"

You weren't trying to be melodramatic; it just all felt like one big loss. You heard Jak sighing beside you, audibly upset by your words as if you were talking about *them*.

"You should just tell her. She went through stuff too—I mean, not like you, obviously. But . . . I don't know. I feel like she'll understand more than you think."

"What do you know that I don't?"

Your tone was sharp, almost slipping out of your control, but Jak did not seem to notice.

"Oh, Whit, so much."

They patted you on the back, chuckling as they said it. You smiled at their humor for a moment.

"She disappeared. And she came back for Ma's funeral, I know that. But then, poof! Gone again. So maybe we're not really friends anymore."

You heard Jak snort in response, their eyes widening slightly, as if waiting for the punch line.

"You know, Whit, sometimes I feel like you hear things, but you don't really listen. Like, we *just* had a conversation about what Chantelle was dealing with, and it was a lot. All I'm saying is she's had her reasons for not being around."

"I listen!"

You knew your response was childish, and Jak responded in kind by shaking their head and holding their arms out, doing a near perfect impression of that Oprah GIF. You scowled, feeling suddenly like you were being told off for expecting your best friend to be around more. And sure, you could have checked in with her after everything, of course. But you were distracted with what was going on with Ma Gloria, with what she'd told you about your father, with the niggling feeling that all was not well and nothing would ever be well again. By the time you'd raised your head above the parapet to look around, Chantelle had literally flown away. Now you were expected to be understanding. Was that fair?

"I didn't know how bad it was with Paris. There was so much she didn't let me in on."

"And what were you telling her?"

You prepared to give Jak a rebuttal but held your breath instead, trying to calm down. Jak wasn't trying to poke holes; they were just fact-finding. You kept an eye on Chantelle, who was now chatting to the bartender.

"Nothing. I wasn't telling her anything—I know that. But . . ." You frowned, trying to understand, to bring your sudden anger back inside. "I just don't get how she would let him take over so completely. Like, of *all* people, I didn't expect that to happen to *her*."

"Well, she probably didn't either."

Jak looked out onto the dance floor. You thought more was coming, but if it was, they kept the rest to themselves. You'd lost sight of Chantelle, who must have revisited you both because you suddenly had new drinks in front of you. "Okay, but seriously, where is she?"

Your voice sounded exasperated, and Jak pointed through the crowd at the sight of a bright green dress lowering to the ground, preparing to twerk. You watched the growing throng of people on the dance floor, and you felt like your legs were buzzing suddenly.

"Go dance, birthday girl."

Jak shoved you with their hip, knocking you out of your trance, reminding you that you often wore your desires all over your face. You smiled back at them, grateful and distant, your mind already on the hard wooden floor, your body waiting to follow.

Chantelle found you on the dance floor, and you were transported back in time for a few sweet moments to what you used to be together. Ordering as many shots at the bar as you could before the money ran out. Being hungover and eating Sunday roasts at your local pub. Bringing way too much food for a picnic in Hyde Park, even though you always ended up struggling to eat because of the flies at the height of summer. Too many nights to count stumbling out of a club in the early hours of the morning, your feet exhausted but happy, marching toward Bagel Majesty for a much-needed energy boost in the form of a hot, toasted meat sandwich.

The nostalgia heightened your senses after you felt the familiar feel of her rings against your hip, like you hadn't spent any time apart at all. So you pulled her toward you to dance, and she obliged. You bopped in rhythm together but never met the other's eye line, choosing instead to point and dance upward, to shake as the music demanded, but still away from each other. You hadn't noticed the physical gap between you get bigger until you twisted around and for a long moment, you couldn't see her anywhere. It was too dark, and maybe she was spinning alone now in her own world, where it was safer. You reached out when you spotted a flash of green again, her luminous dress like a lighthouse above the misty sea of bodies, but you hesitated when you heard Usher's "You Make Me Wanna" spill out of the speakers. You watched in slow motion as two arms reached back out toward you, holding your hands and pulling you further onto the dance floor with them. Chantelle was eye to eye with you in seconds, and you could feel the heat emanating off all the bodies around you, so close you could almost make contact. It somehow revived you a little, and you laughed as she serenaded you with some of Usher's words.

"Before anything began between us, you were like my beeeest frieeend!"

She bopped and swished in front of you comically as you laughed along, grabbing at a moment of joy again. She spun around and you caught her by the shoulders, shuffling along on beat so that she quickly joined your two-step and could see your mouth moving to make words.

"Are we? Still best friends?"

It came out loudly, and you watched her confusion even over the din of the music. And then sadness seemed to take over her features.

"Aren't we?"

You considered dismissing your own question, pretending you hadn't meant it like you did, but that suddenly felt more difficult to do. You shrugged and leaned into her.

"I don't know, maybe not? I want us to be again, though."

You meant it honestly. You felt that hope deep in your bones. Chantelle suddenly looked upset, like she might cry and hit you, both at the same time. You frowned and prepared yourself for the hard conversation that might come next, in the middle of a crowd of people just trying to have a nice time. Chantelle moved away from you slightly but still in earshot.

"We shouldn't talk about this now."

She was closing down the discussion before it began. You jerked back angrily, not willing to let her dictate an important conversation again. But your movement was too fast and erratic, and an unknown body behind you jumped back to avoid making contact, causing you to take one too many steps backward and giving your ankle ample opportunity to choose which direction to twist as you tumbled to the ground.

"Shit, Whitney!"

You heard Chantelle scream as you hit the floor, the circle between you suddenly becoming much wider. Different voices were asking if you were okay, and you felt a pulsating pain in your back. Thankfully you could still move both your legs safely, so it was

mostly your pride that was hurt. Chantelle suddenly came into focus as she knelt beside you, and you realized she was trying her
hardest not to laugh.

"God, Whit, are you okay? You really just threw yourself on the
ground, ya know! Come we go, before people start filming."

You scoffed as she helped you stand.

"Guaranteed someone already did—security's putting a laugh
track on it as we speak."

Chantelle snorted, and it took you both by surprise when you
burst into laughter together. You knew a bruise was already forming on your lower back, and you suddenly felt very thankful you
hadn't hit your head. You made it back to the booth, limping cautiously, and Jak reappeared with many questions for Chantelle.

"Mate, she's fine! She tripped, that's all!"

Chantelle said it loudly and with humor, as if you both hadn't
just been about to start a very public argument. You continued to
make circles with your ankles, feeling the throb already begin. A
bad sign. You looked up as Chantelle edged closer to Jak so you
wouldn't hear.

"I don't think this girl can survive the club anymore, you know."

Jak stifled a laugh, and it even pulled a smirk from you. "You
might be right. Maybe we can go?"

You hoisted yourself up and started putting your jacket on.
Chantelle's face fell, realizing you were serious. She looked longingly back at the dance floor as if saying goodbye to an old friend
but turned back to you with a resolute look on her face.

"Fine, but we're getting bagels first."

You couldn't help but smile—even though it felt more like a
command from Chantelle than a question—but you nodded, confirming your agreement. Jak walked round to the other side of the
coats and handed Chantelle hers before putting theirs on. Then

they stood beside you, putting out their arm so you looped yours into it. You found that with each new hobbled step you took, you were leaning heavier into Jak's side. They held fast to your lower arm, cupping a hand under your elbow, becoming an armrest for you. You felt infirm for a moment but shook the thought away. This wasn't last year. You hadn't fallen under the weight of your own traumas. You had just fallen.

"Bagels'll make you feel better. But after that, maybe we should go to the hospital?"

Jak looked down at your ankle briefly with concern that momentarily sent your anxious mind into overdrive.

"No way, not this late. We'll be there all night."

"Yeah, okay, but if you leave it for tomorrow and it gets worse—"

"I'm cool, Jak!"

You hadn't meant to snap. But your ankle was getting hot, the tendons feeling as though they were vibrating and trying to break through your skin, and you could not imagine anything worse than revisiting a hospital. Not tonight, not like this. You waited for Jak to drop your arm, to let you make your own way to the next stop in retaliation, but they stayed by your side, closing their mouth after your outburst and looking out into the night instead. Chantelle came up on your other side, saving you from the uncomfortable moment you had created. She began to list out loud all the things she would get on her bagel.

"Gotta be salt beef and mustard, obviously. But I might get them to add in some ham and that cheese with the holes. I'm actually starving—your cake was banging, Jak, but that dinner was meh."

Her hands were animated, and she referred to Jak casually now, like there had never been a break between them. It somehow made your distance with her feel even bigger.

"Yeah, it wasn't great. I shoulda just had you over mine."

Jak shrugged as you walked along together, and then you all three looked up at the same time, hearing the tinny sound of the shop's radio before you saw it, playing Aretha Franklin's "Respect." It was a signal that you had reached your destination. The neon sign still buzzed in the shape of a bagel wearing a painted red cape with rubies scattered throughout, as if that one piece of bread ruled over the whole road. On a number of nights out with Jak and Chantelle, you had felt like that bagel's loyal subjects. You chuckled to yourself at the ridiculousness of your thoughts but didn't speak them out loud. Instead, the three of you stood silent for a moment, staring up at the sign.

"Ain't gon' do you wrong while you're gone, ain't gon' do you wrong, 'cause I don't wanna, all I'm askin' is for a little respect when you come home . . ."

"Birthday gyal, just perch out here, and I'll get you something, yeah? I think I already know what, but it's been time, so tell me once more?"

You cocked your head in Chantelle's direction in answer, having let go of Jak to lean against the brick wall.

"Salt beef and mustard, always."

She flashed you a smile and then looked at Jak.

"I'm not even gonna try and guess."

Jak opened their mouth and then seemed to change their mind midsentence.

"I'm not complicated, okay? Also—variety is the spice of life, so I feel like something a bit different tonight, ya know? Yeah . . . okay, I need to look at the menu."

Chantelle threw up her hands in mild exasperation but led the way as they entered the shop together, leaving you outside, leaning slightly off balance and still holding the wall. You readjusted and slid down to the ground slowly, feeling the cold of the pavement through your thin skirt. You surveyed the road in front of you. There were people coming and going, some in the middle of a bar crawl, some looking for food. You were surrounded by restaurants and takeaways open and waiting to provide sustenance for people walking in zigzag formation after joyful moments with friends. You were avoiding looking at your ankle. You knew it was bad. Jak was right that you needed medical attention. But the thought of heading to the nearest hospital brought bile to your throat. It would have to be Ma Gloria's, the one she had worked at, the one where she received her diagnosis, and the one she would have died in if you hadn't respected her wishes and brought her home.

You couldn't deal with this right now, with another painful emotional reminder while you were also in physical pain. You would deal with it tomorrow, put some ice on it tonight, keep it elevated. You would be fine. Not everything needed to be dealt with straightaway.

"But why is that weird? I wanted the cheese with the holes. It was right there."

"Yeah, but you asked for what sounded like 'holy cheese,' and no one knows what that is."

You heard Jak's small laugh as they exited the shop with Chantelle, who was already negotiating which side of her bagel to take a bite out of first.

"I said what I said. Where's Whit?"

Chantelle was squinting across the street for a moment before you alerted them both to your presence.

"Down here."

Your voice came out a little hoarse, and you could already feel that your forehead was damp. Jak crouched down in front of you, handing you your warm bagel with a slight look of disappointment.

"Aren't we a bit too old for this?"

"What, sitting on the ground after a night out? Speak for yourself."

You tried for a grin, but your pain was increasing, and you feared you might have just given them a grimace. Chantelle had taken up a standing post next to you, her mouth full of the bagel but still watching you both carefully.

"You know what I mean. I think we should go to the hospital."

You closed your eyes; it was easier to express your exasperation that way and focus your mind at the same time, now that there were shooting pains in your leg.

"I haven't even eaten my bagel yet."

Jak stood up suddenly, looking down at you as if they didn't recognize who they were speaking to. You felt like a petulant child, but you also saw the wall between you and that hospital, having to overcome some other fear you had developed in the last few months, for the supposed betterment of yourself. Why did you always have to deal with the pain? Why couldn't you just push it aside for one more day? What difference would it make?

"It's gonna make a difference to your fucking ankle, Whit."

"What?"

Had you spoken your thoughts out loud for a moment, or had Jak just read your mind? You stared up at them, waiting for an explanation until you realized that Jak was waiting for you to explain why you were suddenly being so difficult. You were starting to see little white spots in front of your eyes, so you took a bite from your bagel instead, which only seemed to annoy Jak further.

"Chantelle, help me out here?" Jak held their arms out, and you waited for Chantelle to pile on the pressure, but she moved toward Jak instead and said something to them quietly. Jak looked down at you once more, clearly frustrated but trying to hide it. "You know what? There's a new vegan place opened up down the street. I'm gonna go check out their menu. I'll be back."

You watched Jak leave as Chantelle sank down beside you.

"What's going on with you?"

You leaned your head back against the wall, feeling like you had been waiting for this question all night. You nudged Chantelle's black boot with your one good foot and noticed a black mark on your white trainers. Jak had been right about you scuffing them.

"These new?"

"Yeah, Aldo sale." Chantelle stared at you even as you turned away. "So? What, you're scared of hospitals now?"

You felt the truth underneath your tongue; you were trying to dissolve it quickly even though the taste was filling your mouth.

"Not scared, just don't wanna be there. It's not that deep."

You jumped at the sound of Chantelle's "Ha!" as if you'd delivered a surprising punch line. "It's always that deep with you. It's never a small thing, Whit. That's why we love you *and* find you mad irritating sometimes." You felt her shift beside you as you closed your eyes again. "I get it, you know? Your ma was there, and . . . it sucks to go back. But who's that for? Not for you, or her. Imagine what she'd say if you told her you had to amputate your foot because you hurt yourself on a night out and you couldn't be bothered to get checked by a nurse. She'd be piiissed."

You felt her giggle beside you once the smile crept back onto your own face.

"She'd knock my head to be fair, full knuckles on the forehead and say 'Kwasiasem!'"

"Exactly. You know better. So, come we go? And . . . look, if you're scared, that's okay—"

"I'm not scared. I'm just . . . I'm tired, Chan. Tired of feeling like I take a step forward and then something painful sends me five steps backward. Tired of having to fucking deal with everything. Like, maybe I wanna ignore some stuff. Why can't that be okay?"

You hadn't meant to cry, but you felt the wetness on your cheeks, and you hung your head, suddenly embarrassed. You felt Chantelle's arm slip around your shoulders, pulling you closer to her. The sharp pain in your ankle jolted your head up quickly, and Chantelle looked worriedly at your foot.

"I think it *can* be okay. It can. But sometimes we need to go through the hard bit to get to the better bit. Like, talking to you and Jak tonight, it was like something lifted off me. I don't think I knew I was carrying it, but . . . anyway, it was painful, but it helped me. You get me?"

Her words were already unraveling you on the inside, and you weren't ready to admit it. Or had you been unraveling before this and slowly heading toward an inevitable reveal? You needed to consider that Chantelle was honest and continued to tell you the truth now even if it hurt. And it was painful to sit in that and be okay with it and see some way to get to the other side. Your mind was spinning, but you wanted her to know your truth too, the bits you had been keeping from her. You had talked about it in therapy, and the words never came easy, but nevertheless, they came.

"I know I got weird last year, and I pushed you away because, well, you *know* me, right? I *can* get too deep with things, for sure, but then I didn't know how to tell you that he, the Bard . . . he hurt me. In a way that I can't—I mean I couldn't—"

"It's okay. If it's too much right now—"

"No. You're right. If I don't give it air then it suffocates me, right? So, the Bard. He assaulted me and . . . it wasn't like, completely clear to me at the time that that's what it was, but—"

"I get it. I got you, Whit."

Chantelle was squeezing your hand, and you saw in her eyes that you didn't need to say anything more. She knew. She already knew. And she was saving you again even now, not wanting you to fully feel the pain of what you'd been holding in for so long. You squeezed her hand back, hard, as if she were sustaining you, even as you felt your heart beating heavy in your chest.

Silence settled over you both, and you took another bite of your bagel, and another, and another, until it was done, as Chantelle finished hers beside you. You scrunched up your paper wrappers at the same time, giving satisfied sighs before bursting into unexpected laughter. You looked up at the sound of Jak's boots echoing through the narrow street as they headed back toward you, the three of you suddenly the few remaining late-night take-away patrons. Chantelle seemed to jump up effortlessly, her dress staying in perfect shape and hugging all the right places as she stood. She reached both hands out to you, and you didn't hesitate, letting her pull you up to standing on one foot in a short hop.

"You want me to kill him?"

For a second you forgot what she was talking about, as if speaking the thing out loud really had wiped it from your mind. But you laughed and shook your head, trying not to think about the way her face never changed, that she wanted you to know that she was serious if you wanted her to be. You turned to Jak with your most apologetic face.

"I'm sorry—"

They held up a hand to silence you. "It's your birthday, so you get to be an idiot. But only for today." You opened your mouth to argue with their choice of words but thought better of it as your ankle throbbed a reminder.

"Okay, yeah, I'm an idiot. Hospital, yeah?"

You heard a familiar ping from Chantelle's phone, indicating that the Uber was already around the corner.

CHAPTER 28

London, 1996

Gloria

Gloria adjusted herself in front of the mirror, pulling down the red dress she had borrowed from Freda. For her, it was too short, but Freda was adamant she should wear it.

"This red one, I got from Topshop—have you been there yet?" Gloria shook her head, giving the dress itself a discerning look, wondering what mother would wear such a thing. "Try it on. You've got a banging figure. Be a shame not to show it off. Come!"

Freda pulled Gloria toward her bedroom mirror, kicking away the cardigan on the floor that Gloria had been wearing despite the warmth of the house. Gloria did not fight it. She let herself be dressed, be given "a makeover," and slipped on some high heels without complaining. None of the London fashions were unfamiliar to her; she had just never pictured herself in them. She always opted for comfortable shoes, clothes she could get a lot of wear out of, that she could run in. Every so often she recalled the way she used to dominate the district running competitions as a teenager. It was another chance to prove she was the best. And she didn't have to worry about anyone else but herself when she was running; there was always a tunnel of free air released into her brain so that she was just blank, just a shuttle moving forward without a fixed destination, only onward. But since her injury all those years ago, she hadn't been able to reclaim that rhythm, to grasp the joy she had felt without pain soon following.

Now she only found moments of freedom when she danced. This was how Paa Kweku and Freda had convinced her to go to the party, to trek across London and leave Bobo in the capable hands of Freda's mother for an evening; there would be an opportunity for dancing. Gloria was already dreading the journey there, dressed in multiple layers to sit on the Tube—which she had only done a handful of times—to be in close proximity with strangers who didn't seem to realize it was rude to stare. So, she was shocked when they stepped outside and Paa Kweku jostled some keys and opened the door to the car in front of them. It was a small red thing with a few visible dents on the side, but he was beaming with pride at Gloria.

"Surprise! Ford Fiesta—from my cousin Kojo, you know the one who just left London? It's a good one, Glory. We will travel there in style-o!"

He waved his arm, gesturing for her to climb in, and she obliged, bending awkwardly, positioning herself, and trying to ignore the smell of petrol as she sank into the front passenger seat. Freda required no such chivalry getting situated in the back seat. She exclaimed that it was a "lovely surprise" and squeezed Paa Kweku's shoulder at the same time. Gloria kept her eyes on his shy smile but said nothing. Eventually Paa Kweku turned on the radio, the silence mounting with unknown tension.

"Strumming my pain with his fingers, singing my life with his words . . ."

"Ugh, I love this song! So romantic, don't you think?" Freda leaned forward from the back seat to entreat Gloria, who was almost

buried in her thick parka coat. She turned back and smiled, nodding.
Gloria did not want to speak, lest she explode with the way the song
was pointing at her, at Paa Kweku, mocking her a little. Killing her
softly. She was thankful when they finally arrived. The party was
already well underway, the time of night giving everyone an excuse
to let loose. There were no children, as Gloria had expected—just a
small school hall and a DJ. The child of the naming ceremony had
long since been put to bed at home. This was the parents' time to
celebrate and enjoy.

Gloria hesitantly removed her coat as Freda went to grab them
drinks. Paa Kweku was already going around to other people and
introducing himself. Soon enough Freda was on the dance floor,
swaying her hips a few seconds off the beat but apparently not caring. She commanded the space as if she were close to the family
throwing the party rather than a gate-crasher. Paa Kweku was now
on the other side of the room, talking animatedly to a group of
men, some of whom Gloria recognized as Ghanaian. There were
two other white men she didn't know, and she wondered how Paa
Kweku knew them. He was a man of the people, she supposed, and
he had picked up some work in a warehouse to make ends meet
while he tried to get the new branch of Holy Grace off the ground.
He was amassing an array of friends, and Gloria wondered, in spite
of herself, whether there were some women in that number too.
But he always told her about any new person he met and hoped to
invite to a Sunday service, once they found a semipermanent place
to worship. Eventually he would have a flock, a congregation, and
validation that he was making the right decision, choosing something higher than himself, higher than his own desires. She might
feel better able to accept it then, that the decision to remain as they
were had been worth it in the end. Even here on this small island
of infrequent sun, overpriced plantain, and miserable faces on early

morning buses, Gloria still had hopes. She would make a life here for Bobo, no matter what. And she would make a life for herself too.

So when Gloria's namesake proclaimed that at first she had been afraid, Gloria suddenly found herself standing for the song. She already felt the smile creeping onto her face as she made a beeline for Freda, who met her eye with a look of relief, as if she had been waiting all night for Gloria to join in. She spun herself around and tried to ignore the eyes that followed her, the eyes of Paa Kweku and the group of men who were no longer his captive audience. Gloria lifted her hands up in the air, waving to those standing around the edge of the dance floor shyly, waiting for the right song, the right moment to let go. Most were new to London, like her, used to being surrounded by familiar faces in their home countries on the African continent, in the West Indies, open to every shade of deep melanin and a friendly word even from strangers. But this country was different: not as colorful or warm, but still with sparks of possibility for what life could be like, with the right job, community, and love. They were all still finding their feet, just like Gloria. And she would land correctly, she knew that. For now, she would dance. She would sway. She would make a way in this new life, and she would do more than just survive.

CHAPTER 29

London, Present

Whitney

As soon as you walked into the emergency waiting room, the nurse at the front desk recognized you. She had worked with Ma Gloria years ago and then lost touch when she moved from London to Liverpool. Now she was back, and she'd just heard the news about Ma Gloria's passing. You watched her face crumple with sadness as she spoke.

"You probably don't remember me, but my mum—Auntie Maggie—she used to look after you! Now you're all grown up, just like my boys."

She had a kind face, open and soft around the edges. But you had no more emotional bandwidth for a reunion with Ma Gloria's past. You wanted to turn back, to leave that place and its bleach-laden scent, the misery of the waiting room, the bad news behind closed doors. But Jak was practically holding you up at this point, and Chantelle was now leaning on the desk chatting with Nurse Freda. You saw them exchange a conspiratorial laugh, despite the lateness of the hour and the clinical atmosphere. Before you knew it, Nurse Freda had taken you into a side room to triage you before anyone else. After that, you waited an hour to see a consultant, who confirmed that you had a sprained ankle. You walked out half an hour later with a bandage and something for the pain.

"All about who ya know," Jak said smugly in the back of the cab as the three of you headed back to your house. You grunted in agreement. The painkillers had started to kick in, and you felt calmer now, smoother in the throat, as if you had been hovering just above ground all night and had finally landed.

"Wait, wait, wait! Oh my God, I knew it was here! 'Scuse me, Mr. Driver Man, could you park up here, please? Yep, yep, we're just gonna walk somewhere real quick!"

Chantelle was bouncing up and down in her seat, and the driver looked annoyed but slowed down.

"Er, walk where? I can't walk!"

You said it in protest, but there was no real weight behind it. You heard Jak laugh beside you.

"Chan, mate, what are you doing?"

Chantelle had practically launched herself out of the car once it came to a stop. She left the door open for you and Jak to slide out after her, with Jak hoisting you so that you could shuffle over to lean on someone's front wall while Chantelle spoke to the driver.

"What's your name—Omar? Omar, listen, I promise you five stars and a big tip if you please wait here for us, for like fifteen, twenty minutes? See, it's my friend's birthday and she's lost someone really close to her and I think this will make her smile. And Omar, Omar, you can be *that* dude, that got three youngish people home safe and sound, and then you can sleep well with a good conscience about that, right?"

You heard the driver grumble back in agreement, and Chantelle flashed him her best smile before turning back to you both. She looked down at your now-bandaged ankle and for a second seemed to doubt her decision, before reclaiming her determination.

She pointed across the road, toward a surprisingly well-lit side street.

"Down there is something I think you're gonna like, Whit. I couldn't figure out what to get you for your birthday, and then I kept seeing photos of this thing on people's Instas, but I didn't know where it was, and then bam! We're driving past. It's a two-minute walk—or a five-minute hobble. It'll be worth it, though, yeah? What you saying?"

She wore her most sincere look, which you couldn't have said no to if you'd wanted to. And there was something else, something meaningful sitting behind it. You looked at Jak, who shrugged, ready to follow your lead.

"You're the birthday girl."

"I'm down, but there better not be wolves in there."

Jak and Chantelle both stopped to look at you. "Wolves?" They asked it in unison, as if you'd suddenly grown two heads. "How many painkillers are you on right now?" Jak laughed and then kept moving forward with you in tow.

"I'm on however many they gave me, and you know what I mean—wolves! It's a London thing, come on!"

You held up your palms in frustration, unsure why they weren't understanding you. Then you heard Chantelle snort beside you.

"Oh my god, do you mean *foxes*?"

It hadn't been long since the memory came back to you. It was after a night of broken sleep, when you kept hearing Ma Gloria's voice retelling you the story of how you would hide in the garden after dark as a child, when you first came to London.

"I thought I had brought home a wolf."

You hadn't been outside in the garden for weeks, and it hadn't really been Ma Gloria's domain either. She arranged with an auntie from church that her teenage son would come to the house twice a month to tend to the weeds, to the rosebushes that needed some love, to the miscellaneous berries at the back that were toxic to some animals. He did a good job and continued to come after Ma Gloria passed away and you moved back home. You made sure to leave a tenner in an envelope for him outside the back door when he was done. Then one day he didn't come by, and you received a text from his mother explaining that he had a bad cold. Curious, you ventured out into the garden at dusk, to get a lay of the land.

There had been bushes at the far end that he had cut away, replacing the soil with a new batch so something better could be planted. You weren't sure what yet. But you made a beeline for it, the sky creeping quickly toward a deep, dark purple. You knelt into the grass and felt the wetness from a recent rain shower soak through the thin fabric of your trousers. Your hands were deep into the soil before you realized what was happening. You closed your eyes and breathed in that humid scent of earth and leaves and all the living things that would burrow into the ground and keep it going. And you felt your breath catch as the memory pushed its way to the surface with a sudden furor that brought headache pangs.

The smell of smoke. The sound of cars beeping in the distance. The feel of a large hand tugging at your dress, another wrapped around your tiny wrist, holding you in place. The strange pain of it. And then the sound of a child whimpering—you—until suddenly there was shouting and grunts that sounded like a fight. Moments later you were scooped up, safe again.

You remained out there in the dark for what felt like endless minutes, until you returned, at least partially, to the now. You, as an adult, shedding the tears of a three-year-old. You heard the rustle of foxes before you finally stood, taking your tired body back into the house.

Now you stood with Jak and Chantelle, looking up at all the fairy lights, bright white and lighting up the side street. You arched your neck but realized you couldn't make out the whole picture. You were too close. The colors sprayed on the wall were just tiny dots, cells of a larger being. You needed to step away to see it completely. You hopped backward slightly and lowered yourself onto the wooden bench that had been placed there so that people could take in the whole of the artwork magnificently displayed in front of them. Jak and Chantelle did the same, flanking you, all of you unable to take your eyes off the wall. This was a thing you sat down for, that you took your time with. It quieted everything.

You leaned backward into the bench and looked up at the colorful bird spray-painted in dazzling, luminous colors on the brick wall. Its wings were closed, but you could trace the intricate lines of the feathers with your fingers in the air. Its neck was long, elegant, and twisted backward, looking at its own tail with a sharp, oval-shaped eye. There was an egg directly underneath its mouth; the pattern on the shell was of a kente cloth, the zigzag of the design a perfect perspective, almost three-dimensional. The egg looked ready to drop or be swallowed; it floated in the air as if in between something. It was the clock from Ma Gloria. It was her gift of a lapel pin to Pastor P. And it meant something. Underneath the bird, the artist had written the proverb in English. You read it out loud, into the darkness.

"It is not taboo to go back and fetch what you have forgotten."

You felt the fizzy feeling in your sinuses, your eyes blurring slightly from new tears, but you couldn't look away. You let your throat catch, and a slow stream of water fell down your face. But you did not look away. You felt the warmth of Chantelle's hand slipping into yours, and Jak's arm around your shoulder, squeezing you closer.

The sky was a midnight blue cradling a bulbous silver moon, and now it felt like the night before recovery begins, that moment after the pain has subsided, when you can breathe more easily and look ahead.

ACKNOWLEDGMENTS

This story began in January 2020. It has multiple moving parts, helped into its final form by the following generous folks, to whom I would like to dedicate my thanks:

To Sinéad Gosai for always being my first reader, reading every subsequent draft, and cheering me on with honesty and love; there is no me without you.

To my early readers and research helpers: Lauren F. for looking at the therapy bits. Christina Neuwirth for your detailed and tender feedback that helped to make Jak more Jak. Ben A. for the masseuse info and guidance. Alfred T. for the coffee and conversation in Copenhagen. Manaf for the military chat in Accra.

To the orgs: Arts Council England for the DYCP grant that gave me time and funding to develop the book. The History Quill and Louise Hare for sharing her astute knowledge of research, planning, and writing authentic, historical narratives. The Society of Authors for the travel scholarship that took my research to Copenhagen. The Public Records and Archives Administration Department of Ghana (PRAAD), Birch, the British Library, the London Library, City Lit Creative Writing Department, Green Bean Cafe and Old Bank Coffee House for the resources and the space to write.

To Mum—Barbara Kuma-Aboagye—for the conversation and the many more that followed, and for making sure my return to Ghana was exactly what it needed to be.

To Auntie Alberta for your kindness, humor, and hospitality during that week in Kumasi. Gloria, Aretha, and Maame Serwaa came alive because of you. Rest in perfect peace.

To the aunties and uncles: Auntie Adelaide, Auntie Barbara, Auntie Beatrice, Nana Mary, Auntie Nana, Auntie Rita, Uncle Akwesi, Uncle Derkye, and Uncle Nana. Thank you for your openness, for helping to bridge the gap and for passing on lessons that I am still learning today.

To my agent, Maria Cardona Serra, for reading the manuscript in 2022, already knowing what was to come before I'd even finished it, and believing in the kind of books I want to write. This is just the beginning.

To the team at Amistad: Abby West for acquiring the book and continuing to push diaspora voices forward. To my editor, Francesca Walker, for understanding so deeply what the book was trying to say, for hearing my voice and elevating it with your thoughtful and careful edits. To Judith Riotto for your diligent copy edits and huge improvements to my grammar.

To Dapo Adeola for beautifully visualizing what I could not articulate for the cover. Your talent is unmatched. Let's do this again sometime.

To all the other friends, family, writers and creatives who connected, supported and uplifted me during the writing of this book: Abi A., Akim Mogaji, Alex Dane, Amma A., Audrey Brown, Becca Dufie, Bethany A., Bobby Nayyar, Christina Fonthes, Colin Grant, Derek Owusu, Dorothy Koomson, Eloise Faichney, Eva Lewin, Gabriel Gbadamosi, JJ Bola, Jarrod S., Jasmine Richards, Jendella Benson, Joy Francis, Marcelle Akita, Melanie Abrahams, Natasha O., Raph B., Ruth Harrison, Sally R., Sharmilla Beezmohun, Symeon Brown, Tamara Jones, #Twentyin2020 writers, and Vimbai Shire.

To the readers: Thank you, always.

ABOUT THE AUTHOR

Maame Blue is a Ghanaian Londoner, part-time Melbournite, and award-winning author of the novel *Bad Love*, which won the 2021 Betty Trask Award. She has been a scriptwriter on a Venezuelan telenovela remixed for African audiences, and her short stories have appeared in several international anthologies, including *Not Quite Right for Us*, *New Australian Fiction 2020*, and *Joyful, Joyful*. Maame is a recipient of the 2022 Society of Authors Travelling Scholarship and was a 2022 POCC Artist-in-Residence. Maame contributes regularly to *Writers Mosaic* and has written pieces for Refinery29, Black Ballad, and *The Author*. She cohosted the Storymix podcast *Craft & Conversation*, and teaches creative writing for multiple organizations including Arvon, Faber Academy, and City Lit. She lives in London.